# THE
# FOXFIRES
# TRILOGY

# About the Author

E. C. Hibbs is an award-winning author and artist, often found lost in the woods or in her own imagination. She adores nature, fantasy, and anything to do with winter. She also hosts a YouTube channel, discussing writing tips and the real-world origins of fairy tales. She lives with her family in Cheshire, England.

Learn more and join the Batty Brigade at

www.echibbs.weebly.com

# Also by E. C. Hibbs

THE FOXFIRES TRILOGY
*The Winter Spirits*
*The Mist Children*
*The Night River*

THE TRAGIC SILENCE SERIES
*Tragic Silence*
*The Libelle Papers*
*Sepia and Silver*

*Blindsighted Wanderer*
*The Sailorman's Daughters*
*Night Journeys: Anthology*
*The Hollow Hills Tarot Deck*

*Blood and Scales* (anthology co-author)
*Dare to Shine* (anthology co-author)
*Fae Thee Well* (anthology co-author)

AS CHARLOTTE E. BURGESS
*Into the Woods and Far Away: A Collection of Faery*
*Meditations*
*Gentle Steps: Meditations for Anxiety and Depression*

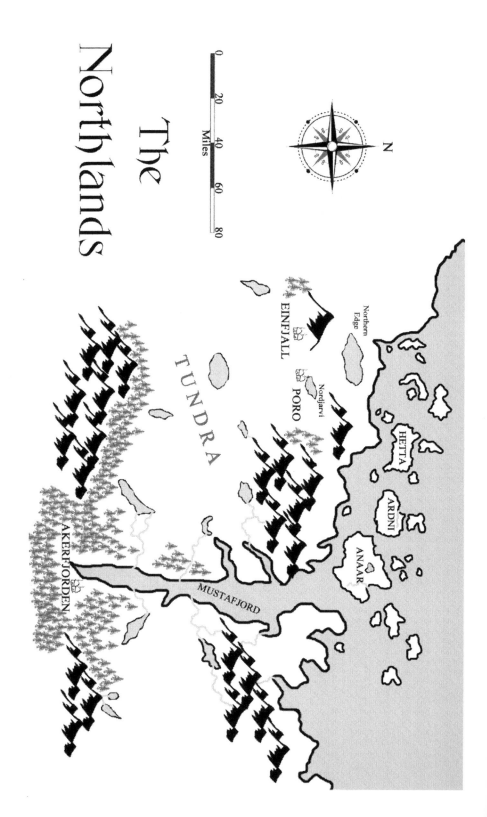

The
Northlands

0
20
40
60
80

Miles

N

EINFJALL

Northern
Edge

TUNDRA

PORO

Nordjärvi

HETTA

ARDNI

ANAAR

AKERFJORDEN

MUSTAFJORD

# The Winter Spirits

## The Foxfires Trilogy
## Book One

*Happy reading!*

*E. C. Hibbs* (signature)

# E. C. Hibbs

This is a work of fiction. Names, characters, businesses, places, events, locales, and incidents are either the products of the author's imagination or used in a fictitious manner. Any resemblance to actual persons, living or dead, or actual events is purely coincidental.

First published January 2020

Cartography, cover design, cover artwork, book production and layout by E. C. Hibbs

Cover stock image from AdobeStock

Author photograph by Allison Page-Hibbs


www.echibbs.weebly.com

Dedicated to the memory of Thomas Hibbs,

The little brother I never met.

Enjoy your dance through the Lights.

# Prologue

At first, Lilja wasn't sure what woke her. There was a strange taste to the frigid air. And it was cold. Far too cold.

She sat up, the soft fur of her sleeping sack falling away into her lap. As usual, she had slept in her coat to keep warm, but even that did little to ward off the chill. The night had sucked the moisture out of her skin; it was numb and tight over her cheekbones.

She eased her eyes open, carefully, in case her lashes had frozen together. There was barely enough light to see by. She couldn't even make out her brother Kari's sack, and he was only lying a few feet away. The cone of interlocking poles which formed the shelter loomed like giant bones all around her, broken only by the smoke hole overhead. The tarp of reindeer skin stretched over the wood was so dark, it was difficult to see where its protective circle ended and the night sky began.

Lilja turned her attention to the hearth, directly under the smoke hole. Only a single tongue of flame was licking at the charred logs.

A frown fleeted across her forehead. Hadn't Kari added another one before he'd gone to sleep? This was the second night in a row that he'd forgotten.

She peered closer. No, the wood was stocked high, like it should be. The fire just hadn't caught.

Rolling her eyes, she wriggled out of her sack and crawled closer, blowing on the embers to try and coax them back to life. When that didn't work, she grabbed another log from nearby and tore off the papery bark, tossing the shreds onto the hearth. Sure enough, the dying fire flared, letting out a waft of thin heat.

Across the hearth, Kari didn't even stir.

Lilja tended the flames as they bloomed back into life, spreading light and warmth through the shelter. She could see the seams of the tent tarp now: sewn together with tendons and sinews, creating a rough patchwork permanently discoloured from years of smoke residue and journeys though the tundra.

From a notch above her sack, her drum hung suspended on a leather thong. The stretched skin was painted with a plethora of symbols, all daubed in red alder bark juice. Her eyes passed over the one in the centre, of the Great Bear Spirit, and a small smile rose to her lips.

She and Kari would need to call to the Bear later, and to the Spirits of the Sea, to ask for fortune in the coming hunt. They had pitched camp close to the coast to fish for char, up here where nobody would walk this deep into winter. As the snows fell thicker and the Sun Spirit retreated more and more every day, all the folk of the Northlands would huddle in their villages and wait for the Long Dark to pass.

All folk, except Lilja and Kari. That was not their way. Theirs was one of wandering, as it had been for years, ever since they were teenagers. Ever since the Great Bear Spirit had brought Lilja back from the dead.

She gazed back at her drum. She was as familiar with it as she was her own body. Since the day she had made it, it had never left her side. Apart from Kari, it was the one thing she still had from her old life. It had grown with her like another limb:

mage and instrument attuned with each other, and as she forged memories, she painted them on the skin so they would not be lost. Even the ones which brought pain, for they were often the most powerful of all.

Her attention strayed to the bottom-most picture. It showed her and Kari: he outside a shelter laying down protective chants, Lilja inside, pulling a baby from its mother. That had happened years ago, in the southernmost village. A poor woman had been in labour, so Lilja was forced to act as her midwife. The child was born healthy, with a glow in its cheeks like the Sun Spirit herself. All the mages present had looked at each other with knowledge they dared not speak aloud, and Lilja and Kari had stolen away as soon as heads were turned.

But lately, Kari had been bringing it up more and more in conversation. There was a strange longing in his eyes when he spoke of it. Lilja had often wondered about the boy herself, and humoured Kari's musings, but she felt it best to stay away. She had learned a long time ago that being around children was not one of her strengths.

She glanced up, over the growing fire, to Kari's sleeping sack. He still hadn't moved.

Lilja supposed she should wake him. There was no point in her going back to sleep now; the two of them may as well feed themselves and the reindeer. A long day of fishing lay ahead.

She picked up another log from the pile – a long thin one – and leaned over the fire to poke him with it.

"Get up, sleepyhead," she said.

The log fell against an empty sack. He wasn't there.

She frowned. Was he feeding the animals?

She threw the last handful of bark on the fire, crawled to the door of the tent and pushed back the flap. The tiniest glow of dawn tinged the eastern sky, but it was upon a land still steeped in darkness. Stunted shrubs stuck up here and there; branches encased in their own crystalline limbs of ice. Snow lay undisturbed and perfect, its whiteness tinted pale blue and lilac by the faraway light.

Next to the shelter, the two reindeer raised their heads to look at Lilja. They were both lying down, their thick fur dusted with snowflakes. There was no sign of her brother.

"Kari?" she called, a note of annoyance in her voice. "The least you could have done was get the shelter warm."

He didn't reply. She craned her head towards the sleighs, in case he was fetching lichen from the bags. The reindeer were able to dig through the snow to find food, but Lilja and Kari always carried a supply for them in case the ground froze.

But he wasn't there, either. The bellies of the sleighs were undisturbed: still covered by the skin tarps Lilja had lashed across them.

"Kari!" she called again, louder this time.

The frozen landscape answered only with silence. Not even an echo of her own voice rebounded back.

Lilja ground her teeth together. Where was he? He'd forgotten the fire again and now hadn't even fed the animals?

Then she tasted that strangeness again, blowing against her face like a wind too faint to truly feel. It was heavy, almost metallic.

Unease twisted her stomach like a knife. Kari had been distracted for the past few weeks, but he wasn't stupid. Something was wrong.

She spotted prints leading towards the forest – the light was so dim, she'd missed them. However, her relief at finding them quickly turned to confusion.

They were *footprints*: clearly marked with the shape of boots. The snow was several inches thick. Why hadn't he taken skis?

She ducked back into the shelter and pulled on her mittens. Then she looked back at her brother's sleeping sack, and realised he wasn't all which was missing.

His drum was gone, too.

That was all the confirmation she needed. He'd left to call to the Spirits. There was nothing strange about that. Like her, he was a mage, after all; it was what they did.

But Lilja couldn't shake off her unease. No skis? Not feeding the fire or the reindeer?

And there it was again: that horrible taste. The air was usually crisp and clear, but now it seemed as though it was cracking under itself. She breathed in through her mouth and immediately wished she hadn't. It lingered on her tongue like blood sucked from a wound. It was wrong, so terribly wrong.

Then, as distant as the Sun, she heard the drumbeats.

Her breath became ragged. What was Kari doing?

She snatched her own drum and held it over the fire to tighten the skin. Usually she would leave it there longer, but now there was no time. Every second felt like an age. When she felt the heat spreading to her hand, she secured the drum on her belt, jamming the antler hammer in beside it.

She manoeuvred the logs in the hearth to ensure they wouldn't fall, exited the tent, and tied the flap down so no snow could blow inside. She didn't worry about the reindeer – no wolves would be this far north. Nevertheless, she checked the rope binding them to the bottom of the shelter, to make sure they wouldn't wander off. Then she trudged around the back, where she and Kari had left their skis. Sure enough, his were still there, sticking up out of the snow. She tied hers onto her feet and set off, after the trail.

She bit her chapped lips together in an attempt to quell the rising panic in her blood. Her heart raced. This was so unlike him. And that pressure in the air was different to anything she had known him drum up before. A mage's power was something both delicate and mighty: a beautiful balancing act with no beginning nor end. But whatever he was doing was too harsh, too coarse.

Nausea welled in her stomach; she couldn't tell if it was from the magic or from her own nerves.

She leaned on each ski as it glided forward, down a gentle slope to the edge of the forest. Even though the trees stretched for miles, here their girths stood thin, and she was able to go on. Overhead, they seemed to melt into the sky, their branches so feathered with ice that they appeared invisible against the white clouds.

The beats of the drum grew stronger the further in she went. They coursed through the ground, reverberated up her legs.

Her heartbeat changed to keep time with the fast, irregular pounding. It squeezed her stomach and she paused, dry-retching into the snow. Nothing came up except bile. Grimacing, she wiped her mouth on her cuff and pushed onwards.

She wanted nothing more than to call out Kari's name, but she knew better than to do that. She could hear his chanting now: he was deep in trance. To snap a mage out of that could be dangerous. If he was in any kind of trouble, the last thing she needed was for him to be so disorientated that he couldn't walk.

She was close now. The heaviness in the air became stronger, until it made her ears hurt. Every time she heard the drumbeat, her hands shook.

Then she spotted him.

He was almost invisible in the low light: standing between two trees, the snow around him churned and uneven. He had his back to her.

Lilja tried to keep calm. She slipped out of her skis and closed the remaining distance on foot. She walked slowly, so as not to startle him, but it was she who was startled.

Kari had built a figure from snow in front of him, carved into the effigy of a human. Two small stones were wedged in its head for eyes; sheets of bark torn from the birch trees lay atop the scalp to serve as hair. He was rocking back and forth, beating his drum crazily, the sound becoming more erratic and unhinged with every moment. Each strike of the hammer sent out a small shockwave, wafting his hair back as though it were caught in a soft wind. His chanting chilled Lilja's blood: both guttural and shrieking, not like anything she had heard before.

She had seen him do something similar when singing to a blizzard, echoing the fitful winds and swirling snow with his voice and instrument, in an attempt to appease the Storm Spirits and still the weather. But he wasn't singing to the Storm Spirits now. He was singing to the effigy, and the mere presence of it almost made her retch again.

She had heard tales of these things, and in the old lore told around fires, they were used for terrible deeds.

But Kari wouldn't be dabbling in anything like that. Not her big brother, who had always been at her side. Her rock, her confidante, her best friend. He was a good man, not evil. He could never be evil.

She reached out a hand, feeling the air. The denseness was still there, but she sensed no resistance against her skin. Kari hadn't even cast a protective circle around himself. That was a novice mistake; one of the first lessons drilled into young mages.

She swallowed, feeling as though a heavy stone had dropped through her entire body. It wasn't a mistake. Kari had deliberately not laid down a circle.

The unease swelled into a crescendo. She had to stop this, now.

She untied her drum and held it before her, ready to begin her own rhythm. The hammer cast a shadow over the picture of the Great Bear Spirit. She eyed it, trying to draw reassurance from the alder painting.

She forced herself to breathe slowly, trying to ignore the disgusting air as it filled her lungs. She could do this. She was Kari's sister, his equal, a mage just as powerful as him. She might not be able to snap him out of whatever horrid trance he had sung himself into, but she could rise alongside him and guide him back, before he had a chance to harm his souls. Once he was lucid, she could demand an explanation.

Then Kari suddenly drew a knife from his belt and slashed his throat.

Lilja screamed. She dropped her drum and ran towards him, not caring about pulling him out of the trance anymore.

With a roar of pain, Kari doubled over, clutching at his chest. He fell to his knees.

Lilja snatched his shoulders and jerked him around to face her. She screamed again.

His eyes were as hollow as a dead tree; his skin drained and paler than the snow. The gash in his throat was deep enough to see the ridges of his windpipe. His beautiful coat of white reindeer fur – the symbol of the mage – was lost in a waterfall of scarlet.

Lilja clamped a hand over the wound in a desperate attempt to stem the flow. Warm blood seeped through her mitten. She wrenched the knife from his grasp with her other hand, in case he tried to hurt himself again. Or her.

No... Kari would never hurt her...

Kari cried out again. Tears streamed down his cheeks, cutting channels through the blood where it had splashed on his face. But with every shriek, his voice became less garbled, as though his vocal cords were somehow unharmed. Then, any semblance of pain left him, and he shoved Lilja away.

She stared at him in horror. For a moment, she wondered if it was even her brother in front of her.

Something small rose out of the gash. It was thinner than a bubble, but sparkled like a star.

Lilja cried out. It was his life-soul. He had ripped it out of himself.

She tried to catch it, but it evaded her hands and flew into the effigy. Kari grinned at her. It was so unlike his usual smile; it turned her stomach. She could sense the darkness he had been drumming up: so thick in the air, she might have been able to cut it with the knife she held. The smell was awful; it tasted like something unearthly and ancient, something beyond even the most experienced mage.

"What have you done?" she shrieked, unable to think of anything else to say.

Kari smiled again, then looked at the effigy. Lilja watched the blood wash through the snow as though it were alive. It surrounded the base of the figure, and Kari lifted a hand.

A rasping snarl came from within the effigy. Then it blew apart, sending clumps of reddened snow in all directions.

A creature unfolded itself from the carnage. Pale skin was shredded about its branch-like bones. An empty mouth opened onto a black throat; within its flat face, two eyes burned like fire. Its fingers were long and tapered into lethal points: so sharp, Lilja couldn't even see their edges. It stank of desolation and death; the clear air around it practically darkened like muddied water.

Terror lent Lilja new strength. She grabbed Kari's wrist and brandished the knife at the creature.

"Run!" she yelled.

Kari pulled himself free.

"There's no need," he insisted. "I'm fine... it worked! I can't believe it!"

Lilja's blood turned to ice. Despite his horrendous appearance, the ragged gash in his throat, what she had seen him doing... those three words unnerved her most of all. There was no pain in his tone. His voice was unchanged – it was exactly the same one she had grown up with, travelled with, laughed with the night before.

She backed away in fright. This was not her brother.

"Have you lost your mind?" she shouted at him. "You have turned against the Spirits! They will punish you for this!"

Kari shook his head earnestly. "Lilja, this is a masterpiece. It's amazing! Look at it!"

Anger filled her.

"It's a demon, Kari! You have made a demon! You have betrayed everything!"

"No, I haven't! This is for mercy!"

He sank down on one knee again, one hand over his heart. Lilja went to help him, but held herself back.

"It hurts..." he rasped. "By the Spirits, it's so strange!"

Lilja immediately understood why he was holding his chest and not his ragged throat. The heart was where a mage's *taika* grew; where the two souls resided, giving a person life. The bodily wound was nothing compared to the one he had just inflicted where no eye could see.

She glanced to where she had dropped her drum. It was a few feet away – if she was quick enough, she could reach it; use it to bind the horrid creature before it managed to hurt either of them.

But as she looked into Kari's eyes, the awful truth finally hit her with the force of an avalanche. He had deliberately chosen to use power how no respectful mage would. All his honour was gone. He had pulled away one of his souls and put it into the demon.

It wouldn't hurt him. It was *a part* of him.

Her vision blurred with furious tears.

"Why?" she cried. "You're a good man!"

"I still am a good man, Lilja," said Kari as blood trickled down his front. He staggered upright and faced her, one hand still over his heart. "You have to understand. This was the only way."

"For what?"

"I need to take back that boy. You remember him? Of course you do. I've been watching him in trance; he is of age now. Imagine the power he holds! Power he has no idea how to harness, too much for a child like him to ever realise. It's better with me... with *us*, Lilja."

He held her hand, the way he always had to comfort her.

"Nothing's changed. It will still just be you and me. I didn't mention this to you earlier because I knew you'd try to stop me. This creature only has half of my blood and half of my souls, true, but I will have it serve you too! Then we can take back the boy, put that power to good use. Think of all the people we'd be able to help! We would be like the Sun upon the earth!"

Lilja stared between him and the demon. Both were leering at her expectantly, each of them with the same dreadful death behind their eyes.

This was not a request. There was one answer, and she knew she could not give it.

"Have you no shame?" she breathed. "You would lay a hand on that boy with this... this monster? We are bound to serve the Spirits! We do not rule and we do not kill! What's happened to you?"

"Lilja," Kari said, "please. I don't want to force you."

Tears rolled down her cheeks and she pulled away.

"No!"

Kari's expression darkened. Lilja set her eyes on her drum and bolted towards it.

Kari raised a hand at her. The demon screeched and loped forwards, snatching Lilja's ankles. She fell onto her front, barely able to reach her hammer. The creature flipped her over and snarled, inches from her face.

Then it bared its ragged claws, sliced down, and blood sprayed into the air.

Lilja clutched her throat. Even though her mitten, she could feel the torn edges of her skin. It had somehow missed her windpipe and blood vessels, but her energy evaporated in an instant.

Kari was going to make this thing kill her. Or worse.

Or worse... *No.* She could not let that happen, never.

Then she remembered the knife in her hand.

She swept it up and caught the demon across the face. It recoiled with a howl; behind it, Kari did the same, grabbing at his cheek.

Gritting her teeth against the pain, Lilja shoved the demon as hard as she could. It didn't dislodge it from her, but it was enough.

She dropped the blade and reached behind her, finding her drum. Blood smeared over the painted skin.

She brought it to her chest, holding the Great Bear Spirit in her mind, summoning all her power. And then, with a cry, she slammed down the hammer.

# Chapter One

*One month later*

In the south of the Northlands, the village of Akerfjorden was abuzz with activity and movement. Conversations and laughter rose on the wind. The cluster of shelters lay nestled between two great cliffs at the water's edge, and people ran between them like ants. It was almost time for the gathering on the fjord's shore, to bid farewell to the Sun Spirit as she dived below the horizon one last time.

Even though the walls of the mage's hut were thin, made only from branches and compacted earth, the noise seemed a thousand miles away. Tuomas could barely make out individual words or recognise his neighbours' voices. The scent of the herbs was muddling his mind. They hung in bundles from every beam; it felt like an age ago when he had scoured the hills with Henrik, collecting them before the first snows fell. Nettle, angelica, roseroot, sweetgrass… their names bled together as much as their aromas.

A thud sounded on the door, followed by mischievous sniggering.

On the opposite side of the fire, Henrik cleared his throat loudly.

"I'll have you quiet, Mihka!" he barked.

There was another bout of laughter, but the sound of footsteps trudging through the snow confirmed there would be no more knocking.

Tuomas couldn't hold back a smirk. Henrik noticed and glared at him.

"Other things on your mind?" he asked.

Tuomas quickly relaxed his face and picked at the fur on his trousers.

"Sorry."

Henrik regarded him with watery grey eyes, the skin around them lined with age. He might be old, but his voice was deep and commanding. And he was a mage. Nobody in their right mind would dare disrespect a mage.

"Would you rather be out there, messing around with him?"

"No. I'd rather be in here," Tuomas sighed.

"Are you sure? Your enthusiasm leaves something to be desired."

Tuomas bit his tongue. "It's just been a long day."

He couldn't help but note the irony of that. This was arguably the shortest day the Northlands would see for another three months.

"Hm." Henrik threw another log on the hearth and sparks spat into the heady air. "And your concentration is fading like the Sun. Well, she is not set yet, and neither are you. So, what was I saying?"

Tuomas tried his best to look invested.

"You were talking about the fire. The drum needs to be held over the fire before it's used. It tightens the skin, and gets it ready to do its work."

"And what is the name of that work? The name of a mage's magic?"

"*Taika.*"

"So you were paying attention." Henrik pursed his lips. "I hope you'll someday listen to the Spirits more closely than you listen to me."

"I do listen!" Tuomas protested.

"If you want to be a mage, you need to do more than stumble your way forward," said Henrik firmly. "One foot in this World, one foot in the others. Strong, wise. Not frivolous, like our dear Mihka out there."

"It would be easier for me to learn if I had my own drum," snapped Tuomas.

"When you were learning to lasso a reindeer, did you do it on a live animal, bucking and running around? No. You used an antler stuck in the ground first," said Henrik. "You can't just jump into this. You need to understand the craft. And you will have a drum when you're ready to use one."

Tuomas rubbed his forehead with one hand.

"Alright, point taken. But I turned fifteen five months ago and we've been doing this ever since. Don't you think I'm understanding?"

"On the contrary, I think you understand a lot more than even you realise," Henrik replied. "But it all takes time. Your *taika* is strong, boy. That's why I insisted you study with me. But it's not just about learning how to use it. You must learn to control it, too."

Tuomas hesitated, to choose his words carefully.

"How am I supposed to do either of those things without the other? When you don't let me practise?"

"Theory before practise. You think magecraft is easy? That you can just pick up a drum and do what you want? Nothing is that simple. So the least we can do with you is *start* simple. You're still young, you think everything can happen overnight. The tallest mountain didn't rise out of the earth overnight."

Tuomas struggled to not roll his eyes. He might be young, but he was still old enough to be a man. And old enough to know that if Henrik had his way, he would spend the next fifteen years sitting here, always listening, never doing.

"Then what about my test?" he ventured. "You've said that every mage must pass a test before they can awaken to their power."

"And you will, in time," said Henrik. He leaned forward so the fire lit his face from below. It made all the lines on his skin stand out like cracks in a dry riverbed. "It might be a sickness you must fight off. Or some life-changing event. Either way, it will not be pleasant. Would you wish that on yourself for the sake of speed? Just to hold a drum?"

He scoffed, then got to his feet, shuffled past Tuomas to the door of the hut and scooped up a handful of snow. He dropped it into the pot over the hearth so it could melt, and threw in some ground herbs to make tea.

"Go on, then," he said. "I can tell you don't want to be here any longer. You're lucky I didn't ask you to assist me at the gathering tonight."

A twinge of guilt pulled at Tuomas's gut, but he decided against apologising again. Something told him it would just put Henrik in a foul mood, and this was supposed to be a night of reverence and celebration. He didn't want anything souring that.

So instead, he bowed his head in respect, bid goodbye, and crawled outside.

He kicked the door closed and pulled on his mittens and hat. It wasn't even true evening yet – only afternoon – but the shadows were long and the light dimmed. The cool air hit him like a wall after the closed space of the hut. Nearby, several other huts squatted close to the ground, the snow between them compacted by the passing of feet. Thin lines of smoke trailed from the holes set into their tops, curling like living things before disappearing into the dusk sky. The air was filled with the aromas of burning logs, simmering stew and baking flatbreads. It made Tuomas's mouth water. All the food would be brought out for the gathering, and the entire village would have a feast together.

A crowd of people were already heading down to the shore, carrying bowls of sautéed reindeer meat and rich berry jams. Over their heads, Tuomas could see the dark surface of the Mustafjord: the great body of water which had carved its way between headlands and through earth centuries ago.

Right here, by its shore, the ancestors had built Akerfjorden; and through the years, new huts had come and gone, as had people. This was only the turn of the latest generation to reside here. A few months ago, they had settled for the winter, the reindeer running wild in the safety of the forest; and would stay here until spring came, when they could follow the animals on their migration to the coast.

It was how it had always been, and how it would continue, long after the youngest baby had grown old and turned to dust in the ground.

Two hands landed on Tuomas's shoulders and gave him a shove. He lost his footing and tumbled into a snowbank.

Mihka's laugh filled his ears.

"It's about time! I was wondering if I'd have to come back next week!"

Tuomas jumped to his feet, brushing snow off his coat.

"You idiot. I've just had an extra lecture thanks to you."

"Well, you can't complain. You're the one who wanted to be a mage," Mihka replied, his eyes shining impishly. "How else was I supposed to remind the old man what time it was?"

"Shush!" Tuomas hissed. "He might be old but he's not deaf!"

"He can't hear me," Mihka whispered back, but Tuomas was still relieved when he didn't press further.

Every child had heard the story of a man in Poro village, generations ago, who had dared to steal a carved antler knife from the resident mage. When he'd tried to escape, a single drumbeat sounded. His feet held fast to the earth and he'd been stuck until morning, when the mage approached and ordered him to admit his crime. The thief had duly returned the knife, along with offering three of his own reindeer in penance, and only then had the mage released him.

They were the first point of call if anything went wrong: curing sickness, managing rites of passage... but they were also the closest any living thing could get to the Spirits. To commune with the beings in the other Worlds was a skill awarded to few, even among those like Tuomas who actively wanted it. Dangerous, thrilling, affirming... so different to the simple monotony of the herding life.

"Come on," Mihka said. "Let's go and get the best spot."

Tuomas swept the last of the snow off his coat in mid-step. Every year, Mihka was determined to have the best view of the gathering, and always insisted Tuomas join him there. Mihka was the son of Sisu, one of the village leaders, so everyone made sure to leave it free for him.

As they passed Tuomas's hut, his brother Paavo appeared, his arms laden with bowls of reindeer stew. Paavo was a brilliant cook and had spent the entire morning preparing his part of the feast. At twenty-five, he was ten years older than Tuomas, and had raised him alone practically since he was born.

"Good timing," Tuomas remarked.

"More than I can say for Henrik," Mihka said. Tuomas elbowed him to make him shut up.

Paavo shook his head in amusement. "I just heard you going past, big feet. You walk heavier than an angry moose!"

Tuomas narrowed his eyes and jabbed a finger at Mihka. "Hey, I've had enough of *him* moaning at me without you starting as well."

"And Henrik," Mihka whispered, then jumped aside with a chuckle before Tuomas could elbow him again.

"Seriously, shut up," Tuomas laughed. "One of these days, he's going to hear you and give you a beating!"

"No, he won't," replied Mihka with a cocky smile.

Tuomas shook his head. "Then the Spirits will. Actually, let's set you a challenge. See if you can make it through the entire Long Dark without having something to say about the Spirit of the Lights."

It was a simple jest, and Mihka laughed as though it was, but Tuomas kept a hint of warning in his tone.

Of all the hundreds of Spirits to aggravate, the aurora was the riskiest. Everyone knew that. The old fireside tales claimed that she was a force to be reckoned with if she was insulted. Apparently, she had once ripped the life-soul out of the founder of the village. Nobody could say why, but the story had reverberated through the generations, like the memory of thunder long after the storm was passed.

Nevertheless, Mihka chuckled again, his eyes shining mischievously.

"So long as she gives us a good display when she comes out."

"That's enough, you two," Paavo said, but there was still an amused glint playing in his eyes. "Now, can somebody give me a hand with these bowls, please?"

The three of them descended the slope which separated the village from the water, Tuomas and Paavo going carefully so as to not spill any of the food down their coats. Washing stains out of them would not be welcomed now the winter was here, and the fjord was frozen over. From this moment on, getting water without having to melt it from snow was difficult.

Most of the others from the village were already there, settling on the snowy bank in the places they always had. A fire had been lit and its glowing tongues flickered against the red sky. The warmth of hearty chatter entwined with the warmth of the flames.

There were only a few families in Akerfjorden, but each one was large, bound together as kin into their community. Everyone exchanged smiles and sincere handshakes as they gathered; children ran among the adults and playfully poked each other with sticks.

In Akerfjorden, as in the other villages which dotted the Northlands, everybody knew everybody and, even if families were not connected in some way, all cared for each other. It was this closeness which had helped them survive since the beginning, when the World Between was made.

Tuomas and Paavo placed the bowls by the fire with the rest of the food, then joined Mihka on a small mound of earth close to the water. Mihka had removed his hat and ruffled the unruly black hair beneath.

They had barely sat down before everyone fell silent. Henrik emerged from his hut and walked towards the fjord. He had daubed ash on his face: long finger-strokes dragged across his wrinkled cheeks. It was a typical ceremonial action, but

Tuomas couldn't help but notice how Henrik's eyes seemed to be glowing from within the dark grey smears. He had put on his trousers of white reindeer fur, and he held his drum in one hand, the antler hammer in the other.

As Henrik passed, Tuomas kept his gaze down, only glancing at him from under his lashes. The mage didn't pay him any attention. He simply strode to the very edge of the fjord, where the iced water met the grey pebbles underfoot. The voice of the waves had long been still. It was probably thick enough to walk on now; the ice fishing could start soon.

All eyes turned to the west. The Sun Spirit bled out across the horizon in a red gash. The Golden One was so far away now, to leave them under the pockmarked face of her Moon sister. She would take her warm glow out of their reach, and all they could do now was bid her farewell, and wait.

Henrik lifted his hammer and began to beat the drum. It was slow at first, but became faster and faster. A chant welled from his chest and spread through the air: a deep unbroken ululation which spoke of complete reverence for the Sun Spirit. He was alone at first, but then others joined in the song, as the light slipped ever further into the fjord. Tuomas started to sing too, keeping his eyes on the sky.

The last spark of summer blinked out, and the stars withdrew from their slumber. Yet the villagers still stood there, still following the beat of Henrik's drum. Tuomas's voice was swallowed into those of all the others. He let himself be lost in the moment, feeling the power to spread through him.

One day, he would do this. He would stand where Henrik did, a drum in his hands, communing with the Spirits.

When he finally opened his eyes, the night had truly come. He always lost track of time on occasions like this. It was so easy to be swept up, to let everything but the song lose its meaning.

When Henrik struck the final beat, the solemnness of the gathering quickly transformed into merriment. Everyone headed to the bonfire, stoking it until the flames grew higher than the tallest man. Sparks blazed into the night like shooting stars. Bowls were heaped with food, laughter echoed around the headlands, hands were joined and everyone danced in a massive circle.

The hours bled into each other. Tuomas let them, allowing himself to get lost in the celebrations. Winter would be hard, as always, and as the Sun Spirit entered the cold with a final blaze of glory, so too would they.

He soon lost count of how many times he spun around the fire pit. The flames filled his vision: ever-shifting patterns of red and yellow; like a snowflake, no two were the same. Dizziness threatened and he pulled his hand out of Mihka's. Mihka didn't even notice; he carried on dancing with endless energy, his cheeks red from the heat.

Tuomas made his way to the edge of the throng. He took off his hat and wiped sweat from his forehead. Paavo was standing to the side with a bowl of stew in his hand.

Tuomas took a second helping of his own, using the blade of a small knife to spoon the chunks of shredded reindeer meat into his mouth. It was lean and a little salty, with the crisp taste of the forest mixed in: traces of the lichen and berries foraged by the animal in the autumn.

He gazed at the sky, taking a deep lungful of the crisp night air. A sudden flicker appeared in the corner of his eye. He blinked hard – the fire must have seared itself onto his vision.

But it didn't go away. And it wasn't yellow like the fire. It was green.

He froze. A faint glow was appearing against the darkness.

His heart skipped a beat and he nudged Paavo's arm. His brother looked at him in confusion, but when he followed Tuomas's gaze, his mouth fell open.

"The Lights!" he muttered.

The green flame swept over the fjord. Tuomas had seen the aurora more times than he could count, but this was special. It was the first time the Spirit of the Lights had danced this winter.

Others had noticed by now and silence fell over the crowd. The only sound was the crackling of the fire as a log tumbled into the embers.

The Lights were growing stronger by the moment, flickering across the sky in eerie waves of blue and green. The stars peeked through the swaying curtains, themselves almost lost against the spectacle.

Tuomas recalled the old legend of a white fox sweeping up the snow with her tail as she ran. The snow burned different colours as it skimmed the World Above, letting the ancestors dance and look down on their living families. It made the aurora, the ever-changing fox fires.

That was the story the first men of Akerfjorden had told to explain what the Spirit of the Lights looked like, but nobody knew how true it was. Tuomas supposed it was a fitting description though. All Spirits demanded respect, but this one was as beautiful and cold as the snow she flung up with her tail, and she knew it.

Tuomas bowed his head. There was a shuffling of clothing as everyone else did the same. On this night, on her first appearance, nobody was about to take any chances.

Mihka ambled over. A scowl was forming on his face

"Of course she had to come out in the middle of the party. They're not even that impressive," he grumbled, just loud enough for Tuomas to hear.

"Shut up, you idiot," Tuomas hissed back.

"I'm serious. She couldn't let the Sun Spirit have all the glory?"

"Will you be quiet?"

Sisu heard the whispers. He strode over and snatched his son's elbow.

"Mihka. This isn't the time."

Mihka threw a disappointed snarl towards the aurora. A restless flash was growing in his eyes, fed by merriment cut short and the attention he loved, unable to be held back now.

"Tell her that. She's got all winter to dance. This is supposed to be for the Sun Spirit."

Sisu brought his face close.

"That's enough! Show some respect!"

"She can't hear me," Mihka insisted under his breath. "And what does she care? What's she going to do, strike me down?"

Tuomas wasn't sure whether he meant it or whether his cockiness had gotten the better of him. Mihka turned his eyes on the Spirit challengingly.

"Go on," he muttered. "I dare you."

The sky exploded.

A peculiar roaring sound filled the air and the Lights shot towards them like an arrow. Women shrieked and leapt aside, shielding their children's eyes. A bolt of turquoise rushed in Tuomas's direction, then a shockwave as strong as a blizzard wind ploughed into him.

He landed on his back, upending his bowl and spilling its contents everywhere. Paavo and Sisu slammed down next to him.

He looked around for Mihka, and a horrified cry caught in his throat.

A few others had fallen over, but in the middle of the commotion, Mihka was still standing – and the Lights had struck him.

The serene green glow was now tinged with a vicious red, and the Spirit was weaving them around Mihka – Tuomas couldn't see her, but he knew she was there; felt her in his bones like the thunder of an approaching avalanche.

"Mihka!" Sisu yelled, barrelling towards his son. But as soon as he came within touching distance of the Lights, he was thrown away like a ragdoll.

Maiken, one of the other leaders, ran over, her hands outstretched towards Mihka. She leapt towards him, only to bounce off the aurora and land in a heap beside Sisu. She tried again, followed by other villagers, but no matter how hard anyone pushed, they couldn't penetrate the Lights. Even Henrik, beating his drum frantically, barely managed to get closer.

The Spirit was too strong. She surrounded Mihka with her fire, restraining him where he stood, jolting him back and forth so fast it seemed his neck would break. He wasn't even screaming. It was so bright, Tuomas could barely see him.

Was he dead?

Tuomas didn't waste time thinking. He leapt to his feet, ran at Mihka, and shoved him hard.

Amazingly, the Lights lost their grip and the two of them tumbled into the snow. Tuomas covered Mihka with his body, screwed his eyes closed, not daring to look.

He felt the aurora behind them; pictured the furious Spirit driving it. The Lights were so close, he saw green and red through his eyelids.

Her power and might flowed through him, cold, as though he'd fallen into a freezing lake. It was something not of this World; too icy to be anything but a Spirit.

He gritted his teeth, waiting for her to strike him too.

But nothing happened. There was a flash, and as quickly as the Lights had come down, they were gone.

Tuomas inched his eyes open, trembling with fright. The sky was empty, and Mihka stared silently up at him, barely breathing, his sooty hair now white.

# Chapter Two

Everyone hurried back to the village, keeping their eyes fixed on the ground in case the Spirit of the Lights was still watching. If she had struck Mihka – the son of one of the leaders – then who might she come after next?

Tuomas clung tightly to Paavo. His legs moved as though separate from his body, only going through the motions of walking. His mind blazed.

What had just happened? What was wrong with Mihka? He could see his friend up ahead, bundled in his father's arms, followed closely by Henrik.

What had the Spirit of the Lights done to him?

The bell of the lead reindeer sounded from somewhere in the forest, along with the low faraway thunder of hundreds of hooves moving over snow. The herd was spooked. They knew something had happened.

Henrik pointed at his hut, and Mihka was quickly taken inside. Tuomas strained to see, but Paavo pushed him through the door of their own shelter. Paavo had left the fire piled high while they were out, so it still burned healthily and the interior was deliciously warm and light.

But the comfort was lost on Tuomas. He still felt the ghostly chill of the aurora at his back.

"Are you alright? Are you hurt?" Paavo asked, checking Tuomas's face.

"I'm fine," Tuomas assured him. "You're not. You're bleeding."

He touched Paavo's temple and his fingers came away red. Paavo winced at the touch.

"I must have landed on a rock. I'll be fine, it's not deep," he said as he examined it himself.

Tuomas nodded in relief, but then it gave way to frustration. He kicked at one of the stones surrounding the hearth.

"Idiot! What was he thinking?"

"Why? What did he do?"

"He insulted them – the Lights! That's why she came down! Why she only went for him!"

Paavo frowned. "Wait… how did you do that? Push him away? No-one else could break through."

Tuomas's throat tightened. "I don't know..."

The door swung open and a face poked through the frame. It was Aslak: one of the older herders.

"Are either of you hurt?" he asked.

"We're fine," Paavo replied, wiping the blood off his cheek. "What's the matter?"

Aslak propped the door open with his shoulder.

"Can you come with me to check on the herd? If they're startled, we'll need a few men to calm them down. Maiken and Anssi are heading up there now."

Paavo nodded and grabbed a hat, pulling it on in mid-step. Halfway out the door, he glanced back at Tuomas.

"Will you be alright here?" he asked.

"Yes, go on," Tuomas insisted.

Paavo held his eyes for a moment. "Stay inside."

With that, he disappeared, kicking the door shut behind him.

Tuomas glanced about in agitation, digging his fingers into the thick fur of his sleeping sack.

*Stay inside?* It was the sensible thing to do, but was Paavo honestly serious? Stay inside, when he had no idea what was happening with Mihka?

He managed to sit for a while, until silence fell. Everyone must have hurried back to their huts. He crawled to the door and opened it a crack to check.

There was nobody in sight. He threw a glance at the sky. A thousand stars blinked back at him, but no Lights. He was safe.

Seizing his chance, he slipped out and crept towards Henrik's. The powdery snow muffled his footsteps a little, but he was still careful, placing his feet softly until he arrived at the side of the hut. He pressed himself against its turfed wall.

Henrik was chanting softly, accompanied by slow, harsh beats of his drum. The sound he made was unlike any Tuomas had heard: mournful, beseeching – desperate, even. It echoed all the uncertainty of the night.

After a while, the chant stopped. Tuomas knew Henrik would be coming out of the trance he'd sung himself into. He waited, listening hard.

Then a new voice spoke: Sisu.

"Can't you wake him?"

"I'm afraid not." There was a dull thump as Henrik put down the drum. "It is as I suspected. His body-soul is intact, but his life-soul has been taken."

"Taken..." Sisu repeated. "How? By one of the ancestors?"

There was a hint of hope in that last question, but even from outside, Tuomas knew Henrik would be shaking his head. Only one kind of being had the power to take a soul.

"The Spirit of the Lights. Your boy has offended her. She's stripped the life-soul away as punishment."

A horrible silence descended. Tuomas's heart pounded behind his ribs. Whether it was a human or an animal, nothing could survive without both of its souls, not properly. When the mages entered trances to commune with the Spirits, the life-soul travelled away from their body, letting them draw closer to the one they needed to speak to – but it always returned; they always woke up. To have it *stripped away*...

"But... he was only playing!" Sisu insisted, his words trembling. "He didn't mean it... he was just being mischievous! You know that, surely!"

"Yes, *I* know what Mihka is like," assured Henrik, "but Spirits won't think that way. You see, they are pure energy, Sisu; neither completely good nor bad, just as nature is neither. They don't have physical bodies like us; they are formless, unbound. Human emotions are beyond them. Aside from pride, perhaps."

"What are you saying?"

"She has been insulted, and has responded in kind. Or, what she sees as in kind. This attack wasn't pre-meditated, it was purely on impulse."

"So what do we do?" asked Sisu.

"She must be appeased."

"Well, you're the mage. Can you do anything?"

"She won't have it from me. She is angry, Sisu – she's one Spirit I have rarely spoken with, and she almost threw me away the moment I approached."

"But we need to get him back... he *must* wake up! I know I've spoiled him, but he's the only family I have left."

"I know."

For a moment, Tuomas forgot to breathe. This couldn't be happening.

Then Sisu spoke again. Tuomas had to strain to hear him; he was so quiet.

"The wandering mages. Do you remember them? That brother and sister?"

"Of course I remember them. How could I forget?"

"We could seek them out. Their *taika* is so strong… especially the woman. We all know that from the last time they were here. If you can't reach the Spirit, they must be able to."

"I agree, they probably could," said Henrik tightly, "but it's been fifteen years since they were here. I haven't even seen them on the migration routes since then."

"I know they're solitary, but they can't be impossible to find."

"Be careful, Sisu. They are powerful mages – *too* powerful, in my opinion."

"We need all the power we can find if we want any hope of getting Mihka back," said Sisu, firmer now. "I don't care what they ask for – they can have all my belongings and reindeer if they want. But I am not about to let him stay like this forever!"

Henrik let out a sigh. "Alright. But on one condition."

"What? I should go looking for them?"

"No. Tuomas should. You know my reasons."

Tuomas drew back from the hut in alarm. They wanted *him* to go? Why?

He held his breath, waiting for more, but all that came was Sisu's conceding sigh.

"Very well."

Before Tuomas could stop himself, he hurried to the door and pulled it open. Henrik and Sisu looked up in surprise.

"How long have you been there?" Henrik asked tersely.

"Long enough," said Tuomas. "I'm sorry, I was so worried. And then I heard you in a trance and knew not to disturb –"

"Never mind that, come in here," said Sisu.

Tuomas quickly obeyed, shutting the door behind him. His eyes immediately found Mihka. He was lying in front of Henrik, covered up to his neck with a blanket. The men had managed to close his eyes, but his hair was even more jarring in the firelight flickering from the hearth. It was as white as snow, paler than hair Tuomas had seen on the oldest man.

The sight chilled him as though the aurora was behind him again. For all of Mihka's troublemaking, he was still his best friend. He didn't deserve a fate like this.

He faced Sisu, hoping he looked more confident than he felt. Sisu stared at him, his dark eyes appearing even darker beneath his thick black hair. His tunic was adorned with pieces of antler jewellery and bone beads: the sign of a village leader.

"I'm sorry I listened in," Tuomas said.

Sisu grunted, not impressed with his eavesdropping, but then his face softened as he glanced back at Mihka.

"Thank you for getting him away from it," he said. "But now we need your help again."

"What must I do?" asked Tuomas.

Henrik was still glaring at him disapprovingly. "It's simple enough. You were the one who protected Mihka from the Lights. You saved him. The Spirit stopped her attack because of you. So you are the one best suited to find how to appease her."

Tuomas glanced between him and Sisu. "Is that your reason?"

Henrik's eyes became harder than stone.

"Mind your tongue. You have a hand in this, in some form, so you have a hand in undoing it. Do I make myself clear?"

Tuomas nodded. Now wasn't the time for prying. There were more pressing matters to deal with.

"Mihka means a lot to me. I'm the only friend he's got." he said. "I need to look for two mages?"

Sisu nodded.

"They should be in their late twenties by now – the last time they were here, they were younger than you. They are called Kari and Lilja."

"Which is their village?"

"They don't have one. At least, not anymore. They left years ago and now they wander wherever they want."

Tuomas threw up his hands in exasperation. "Then how am I supposed to find them?"

"Good question," Henrik muttered, with a pointed glance at Sisu. "Be wary of them, boy. They're a strange couple."

Then he mellowed and checked Mihka's temperature with the back of his hand.

"Can you be ready to leave tomorrow?"

Tuomas nodded. "I'll find them. I won't fail you."

Henrik lifted his hand from Mihka's forehead.

"I'm not the one to fail," he said. "But, in any case, your wish is materialising: an awful event has befallen us and it is your responsibility to come through it. So, take a good look at your friend. As of this moment, consider him your mage test. You have a terrible Spirit to appease before this is over."

The words fell upon Tuomas like stone, and the gravity of the situation truly dawned on him. But as he gazed down at

Mihka – seeming so much like a corpse – determination began to flow through his veins.

He would do it, and by the time he was home, Mihka would be awake, and he himself would be a mage at last.

# Chapter Three

The next morning, Tuomas woke early, alert as soon as he opened his eyes. The fire in the hearth had burned low, leaving the hut gloomy, but he could still tell that Paavo's sleeping sack was empty. That was nothing out of the ordinary – his brother was an early riser.

He pulled on his sealskin shoes and fur coat, lifted a rope off the central beam, and slipped outside. It was still dark, but that was to be expected. The brightest it would get would be a pale bluish twilight around midday. Luckily, the Moon Spirit was waxing overhead, giving just enough of a glow for him to see by.

Drawing his neckline tight against the cold, he hurried off into the forest. The trees loomed straight and tall, black save for one side, which were dusted by snow that had blown in on a northern gale several days ago. It made for a land of stark contrast: no grey anywhere; edges either softened with snow or harsh with ice. The silence was absolute. There wasn't a single breath of wind to stir the spruce branches, nor any cries from animals to herald a new day. In all appearances, time had frozen.

But not for Tuomas. Urgency drove him on, through ankle-deep snow, until he found the reindeer herd. Even if they hadn't been wearing bells around their necks, the air was slowly filled with the clicking sound of tendons sliding over knees. It was said to be a way for the animals to find each other if they were ever separated in a blizzard. But it helped the herders to find them just as much.

A large group of reindeer stood together for warmth, using their wide hooves to dig into the snow in search of lichen. Some had already found patches and were nibbling away contentedly.

Tuomas looked over them, searching for one of his. Although the herd as a whole belonged to Akerfjorden, each reindeer was owned by a single individual. Every herder had their own unique mark, which was cut into the animals' ears while they were still calves. It was as distinctive as a fingerprint, and Tuomas, like everyone else, could recognise his instantly.

He looped the rope into a lasso. After circling them a few times, he spotted what he was after. Near the edge of the group was a strong young bull with pale grey fur, which he'd been training to take a sleigh for the previous few years. Perfect.

He approached slowly, never taking his eyes off the reindeer. Then he raised the rope and threw it.

The noose landed around the bull's neck. It kicked out in fright and the other deer bolted a few feet away.

Tuomas reeled himself closer to the bull, letting it become used to his presence. It stared at him with huge black eyes, snorting indignantly. When it realised it couldn't escape, it calmed down, and he began to lead it back along the trail of footprints he had left.

When he reached the edge of the forest, he paused for a moment and looked down upon Akerfjorden. It always seemed smaller from up here, dwarfed by the high cliffs of the Mustafjord.

The giant stone walls reared on either side, glazed with ice. At the back, where he stood now, the ground rolled upwards in a soft incline, bound in place by trees older than the oldest villager. The huts squatted in their little clusters, dusted white with frost and snow; on the outskirts, storage houses stood on thick stilts to keep their precious bounty of food and tools off the ground. Fire pits sat here and there; wooden frames hung by them, draped with strips of fish and reindeer meat left to dry in the heat. It was a perfect location for a winter camp: protected from the wind, close to water, with a stock of wood to last the entire Long Dark.

Tuomas made his way down, leading the bull in his wake. The village was awake now, many of his neighbours already outside. Some were going about the morning chores: carrying logs from the woodstores or fetching clean virgin snow to melt into water. But most were waiting for him.

Their faces were tight with apprehension – no doubt, they were remembering the previous evening, when he had pulled Mihka away from the Lights. The only one who had managed to free him.

And now it was up to him, setting out alone, to bring the life-soul back.

He wasn't surprised that news had spread so quickly about Mihka's condition. In such a small community as this, everyone knew everybody else's business. Just one glance at his neighbours told Tuomas they were aware of what was going on.

A knot of nerves began to grow in his belly, but he forced himself to ignore it. There would be time to dwell on his task later. Now, he needed to be strong.

A figure approached him. In the dim glow of a nearby fire, Tuomas recognised it as Aslak: the herder who had fetched Paavo the night before. He was hauling a sleigh behind him, the seat already covered with a warm reindeer pelt.

Tuomas smiled gratefully. It was his and Paavo's sleigh, which had borne them both across the Northlands on every migration he could remember. Aslak must have dragged it out from behind their hut while he had gone into the forest.

"Give me a hand with this," Aslak said.

Tuomas led his reindeer into position, then he and Aslak hitched the long birch poles at the front of the sleigh to a harness around the animal's chest. They had no sooner finished when the other villagers came forward and began depositing goods into the back. There were reindeer skins, new fish hooks, food parcels, arrows, a pair of skis, and the poles and tarp for building a tent.

Tuomas thanked them all graciously, and they answered with smiles and handshakes. Then the crowd parted and revealed the three Akerfjorden leaders: Anssi, his cousin Maiken, and Sisu. Beside them was Henrik, dressed from head to toe in his white mage furs. He was clutching a bundle under one arm.

Tuomas lowered his head respectfully as he walked closer.

"You can do this, boy," Henrik said, his usually deep voice now soft and reassuring. "You have the makings of a great mage in you. Don't be afraid to ask the Spirits for help. They will guide you."

Tuomas bit his lip. He wasn't sure how open the Spirits would be to him after knowing one of their own had been insulted.

Henrik seemed to read his mind.

"Show them respect and they will respond in kind," he whispered. "You know yourself; few Spirits are as feared as the one we saw yesterday."

"That doesn't help much," Tuomas admitted.

Henrik grimaced. "I know. I won't tell you to not be afraid. But you know this land – it is your home, your heart."

He pushed the bundle into Tuomas's arms. "Here. You haven't made your own yet, and you will need one."

Tuomas frowned. He untied the cord at the top and let the soft skin parcel fall away. A gasp caught in his throat.

It was Henrik's drum.

"No, this belongs with you," he said, going to give it back, but Henrik stood firm.

"I'll keep myself busy watching over Mihka and make another."

"But what about your *taika*?"

"Still not listening, I see. It will cross over to a new one. Drums can be passed on, just not destroyed. Remember that."

"But it's personal. Sacred to a mage!"

"Yes, a mage. As you will hopefully be before this is over. And you will need it. It's vital that you channel your power and stay in control of it – this is the best way to do that. Just always remember to cast a protective circle around yourself before you start to work; it will keep you from harm and trickery. I hope that if there's only one of my lessons you listened to, it was that one!"

Henrik kept his hands behind his back so Tuomas couldn't force the drum back into them.

Disbelief stabbed at him. Hadn't it been only yesterday that they had argued about him not having his own? And now Henrik was handing over the one he'd carried since his own youth? That alone was enough to set a new wave of anxiety racing.

Tuomas had never struck a drum in his life, and now he had to take one with him? *This* one?

He opened his mouth to protest again, but Henrik cut him off.

"Head north. Kari and Lilja were always in the opposite places to everyone else, and I suspect nothing has changed. Go over the Mustafjord and follow the treeline towards the tundra."

Grateful for something else to focus on, Tuomas nodded. He could deal with north. The further north you went, the less safety there was; and to venture too far, especially in winter, was ill-advised. On the one hand, it was stupid to travel during the Long Dark anyway, but on the other, everyone else would think the same. Wandering mages or not, this brother and sister would need to find shelter somewhere.

Then he looked around, and realised someone was missing.

"Where's Paavo?"

Maiken glanced at the other leaders, then back to Tuomas.

"Was he with the herd when you went up there?" she asked.

Tuomas shook his head. "No. Aslak, have you seen him?"

"No. I'm sorry," replied Aslak.

Henrik leaned close to Tuomas and spoke in a whisper.

"Don't worry, he's somewhere. But it's a clear sky; you will have a cold journey. You must leave now and cover some ground before you make camp."

Tuomas's stomach twisted. Going away was one thing, but without saying goodbye to Paavo? Where was he? Early riser or not, this was unlike him.

But he knew Henrik was right. He couldn't linger, for Mihka's sake. The sooner he left, the sooner he would be home: a fully realised mage. And then he could tell Paavo all about it.

That gave him new confidence, and the anxiety was finally quashed. He drew his shoulders back, grasped the reindeer's harness and walked it to the edge of the village, facing out towards the frozen fjord. The sleigh's runners left deep lines in the snow behind him. He climbed inside it and drew a thick fur blanket over his legs.

*Paavo's fine*, he told himself. *He knows this place as well as anyone, and he's not stupid. He probably just didn't want to see you go.*

He jumped when Sisu appeared beside him, holding a freshly-lit torch. But he didn't pass it over straightaway, instead extending his other hand. Stark against his grey mitten was a lock of white hair. Tuomas knew instantly it was from Mihka.

"A token. Don't forget who this is for," Sisu said. His small eyes shone with unshed tears beneath the patterned brim of his hat.

Tuomas bowed his head respectfully. He took the torch, then the hair, sealing it inside a small sealskin pouch at his belt. Now Mihka – and the importance of the journey – would be with him always.

"I'll be home before you know it," he said. "Take care of yourselves. And give my love to Paavo."

"I will," said Sisu. ""Go in peace."

"Stay in peace," replied Tuomas.

Before he could begin doubting himself, Tuomas held the rope in his spare hand and gave it a snap. The reindeer took off through the snow. Tuomas kept his eyes straight ahead as he sped along the ice of the Mustafjord, so he couldn't look back and see the village shrinking into nothingness.

Soon, all the cries of farewell disappeared, and he was alone. There was only the steady jingle of the reindeer's bell to break the silence, and the silver face of the Moon Spirit staring down from the World Above.

# Chapter Four

The sleigh moved slow and steady over of the frozen water. Rocks and trees flew by on the nearby shore, their branches crystallised in feathery ice.

Tuomas regarded them as he passed. Soon the snow would fall so heavily, those same trees would bow under the weight of it, until they didn't even look like trees anymore. At least some of the bark was still visible. By the time of the next full Moon, even that would be gone, hidden beneath laden branches.

His attention strayed to the rocky walls of the headlands. The size of the Mustafjord always took his breath away. It was a huge beast, curling left and right, framed by high ridges and frosted cloudberry bushes, their precious golden bounty long gone. He knew he would have a small supply of them in his donated food parcels, along with other berries and wild mushrooms, but they were precious – he would save them.

The midday twilight came and went. The faint glow stretched everywhere and yet left not a single shadow. The land briefly turned a soft violet, then blue, and then darkness fell once again. A wisp of cloud drifted across the Moon Spirit.

Tuomas felt his eyelids beginning to droop, and the reindeer was slowing. It was time to stop.

He was still on the fjord, but the banks were high and rocky – there was no way he would be able to scale them. But he spotted a cluster of trees sticking out from the shore on a small lip of earth. It wasn't much, but it would do for a few hours' sleep.

He hopped out of the sleigh and unhitched the reindeer from the poles. Then he took the animal by the harness, guiding it off the ice and into the thin birches. He was at the edge of the forest here; it would provide a little shelter from the open expanse of the fjord, and gave enough space for a fire to breathe without leaving them too exposed.

He took the long poles from the back of the sleigh and stuck them deep into the snow, binding them together at the top with rope. Then he draped the reindeer skin tarp around them, securing it where he could, leaving a smoke hole in the middle. Once his shelter was up, he threw some furs onto the floor.

He cut down a small birch sapling, thanking the little souls inside for their sacrifice, and made quick work of it, chopping it with an axe. He imagined the life-soul drifting up in the arms of the Spirit of Passage, going to rest in the other Worlds before it returned to a new body. It could be a mosquito, a wolverine, another tree, or perhaps a human child. None were more important than the others: they were all alive, all relying on their neighbours in nature to survive.

He held his torch to the bark, and soon a fire was burning in the centre of the tent. It didn't take long to make dinner: carving flakes off some dried reindeer meat and letting them stew in water melted from the snow. Then he brewed himself some herbal tea and rested his back against one of the sturdy poles, lifting the food to his mouth on the blade of his knife.

It suddenly struck him how alone he was. Being in his own company was nothing new, but it was always with the knowledge that a neighbour was close by. Even on the herd migrations, when the entire village slept in shelters like this for weeks at a time, the community remained together.

Akerfjorden, as a place, wasn't home. Its *people* were home. And without them, Tuomas felt like a tiny speck on the surface of the huge white World.

To distract himself, he recalled an old fireside story: the legend of how their winter settlement came to be. Generations ago, a powerful man known only as the Great Mage had lived. His name was lost to time, but everyone knew his story, and held it as close to their hearts as any event within living memory.

He'd led the ancestors out of the north, across tundra and through forests, to where the Sun Spirit would return her glow first after the Long Dark. But he died less than a mile from his destination; fallen through the ice underfoot and never resurfaced. Those who had followed him claimed they had seen the white fox of the aurora sweep down and pull his life-soul out of his chest. They said she had taken it back into the World Above, filling the fjord with her Lights. The story varied about whether that had been the event which made him drown, but from that moment on, the villagers of Akerfjorden had named the Mustafjord in his memory: The Black Water.

A shiver ran down Tuomas's spine. *That* was the best story he could have thought of for comfort?

As a youngster, it had been one of his favourites. When the old women told it, he would shuffle close and soak up every word, imagining the tale playing out in the shadows cast by the fire. It was exciting; an adventure, unlike anything to be found in the monotony of Akerfjorden. A legend of Spirits and mages, and of two celestial children, swapped between night and day in the formless World Above.

Now, it left him cold, with a bitter taste in his mouth. His imagination lingered on the image of the Lights tearing out the Great Mage's life-soul, then shifted to memory: Mihka hanging there in her freezing grasp...

Suddenly restless, he put down his half-eaten meal, crawled out of the shelter took a huge lungful of air. The temperature had plummeted since he had made camp, and the hair inside his nostrils froze with each inhale. His reindeer was nowhere to be seen, but he could hear it: bell tingling as it foraged for food. It wouldn't go far.

He trudged over to the sleigh and started to draw the tarp over it. He had left some of his belongings inside – there was no point unpacking everything when he was setting off again in a few hours. But it was better to cover them in case snow fell during the night.

Then his eyes settled on the bundle Henrik had given him. He pulled the drum closer and drew back its covering.

It truly was a beautiful thing: as wide as the span of both his hands, carved from a circular birch frame with reindeer skin stretched taught across its mouth. The skin was painted with a lifetime of symbols, the head of the Great Bear Spirit sitting in the centre. Henrik had made and decorated this himself, to showcase his individual powers, and harness the heartbeat of the earth.

How would Tuomas paint his own drum, when he made it? There would be images of himself and Paavo; that much was for sure. And of their parents. Tuomas had never known them, but they had given him life, and that was something to revere.

He imagined beating the drum before a roaring fire, singing to the Spirits, passing down stories and histories to the next generation. There would be tales of ancient wicked mages who wore other people's skin to trick them; of ones able to walk through flames to travel miles in seconds, or weaving illusions out of snow or shifting light. Henrik used to do that when he was younger, to entertain the children, but as age bent his back and stiffened his joints, he'd limited himself to only what was necessary.

That was why he needed an apprentice. And Tuomas had been so eager to fill that place.

He noticed movement out of the corner of his eye. The sky began to tremble and dance, and a green curtain swam into life.

Tuomas turned away, instinct getting the better of him. But as soon as he did, his heart burned with rage.

There she was, right there, above him: the Spirit who had swept down and stolen Mihka's life-soul.

The drum was still in his lap. He ran a hand over it, feeling the smoothness of the skin and raised edges of the dried alder paint against his palm.

A thought struck him. Why should he have to wait to find those two mages? If he was the one who needed to appease the Spirit of the Lights, then why not just do it? Wasn't it enough of a test to see poor Mihka's white hair and pale face?

He didn't pause to wonder if it was a bad idea.

He rushed to the shelter and held the drum over the fire, as Henrik had taught him to do. Then he came back outside and ran onto the ice, so the black sky and green Lights stretched all around him. Then he spun a circle of protection, raised the hammer, and struck the skin.

The sound vibrated through him; so strong, he almost fell to his knees. But he stood his ground and hit it again, finding a rhythm, riding it like a kayak in a stormy sea. An angry chant poured from his throat, deep and guttural, and he willed himself to rise up, out of his body. Up, into the World Above, where he could see the Spirit and demand an explanation; ask her what she needed for her appeasement.

Why did she have to be so arrogant, so easily offended? Why should she be feared? By what right did she snatch away the soul of a fifteen-year-old boy?

He knew this wasn't the way to connect with a Spirit, but he didn't care. He wanted her to feel his fury.

He let himself float higher, imagining himself leaving the earth, charging into the sky like an enraged bear. The drum's beat swallowed him, surrounded him in its thunder.

He grew heavy. He went to fight against it, but it felt right, to let out how much he resented everything that had happened. Mihka did not deserve this, nobody deserved this...

His chant transformed into a furious scream. He drew his *taika* down, pulling it towards his core. This was not like anything Henrik had described. He had never felt anything like this, but it was so perfect, so strong...

Another scream joined his: shrill, otherworldly. Then he ran out of breath and collapsed on all fours.

He sat up, and fright froze him to the spot.

The sky was as clear and dark as it had been before. All traces of green were gone. But lying by the entrance of his tent was a figure: slender as a sapling, completely white, clad in fabric which seemed to be made from starlight itself.

It rolled over and revealed a thin feminine face. Two large pointed ears, like a fox's, protruded from long hair as colourless as the snow.

She looked straight at him. Her irises were the raging hues of the aurora.

Tuomas's heart thundered. He couldn't move. He glanced between the drum and the girl, unable to believe his eyes.

She leapt to her feet and flew at him. He recoiled in panic, throwing up his arms to protect himself.

She paused inches from his face, blocked by the circle he had cast. But that invisible barrier, thinner than birch bark, didn't fill him with any confidence and he trembled like a terrified child.

What had he done?

"How dare you!" the girl shouted. "Put me back!"

Tuomas stared at her, too scared to move. She bared her teeth and her eyes shone red: the same colour as when the Lights had struck Mihka.

"Return me to the sky!" she demanded. "Now!"

Her ferocity shocked him into action. He hit the drum desperately, striking out a tuneless beat. But his hands trembled so much, he dropped the hammer.

The girl snarled. "A fine mage you are trying to be! Put me back!"

"I... I can't!" Tuomas stammered. "I'm not a mage yet..."

"You brought me down here! You put me back!"

"Please, I can't!"

She locked eyes with him. The redness blazed across her face, throwing strange shadows onto cheekbones which might have been chiselled from ice. Everything about her spoke of coldness, control, authority. The longer she glared, the more Tuomas's fear grew.

"You summon a Spirit – confine a Spirit – and do not even know what you did?" she said incredulously. "You should have the power!"

Tuomas frowned.

"What? But I told you... I'm still training!"

"But you should know!"

There was a swooping motion behind her, and Tuomas noticed for the first time that a bushy white tail had appeared from beneath her skirt. He regarded her ears again, and realisation gripped him.

Fox fires.

Somehow, he had trapped that very Spirit in human form.

"It was you..." he muttered. "You took Mihka's life-soul!"

The Spirit didn't even blink. "He insulted me."

Tuomas was tempted to yell, but held it back. Anger had brought this furious entity down from the World Above. She only looked the same age as him, but he knew that was in appearance only. This being was older than the mountains, colder than the deepest frozen sea. She was one of the most feared and revered of them all.

Henrik had said, mere hours ago, to respect Spirits and they would respond in kind. He hoped with all his might that the old mage's words were true.

"He was just being stupid," he said carefully. "Return the life-soul to him. Please."

Her frosty expression didn't change.

"That is not possible for the time being. Because of you."

"What do you mean?"

"You ripped me out of the World Above, you fool! How am I supposed to do anything down here?"

She regarded her body with disgust.

Tuomas thought quickly. He'd never even thought something like this was possible, least of all by him. But the deed was done now, and he needed to appease her. If he returned her to the World Above, surely she would grant his request.

He let out a shaking breath.

"I'm on my way north to find the wandering mage siblings. Kari and Lilja. They'll be able to help you more than me. They... they can put you back."

The girl glowered at him.

"*You* are the one who owes me a debt. You interrupted me from punishing that insolent boy."

Tuomas gritted his teeth.

"He didn't mean anything by it!"

"Is that so? You heard his insults as well as I did."

"That's honestly your excuse for stripping him of his life-soul?"

Her eyes narrowed dangerously.

Tuomas took a step back. She might not have spoken, but her threat was real, and he couldn't allow himself to forget it.

No matter she was in a physical body; she could crush him under her foot like a snowflake if she wanted. And the circle might be protecting him now, but he wouldn't be able to stay inside it forever.

"Please," he said, not caring about the frightened croak creeping back into his voice. He held up his hands, trying to placate her. "Please, why don't you come with me, to the mages? They can help us both. And if I owe you a debt, the least I can do is get you home."

The Spirit regarded him with a cold glare. "Brave words."

Tuomas looked at her imploringly.

"I'm sorry. Honestly, I am. I didn't mean to do this to you... I only wanted to talk."

"You wanted to *demand*, without thought of the consequences."

"When this is done, you can take whatever you want from me. Just let my friend have his life-soul back."

The girl stayed where she stood. Her face was unreadable.

It was then that Tuomas realised she was actually standing *on top* of the snow, as though she weighed no more than a feather. There weren't even any prints behind her from when she had run towards him.

"Very well," she said coolly. "I will come with you. But only when I am back in the World Above can I grant your request."

Tuomas swallowed his nerves. He didn't want to have her with him any longer than necessary. For as respectful as he tried to keep himself, he couldn't hold back a shiver of fear.

"Please, don't hurt me," he said.

She didn't reply except to flick her tail back and forth.

Realising he wouldn't get a moment of sleep now, Tuomas inched past her, and felt the protective circle dissipate as he stepped outside it.

He eyed her warily, expecting her to attack again, but she didn't. He let out a relieved sigh and pulled the tarp off the tent, then kicked snow over the fire to extinguish it.

A short time later, the entire shelter was collapsed and heaped back into the sleigh. He fetched his reindeer from the trees and tied it to the poles with trembling fingers. Finally, he picked Henrik's drum out of the snow and strapped it around his waist with a leather rope: the same he had seen his mentor do all his life.

The Spirit watched in silence. Tuomas threw her a wary look before taking the harness and guiding the reindeer forward. Only when the sled began to move did she follow, walking so softly that Tuomas might have forgotten she was behind him, were it not for the feeling of her ethereal eyes boring into the back of his head.

# Chapter Five

The miles fell behind them as they followed the unkempt forest trails where the trees stood a little further apart. The runners of the sleigh snagged on roots, and on a few occasions, Tuomas had to hack them free with his axe. It was difficult to see in the darkness, but soon enough, the faint blue glow of faraway daylight seeped across the snow. It wasn't much to work by, but he was grateful for it.

He heard a faint groan and turned to look at the Spirit. She was leaning against a frost-caked tree, her eyes screwed shut.

"Is something wrong?" he asked, as respectfully as he could.

On the tree, her fingers curled into a fist. Even that gesture, full of discomfort and irritation, remained as graceful as her dancing Lights.

Realising she wasn't going to reply, Tuomas released the reindeer harness and approached her.

At the sound of his footsteps, she opened her eyes and glared at him. Their colour bounced between striking green and blood red.

That was warning enough to not come closer. He stopped in mid-step, but didn't look away from her. What was wrong? She seemed weakened, as though if she took another step she would stumble.

His gaze strayed to the faint blue of the snow, and an idea struck him. Even though it was the Long Dark, the Sun

Spirit was still close enough to throw a little light over the land. And the aurora was a thing of the night.

"Is it the light?" he asked softly.

The Spirit still didn't answer.

Tuomas wrestled with himself. He knew he was right, and she wasn't going to move another step until the true night returned. But there was no time for this.

"Spirits forgive me, I'm truly sorry," he muttered, then stepped forward and picked her up.

Even though she weighed nothing, the girl went as stiff as a board.

"Release me!" she snapped. Her ears drew flat against her scalp.

Tuomas hurried to the sleigh, kicked a food parcel out of the way, and set her on the seat. As soon as she was inside, she raised a hand. It glowed a threatening bright green.

"How dare you!" she snarled.

"I was only trying to help," he protested. "If you put the blanket over yourself, it will keep the light away. I'll let you know when it's dark again."

"I will *know* when it is dark," she said pointedly, but nevertheless lowered her hand and laid the blanket across her legs.

Relieved she had taken his advice – and not ripped his own life-soul away – Tuomas returned to the reindeer and continued the trail. Once they were on a straighter part of the path, he glanced back over his shoulder.

"Forgive me for asking this," he said, "but is there a name I can call you?"

The girl looked startled – even a little upset. But before Tuomas could question her, she pressed her lips together and turned her face away, her expression stoic once more.

"That's fine," he said, trying not to sound frustrated. "I'm called Tuomas."

"No, you are not."

He frowned. "What do you mean?"

But there was no answer. She simply drew the blanket up over her head.

Tuomas gritted his teeth and trudged on in silence, his shoes sinking into the soft snow. It was powdery and crisp, falling off him as soon as he moved. The freezing air made it too cold to be wet, to cling to anything. He considered fetching his skis, but that would mean going over to the sleigh – to the Spirit – so he decided against it.

The dim light grew until it transformed the land into a blanket of cold pastel blue. Despite being surrounded by the trees, it seemed brighter to Tuomas now than when he had been in Akerfjorden. He fancied that, just below the horizon line, the Golden One was lingering, as close as she could come to them in the Long Dark.

He tried to keep his attention on the trail, but every now and then, he glanced at the sleigh. The Spirit was still covered by the blanket, so motionless, she seemed barely alive.

He wondered if she was even alive, really. Was a Spirit a living thing? Looking at her like this, hidden by fabric, he could almost imagine that figure was the outline of his food parcels and rolled-up hides. Might it be that he'd imagined it all?

He heaved a long sigh and looked away. There was no use in pretending. She was there. And Mihka still needed the wandering mages.

He could kick himself. This little escapade was going to cost his friend valuable time. What if the Spirit was lying about returning Mihka's life-soul? What if she refused, in retaliation for this second insult? What if she decided the debt should be paid by carrying Tuomas himself away with her? She had already threatened to, in all but words.

He shuddered. What had he done? How could he have been so stupid?

As quickly as it appeared, the twilight began to fade. Tuomas gave a tug on the reindeer's harness to make it stop, and then pulled his torch from the edge of the sleigh. He uttered a silent thanks for thinking to store it there; it was the furthest corner away from the Spirit. He wrapped wool around the end, laced with dried grass and fragments of birch bark, and struck some flint. A flame flickered into life, and he pressed on again, torch in hand, keeping his eyes peeled for somewhere to make camp.

"It's dark now," he said quietly.

She didn't respond.

They moved down a small slope and came to the bend of a river, long frozen over. A thin layer of snow covered it, crowned with a sheen of hoar frost.

Tuomas scanned the far bank. There was a clearing between the birches, just large enough to take the sleigh and tent.

He made the reindeer stop, and edged forward, placing one foot on the ice to test it. It groaned a little, but took his weight. He jumped up and down to be sure – it still held him. Before his nerves could fail him, he seized the harness and hurried the reindeer across.

When they reached the other side, he unhitched the animal and it wandered to the edge of the trees, beginning to paw at the ground in search of moss. Tuomas stuck the torch into the snow and tugged his mitten off with his teeth. He wiped at his brow, letting out a weary groan. He supposed they had managed just over ten miles since his last camp.

There was a snap of fabric behind him as the Spirit threw back the blanket.

"How are you?" Tuomas asked in a small voice.

She glared at him, but kept her mouth shut.

Deciding better than to press her, Tuomas dragged the tent poles out of the sleigh. The Spirit shuffled indignantly as they knocked against her. He muttered an apology, then positioned one of the poles, ready to drive it into the snow to form the first part of a shelter.

He caught a movement in the corner of his eye. The reindeer's head had shot up, its ears erect.

Reindeer had better senses than any man. Something was coming.

Tuomas snatched the torch and held it before him. The snow muted sounds, but there was still just enough light to see by if he looked carefully. He stood still, straining to pick up on something, anything.

Then he heard a low growl to the left. The reindeer snorted in alarm. Tuomas spun around, and fought back a wave of panic.

A wolf was standing there. And as soon as he noticed it, more began looming out of the shadows.

There were only three of them, but that didn't bring Tuomas any comfort. Just one would have been able to bring down his reindeer. A trio would likely kill them all.

He knew better than to flee. That would only awaken the chase in the beasts – they would run him down in no time. The only chance was to stand his ground, use the torch, and make a scene; try to convince them he wasn't worth the effort.

But his reindeer wouldn't think that way. He could tell by its agitated movements that it was going to bolt at any moment.

"Spirit, please calm him," he begged, trying to keep his voice from wavering. "If he runs, it's the end for all of us."

He heard the creak of the sleigh as she slid out of it, then she appeared in his peripheral vision, laying one white hand on the reindeer's neck. It didn't look much calmer, but stood still, and that was an improvement he was willing to take.

One of the wolves approached, lips peeling back to expose its ferocious teeth. Tuomas waved the torch at it threateningly.

"Get away!" he snapped.

The wolf snarled harder, its eyes gleaming.

Tuomas had never been more grateful for a torch. Fire was the one thing wolves were afraid of. But he still cursed himself for leaving his bow and arrows in the sleigh. Why had he been walking with the drum strapped to his belt instead of those? He was an idiot, and now his stupidity might have cost them everything.

One of the other wolves lunged at the reindeer. It bellowed in alarm, kicking out with its hind legs. The third one went for the Spirit.

Tuomas drew his largest knife and threw it. It grazed the wolf's shoulder, then thudded into the snow at its feet. It growled in pain, but resumed its attack.

The reindeer squealed in terror as the wolf harrowed it. The sound tore at Tuomas's ears. He had marked that one himself just a few years ago, as he had marked its mother. The reindeer were dearer than most of his possessions. And now this one was in danger.

A wave of anger surged through his blood. He leapt forward and swung the torch, smashing the flaming end into the wolf's muzzle. It yelped and fell back.

Tuomas let out a sharp laugh of triumph.

"Get away!" he yelled, brandishing the torch even harder.

The wolf growled again, but it was definitely cowed. He sprang at it again to show his strength. Then, before he could doubt himself, he edged towards the reindeer and the Spirit, lashing out at the other wolves.

But as soon as he turned his back, the first one reappeared and threw itself at him.

The Spirit thrust her hands at the wolf and caught it in its narrow chest. A burst of spectral light burned into Tuomas's eyes.

He turned away with a startled yelp. It was as though he had looked straight into the Sun. Strange shapes danced behind his lids; his balance spun and his heart thrummed in his ears. When he eased his eyes open, he was shocked to see the wolf had been hurled back towards the trees by the blast. It lay in a heap, knocked unconscious.

He stared at the Spirit.

"What was that? What did you do?"

Before she could answer, a shockwave flew past him, like a gust of fierce wind. It hit one of the other wolves and flung it onto its side. The last wolf let out a whine of defeat and the two of them ran off across the frozen river, disappearing into the trees.

Tuomas turned to the Spirit. "Are you alright?"

She nodded as though nothing had happened, and softly patted the reindeer, trying to calm it down.

Tuomas held the torch aloft and crept in the direction the wave had come from.

"Who's there?" he called. "Show yourself!"

For several long moments, nothing happened. After what felt like the entire winter, he saw movement among the black trees. A figure walked closer, shouldering a bow in mid-stride.

It stepped into the glow of the torch, revealing a short stout woman, a freshly-shot ptarmigan hanging by its feathered feet from a rope around her chest. She wore a coat of reindeer fur, the body tan and the sleeves pure white, bound at the waist by a thick belt intricately woven with coloured fibres and beads. It was unlike any clothing in Akerfjorden. Tuomas recognised some the patterns as being from Poro village, up in the north, but there were others which he had never seen before. She must have added them herself.

In her hand was a drum – Tuomas realised she must have struck it and sent the shockwave. Only a few mages were able to do that. Powerful ones.

She scanned her eyes over him, then they shifted to the Spirit and widened in alarm. Even from this distance, Tuomas could see a twinge of fear in her face too.

"White Fox One," she gasped. "Is that your doing, boy?"

Tuomas hesitated. He doubted he would have trusted Paavo with what he had done, let alone a stranger.

"Who are you?" he demanded.

She looked him up and down again before answering.

"My name is Lilja."

# Chapter Six

"You're Lilja?" Tuomas asked.

The woman nodded.

"I heard a commotion and came to see what the matter was. Those greylegs have been creeping about for a few days."

She paused, glancing critically at him.

"You don't look as though you're in any fit state to have fought them off, either. When was the last time you slept?"

Despite his relief, Tuomas couldn't help but feel like a chastised child.

"It's complicated," he said in the end.

"So I see," Lilja remarked, throwing a pointed look at the Spirit. "So this *is* your doing?"

"It was an accident," Tuomas hissed.

"There are no accidents," she replied. Her eyes lingered on the Spirit; her shock barely hidden. "Daughter of the Moon?"

The Spirit drew her shoulders back with pride. "I know of you too, Lilja Bear-Mage."

Lilja bowed her head low. After a few moments, she straightened up and walked towards Tuomas.

"Alright, come with me. My camp isn't far."

Tuomas approached the reindeer, grasping the poles of the sleigh and dragging it closer in mid-step. He was about to bind it into place when Lilja slapped his hands away.

"No, I'll do this. You get in. Best to move quickly, and you're tired."

Tuomas threw a nervous glance at the Spirit.

"I... It's fine. I'll walk with you," he said.

"No, you won't."

Lilja didn't even turn around. She tied the staves and then looped a lasso around the reindeer's neck.

"I said get in. Both of you."

The Spirit's eyes flashed an angry red.

"You speak to all of my kind this way?"

"Forgive me, but with all due respect, you're not in the World Above right now," Lilja said. "The quicker we move, the quicker we can sort this out."

Tuomas was taken aback. The Spirit had a point. He doubted Henrik would be so blunt with one such as her. But Lilja seemed different, almost careless. Was she honestly so confident that she would risk an insult, however veiled? If a flippant criticism was worthy of having a life-soul ripped away, he hated to think what sarcasm might invoke.

To his surprise, however, the Spirit didn't respond, and climbed into the sleigh. He stepped in beside her and sat down, painfully aware of how close they were. He threw her a cagy glance before covering his legs with the blanket. He didn't bother asking if she wanted to get under it too.

She might not have risen to Lilja's comments now, but maybe that was simply because she was trapped in human form. Would she be so restrained once she was back in the sky?

Lilja gave the lasso a tug and urged the reindeer on. The sleigh jolted forwards, then settled into a gentle slide as they moved back under the cover of the spindly trees.

Suddenly aware of how exhausted he was, Tuomas let his head roll back onto one of his skis. The hard edge dug into his neck, but he didn't care. The last thing he saw was the night sky, before it swarmed its darkness around him and pulled him down into a deep sleep.

When he opened his eyes, he immediately looked at the Spirit. She was still facing away from him, legs pulled up to her chest. At first glance, he wasn't sure if she was even breathing. But then she turned her eyes on him. Their black depths were edged with a fine hint of turquoise.

"How long was I asleep?" he asked.

As he expected, she didn't reply, so he instead looked at the sky. The stars had moved, and he used that to judge. A little over an hour.

"I thought you said your camp was nearby?" he called to Lilja.

She didn't look at him; just carried on walking beside the reindeer.

"It is. We're almost there," she replied. "I was out hunting when I heard you. That's how I got to you so quickly. No prey comes that close to a shelter."

Tuomas glanced at the ptarmigan she was carrying. The only time one of those had actually come to him, rather than him pursuing it, was a few years ago. He and Paavo had pitched a tent while hunting, which unbeknownst to them, had been in the middle of an aggressive male ptarmigan's territory. It had harassed them and snapped at them with its peculiar yelping call, which was only silenced when Paavo took a shot at it.

Akerfjorden had eaten well that night. Any food during winter was not to be refused, especially when it practically offered itself to them.

Tuomas smiled at the memory, but it soon dimmed as he recalled Paavo's face. Already he was missing his brother. Was Paavo feeling as bad about not saying goodbye as Tuomas was?

*Don't fret,* he told himself. *You'll be back before you know it. Then you can tease him about it all until the end of the Long Dark.*

He moved his attention to the surroundings. Tree boughs were laden with snow, and every now and then, there was a muted thump as a pile of it slid free and fell. The white ground around the roots was untouched; no wolverines or moose had come by here. There was only the single line of footprints which Lilja had left when she had come in search of them, which they were now following back.

They broke free of the trees and entered a small clearing. Small shrubs poked their thin branches through the snow, spindly edges glistening with tiny icicles. In the centre of the glade was a tent, a sleigh parked outside it with a sheet covering its cargo. The flap of the shelter was closed, but the welcoming orange glow of a fire lit up the hide tarp from within.

Lilja drew Tuomas's sleigh alongside her own and released his reindeer. It immediately trotted over to where her own two were grazing, and joined them in nibbling at the white lichen they had uncovered beneath the snow.

Tuomas tied a rope around a tree, then attached it to his reindeer's harness. None of them would stray far with wolves in the area, but Lilja had also tethered her animals – neither of them was willing to take any chances. At least this way, if any greylegs came back, the animals would be close enough to defend easily.

Lilja headed for the tent and he followed her. He hesitated at the entrance, waiting for the Spirit to come too, but she remained seated in the sleigh, her eyes turned to the sky.

For the first time, Tuomas's wariness of her subsided into a wave of pity. He had been so angry with her for stripping Mihka's life-soul away – but he had done the equivalent to her.

In a fit of rage, he had torn her from her home in the World Above, and trapped her.

Biting his lip guiltily, he ducked through the flap and let it fall shut behind him.

Lilja had her back to him as she hung her ptarmigan on one of the tent's beams to pluck and clean later. Then she took another piece of meat from beside it, freshly skinned and gutted. Tuomas could tell from the shape of it that it was a hare.

Without a word, she skewered it and placed it over the fire. Blood dripped from the punctures and sizzled as it hit the warmed hearth stones. She turned it occasionally to seal it, then left it to cook through, before hoisting a pot of water close to the flames to boil. When it began to bubble, she threw in some herbs.

The delicious aromas of simmering nettle filled the air and made Tuomas's stomach rumble. He realised how little he had eaten since leaving Akerfjorden. He had barely managed half of his last meal before he had rushed outside and summoned the Spirit.

He looked at Lilja across the fire.

"I was sent to look for you."

"And you found me. Or, should that be, *I* found *you?*"

She stirred the tea with a ladle made from the carved shinbone of a reindeer. The craftsmanship in it was extraordinary – Tuomas guessed she had a lot of free time to create, as practically every single one of her belongings was decorated in some way.

"You and your brother, Kari," he carried on. "Where is he?"

Lilja stiffened. "Gone."

"What do you mean? He's dead?"

"Gone."

74

Lilja threw him a harsh glance which told him not to press further. Then she laid her bow and drum behind her, pulled her hat off and shrugged out of her coat, revealing a bright tunic woven about the cuffs and hem with intricate patterns. Like the coat, they were different from the ones he had seen on clothes in Akerfjorden, but equally as beautiful. Now he could get a good look, he recognised the patterns. They were in the shape of a reindeer, its antlers rising in glorious splendour. She was definitely from Poro. Or, she had been, once.

Like Sisu had said, she was in her late twenties, a couple of years older than Paavo. That was old enough to be a woman, of course; to be married and have children. But she looked as though she had no intention of doing either of those things. Tuomas had never seen anyone who seemed so content in their own company. She moved with the subtle confidence of knowing herself and surroundings perfectly, and when she spoke, her voice crackled, as though she hadn't used it in a while.

Her hair was a fine sandy blonde, woven into two long braids which tumbled over her shoulders. A pair of brilliant blue eyes sat quite far apart in her face. Just visible under the neckline of her tunic was a long scar. It reached across her throat from left to right, and the flesh had a pinkish tinge; it hadn't long healed over. She noticed him staring and quickly tugged her collar up to cover it.

Tuomas frowned. What could have caused a wound like that?

His eyes wandered the shelter, and found her drum, propped up against the side of the tent behind her. It was a little larger than Henrik's, but decorated just as carefully, with an array of new spiralling symbols he hadn't seen before. The Great Bear Spirit sat in the centre, as it did on all drums, but it was also painted to the side, hovering over the figure of a bedridden child. Opposite that was another child, this time standing alone in the middle of a lake. And in one corner there was a dark red mark, smeared clumsily, as though with the fingers. It looked like blood.

Lilja made a deliberate clatter with the ladle against the pot.

Snapped from his reverie, Tuomas watched as she poured two helpings of tea into cups made from hollowed burrs. She handed one to him and he drank gratefully, letting the welcomed warmth spread through his body.

"So... why are you out here by yourself?" he asked.

"I'm a wandering mage. The clue's in the name," she replied, idly turning the spit with one hand. She took a sip of her tea, then lowered the cup into her lap.

"I was actually on my way to complete a very important errand. But then I saw the Lights strike the earth, and I knew I had to make a diversion. The way they behaved... we both know it wasn't natural."

Tuomas lowered his eyes.

"No. It wasn't."

"But I wasn't expecting to see what I did when I found you," said Lilja. "The Spirit of the Lights, standing in a physical form. Bringing her into the World Between requires powerful *taika*. So, in that respect, I'm impressed. No wonder you tired so quickly."

He frowned, not sure whether to take that as a compliment.

"I didn't mean for it to happen. I was angry."

"Unchecked anger is dangerous. You need to harness it if you're to be a mage. I take it you're training to be one? I noticed your drum as much as you noticed mine."

She sounded so much like Henrik, Tuomas couldn't suppress a half-smile.

"I'm not off to a great start."

"All of us need to start somewhere," said Lilja. "Anyway, it's a good thing I ran into you. It means I no longer need to carry on with my errand."

"Why?"

"Because I've already found who I was looking for."

Tuomas set down his cup.

"Me?"

Lilja nodded. "I understand your alarm, but why do you look so angry, boy? Should I be worried? Are you going to chant me somewhere I don't belong, too?"

"No... I mean... I came out here because we need your help!" Tuomas cried. "Forget why you were looking for me! You have to come back to Akerfjorden!"

"No," she replied, cutting across him. "You're more important than whatever is happening in Akerfjorden. I take it Henrik's still alive and kicking? Any mage can sort reindeer problems, or illness, or whatever's happening down there."

Tuomas shook his head at her flippant tone. "It's nothing to do with the reindeer!" he insisted. "It's serious! It's the son of one of our leaders – my best friend!"

"Who got exactly what he deserved."

Both of them looked around to see the Spirit standing at the entrance, holding back the flap in one hand. Her face was set in a cold mask of determination.

"He and I have an agreement," she said to Lilja. "He appears to be unable to put me back in the World Above. So you will do it. Now."

She turned her eyes on Tuomas. "And once I am back, I will spare your ignorant friend. Is that not what you wanted?"

Without another word, she disappeared back into the snow.

Lilja blew out her cheeks, then lifted the hare away from the hearth.

"Well, I suppose dinner will have to wait," she muttered.

She grabbed her drum and held it over the fire. She moved almost idly, with none of the weight which Henrik would use – practically dangling the instrument on two fingers as though she didn't care if it fell.

But as soon as it drew near to the flames, Tuomas felt the air change. It became sharper, headier, swimming with untapped magic. He felt like he could have cut it with a knife. He sensed fresh summer flowers casting their scent on the air; the heathers of the tundra bursting into colour beneath the never-ending light of the Long Day; a sound of childish laughter on the banks of a lake.

It was unlike anything he had sensed from Henrik. No matter how she acted, this mage was powerful.

Lilja tucked the drum under her arm and crawled outside. Tuomas followed her, watched her beat out a protective circle with her antler hammer. She sat in the middle, drum cradled in her lap like a child, her eyes on the starry sky.

Tuomas looked for the Spirit. She was standing beside the sleigh, staring intently at Lilja. Feeling his gaze, her eyes flickered to him.

He had the sudden urge to look away, to break free of those inhuman colours which danced and reflected on her pale skin. But he didn't. Somehow, however silently, he had to let her know he was sorry for what he had done.

She continued looking at him. Then her features softened, as though she had read his thoughts.

The drumbeats started. It was simple at first but gradually grew faster, adding in smaller beats that reverberated through the snow.

Lilja began to chant.

The sound poured from her like water. It was as though a new voice had taken over her – it sounded nothing like how she spoke. There were no words; just a stream of deep, rolling hums, echoing through the silent forest with a power which sent shivers down his spine.

He marvelled at the *taika* gathering around them, swimming about his limbs and into his lungs. He felt his souls loosening inside his body, and strained to keep them close. He didn't want to fall into a trance, not while the Spirit was still there.

Instead, he focused on her. She had her arms raised, like a child begging to be borne up in the arms of a parent.

Lilja's chant became mellow as she sung herself deeper. She rocked back and forth, still keeping the beat of the drum. Tuomas watched as the skin vibrated, the symbols bouncing with each strike of the hammer. Her voice was richer than Henrik's; the drum's timbre was deeper – unlike any mage song he'd ever heard. He found his hands digging into the snow, seeking some kind of anchor, lest he get pulled away with it.

Then silence fell. It was so sudden, Tuomas worried for a moment that his life-soul had slipped away. He quickly ran his hands over his body, and found it solid. Good. That meant he was still there, still lucid.

The swarm of *taika* evaporated, leaving only the cold night air in its place.

Tuomas looked at Lilja. She was on her feet, eyes scanning the sky. Her brows knotted into a confused frown.

Tuomas glanced around for an aurora, but saw nothing but stars.

"Did it work?" he asked tentatively.

The words were no sooner out of his mouth when the Spirit stepped forward and flung a green flash past him. It hit Lilja's circle and rebounded into the trees.

"I told you to put me back!" she shouted.

Lilja shook her head. "I'm sorry. I tried."

The Spirit's eyes turned blood red. Tuomas shrank back in alarm.

"Can't you try again? Please?" he muttered, wishing he could be inside the circle as well.

"There's no point. If it didn't work this time, it won't work at all," said Lilja firmly. "I'm sorry, but it seems I don't have the power. That's some pretty strong *taika* you've used, boy."

Tuomas stared at her.

"But… you're the wandering mage! Henrik said how strong you are! You *must* be able to do it!"

"Must I?" Lilja snapped. "Well, it turns out I can't. So stop pressing me."

"You said you would put me back!" the Spirit raged.

Without warning, she raised a hand and flew at Lilja, inhumanly fast. Her entire arm glowed with a ferocious aurora.

Tuomas's heart leapt. He knew what she would do; could see Mihka in front of him again, jolting back and forth as his life-soul was ripped away…

Barely thinking, he jumped between them and seized the Spirit by the wrists.

Her power and fury shot through him like electricity, and the two of them were thrown away from each other.

Tuomas landed on his back. He gasped; it felt as though he had been struck by lightning and swallowed by an avalanche at the same time. He sat up as fast as he could, in case the Spirit tried to go after Lilja a second time.

Instead, he found her also on the ground, the anger on her face replaced with shock. To his relief, the Lights had disappeared from her hands.

He rolled onto all fours and crawled over. His entire body trembled from the impact with her.

"Are you alright?" he asked.

She glowered at him, but didn't attack again. The redness in her eyes had also gone, now replaced with a ghostly turquoise.

"Yes," she said.

"There's no point trying to hurt Lilja like that," he said in a low voice. "If she says she can't do it, we have to accept she can't. We'll figure something out. I promise."

"You *promise?*" she scoffed, but it wasn't as harsh as it could have been. "You are the one who trapped me here in the first place."

"I know. But it's just as important to me that you go back. If you don't, I lose my best friend, and I fail my mage test."

Tuomas sighed, trying to stop his arms shaking.

"I know he's a troublemaker, but I care about him. I hope you can understand that. I will find out how to send you back to the World Above; I swear it on my souls."

The Spirit pursed her lips, but nodded in assent.

Tuomas stood and dusted off his trousers. When he got his trembling under control, he held out a hand out for her. To his surprise, she took it and allowed him to help her up.

He realised that this was the first time he had actually touched her, besides when he had bundled her into the sleigh, and he marvelled at the smoothness of her skin. He was used to roughness and calluses: an occupational norm from a lifetime of herding and moving camps along the migration. But hers was like ice, completely pure and unblemished, and as cold as the snow she resembled. It was inhuman, otherworldly, yet strangely beautiful.

Lilja broke her circle and busied herself with shoving everything back inside the shelter. When she removed her torso from the entrance, she brought a small axe with her, and tossed it at Tuomas.

"Go and get some wood," she said.

He frowned at her abruptness – she didn't even seem shaken from the attack. But he decided that after everything that had happened, a short time alone was more than welcome.

He took the axe with a shrug and trudged away towards the trees.

# Chapter Seven

The Spirit watched him go. The darkness swallowed him, leaving only a trail of footprints in the snow. It seemed to stretch on forever between the trunks: a pristine unbroken blanket, too perfect to have been laid by anything but the Spirits. The low light of the fire inside the shelter hit the tiny flakes; they sparkled like stars, and for a moment she was reminded of the sky above.

The soft thuds of landing axe bows reached the Spirit's ears. When it was clear they were alone, Lilja approached.

Her pointed ears twitched, but she didn't move to attack again. Lilja noticed and gave a grateful nod.

"With all due respect, striking me would have done you no good, White Fox One," she said.

"It would not have hurt, either," the Spirit glowered, not bothering to mask her anger.

The corner of Lilja's mouth turned up in a wry smile.

"True. But you're not the Spirit of Death. You're of the ancestors, of light in the darkness. The Daughter of the Silver One. I understand your anger, but underneath all that, you couldn't take a life. Not really."

She raised her chin. "Is that a challenge?"

"An observation."

"I took a life-soul."

"Hardly the same. The boy you stole it from still lives, in some limited form," Lilja pointed out.

Her tail flicked from side to side irately, but then she lowered her eyes in agreement.

"Why can you not put me back?" she asked, the sharp edge disappearing from her voice. "I *must* go back. Please."

Lilja offered a small smile. "I know. You don't belong down here. But I wasn't lying to you. I can't do it."

"Why?"

"Because I'm not the one who summoned you. His power is stronger than he realises. You know that as well as I do."

She scoffed. "He tried to put me back and had just as much luck as you."

"He was probably frightened," said Lilja. "No mage can do their work if they are scared. Especially not a mage in training. And if your display just now is anything to go by, I'd imagine he *was* scared. You are not only revered down here; you are feared."

A flash of guilt coursed through her mind, but disappeared just as quickly. That was how it should be. Nobody should dare disrespect the Spirit who brought light in the middle of the longest night, who cared for the ancestors who chose to dance with her. Any of her displays firing through the sky were cause for admiration and gratitude.

She deserved that. To be loved and feared were one and the same. Especially since she could so easily leave them all in darkness, forever wondering, staring up at the World Above and never seeing a thing.

But then… how would *she* see? How could she look *down* on the World Between, to watch over…

She cut off that thought before it could hurt her.

"So, what would you suggest?" she asked coolly. "You have dealt with Spirit matters before, Lilja Bear-Soul; I have connected with you in the World Above several times. Of all the mages I could be speaking with, you are the most fitting for this."

"I'm honoured," Lilja said, the tiniest hint of sarcasm in her voice. "But that's not entirely true, is it? There *is* one more fitting here. And to see the two of you together like this... that's something else."

The Spirit's eyes widened.

"You know about him?"

"Of course." Lilja's glanced in the direction of Tuomas's footprints. "I take it he doesn't know."

"I doubt it. I recognised his life-soul as soon as I saw him. But... he did not know me."

Lilja's expression softened.

"Time has passed, White Fox One. To be perfectly honest, I would have been shocked if he *had* recognised you."

She let out a sharp exhale. "Well, it matters not. I will return to the World Above and he will stay here."

She looked at her hands, turning them over and inspecting the sparkling flesh.

"Maybe it is for the best that he does not remember. I just need him to help me."

"You're lying to yourself," Lilja said abruptly. "With all due respect."

"What do you know about it?"

"Enough to know how hard it is to lose that one person you think will be with you forever."

"Forever?" she repeated scornfully. This woman was human – her concept of forever was mere seconds to a Spirit. And yet it did seem like forever since things had been different.

She turned away. All these thoughts, walking here like this... it stung her, deeper than she had thought possible. She was a Spirit, older than any living thing upon the earth; infinite, at one with her entire being.

So why did her chest feel as though it would cave in on itself?

Lilja slid her shoulders inside the tent to place the hare back over the fire. As she held the flap aside, the Spirit caught a glimpse of the hearth. The flames were still going strong, and bundled in a dark corner under a blanket was a pile of birch logs.

"You did not need more wood," the Spirit said.

"No, I just wanted to talk to you alone," Lilja admitted softly. "It's your decision, how you spend your time down here, but he's going to find out eventually. And I wouldn't assume it's my place to tell him."

For some reason, that was more than she could bear.

She didn't wait for Lilja to withdraw herself from the shelter. She turned on her heel and ran into the trees, running on top of the snow.

This was all too much: to be trapped down here in this strange body, to be walking on the same level as humans. The cold air bit at her skin and the wind dragged invisible fingers through her hair. They were strange sensations – every touch, no matter how light, was alarmingly close.

It was unlike anything she had experienced. In the World Above, her home of no boundaries and no weight; there wasn't any need for a body. Up there, she was free, wandering in her green rivers of light, always half-watching the faraway World Between. To be here, in this single specific form, cut off from all she had ever known…

She slowed to a walk, inspecting her body as she wandered through the forest. By all accounts, it was perfect: humanlike, yet unmarred by the harsh life humans led down here. Her skin was smooth, her hair fine, merging seamlessly with the soft fur on her ears and tail.

At least that was something he had gotten right. As formless and nameless as she was, the fox was as close as a mind could come to perceiving her.

After a while, the trees thinned and she stepped out into another clearing. The temperature had dropped, and a cold ring appeared around the Moon Spirit. The snow glowed blue, forming a thin crust of frost – she felt it under her feet with every step. Even the air was frozen: tiny water droplets had crystalised and hung glittering all around her.

The coldness didn't bother her at all, but the frost was sharp, so she sank to her knees. As she nursed her toes, she allowed herself to look around, and couldn't help but marvel at the beauty of the icy land.

The pines and birches stretched high, their boughs coated with the perfect amount of snow they could hold; every harsh angle softened beneath the sparkling powder. Anywhere devoid of snow was coated by a layer of ice, which shone even in the low light. Silence stretched all around – there were no signs of any animals. Even the wind ceased, until she was left in a perfect stillness which could have stretched away to the ends of the earth.

Her face, usually so expressionless, formed a small smile.

It was stunning; she couldn't deny that. She hadn't seen it like this before: first-hand, down within the forest. The view from the World Above was completely different. And despite the discomfort of her physical body, the harshness of the surroundings as they touched her skin and bombarded her senses... perhaps it was worth it, just to witness this land.

She turned her eyes to the sky. The stars shone down upon her, and sadness ached within her chest. They were missing her; all the ancestors and the Spirits of winter. She was their leader – she felt them calling for her. No Lights could dance while she was trapped down here. There wasn't even a Milky Way to lay its path through the sky. They were all alone, and so was she.

Her gaze turned to the Moon Spirit. Her mother's face was full, and cold eyes were on her.

Then she heard the formless and wordless language which only Spirits and mages could speak.

*Foolish White Fox One. You are just as feared as I, and for what? To punish a stupid little boy? Look where it has gotten you!*

*I will come home,* she snarled back.

*How?* said the Moon Spirit. *Will you tell him the truth? And hurt yourself even more in the process?*

*Oh, yes, Silver One, you would enjoy that,* she snapped. *You can speak nothing of truth. If you had not been dissatisfied with your own truth in the beginning, he wouldn't even be here right now. He would still be with his own mother. Not here. Not like this.*

*Strong words from one who cannot even ignore an insult,* the Moon responded coldly. *You always held yourself so mightily. I am the symbol of the Long Dark, which brings blizzards and lean hunts… and yet they fear offending you more than me. For as terrible as I am, I have never taken a life-soul. I have never been bound to their realm. Look at where your pride has left you!*

The words struck her. She turned away, shaking with fury and guilt. No, she was the majestic aurora, the Spirit of the

Lights! She was powerful and beautiful, no matter where she was or how she appeared!

*I will come home*, she repeated again, *with or without his help.*

Her pupils shrank into a haze of flashing green and blue. The colours filled her from head to toe. Unable to stay still any longer, she took off at a sprint, her ears flat against her scalp.

As she ran, her tail swept at her heels, bringing up bursts of snow. They hung in the air, forming a trail behind her, waving into a tiny aurora.

Tuomas made his way back towards the tent, his arms piled high with freshly-cut wood. Lilja's axe hung at his belt, tied there with a strip of leather.

He followed his footprints through the trees until they became sparse, and the shelter appeared, highlighted orange from the fire inside. The reindeer were lying close to each other, still tethered to the tree. Their ears swivelled towards him inquisitively as he passed, but upon sensing he had no food, they returned to their rest.

Tuomas paused by the sleighs. The Spirit was nowhere to be seen, and he doubted she would have gone into the tent. Somehow, he suspected she would want to stay away from anything warm. She was, after all, a thing of winter.

"Don't worry about her," Lilja called from inside the shelter. "She'll come back when she's ready."

Tuomas hooked his foot under the flap and held it wide enough to throw the logs inside. He crawled in after them and shoved them towards the skin wall, then settled opposite Lilja.

While he'd been gone, she had retrieved his sleeping sack from his sleigh and laid it out. The gesture took him by surprise – it was a courtesy given by a host to welcome someone into their shelter. No matter that she had no people; she had still done it.

He offered her a grateful smile, but she was too preoccupied in piling some of the wood on the fire. She arranged it in a cross-hatch manner, to burn steadily through the night. Then she handed him half of the hare, now fully cooked.

His mouth watered. He thanked the Spirits before taking a large bite out of the rump. Lilja did the same, muttering courtesies under her breath. They ate in silence, pulling off every scrap of meat, then withdrew their smallest knives and split the largest bones lengthwise to pull out the juicy marrow within.

"Where did she go?" Tuomas asked eventually.

"Into the forest," said Lilja. "Are you worried about her?"

"I'm responsible for her."

"No, you're not. She's a Spirit. She can take care of herself."

Tuomas grimaced, remembering how she *took care* of Mihka.

"Well, I owe her. I need to appease her," he said.

"That's not the same as being responsible for her," Lilja remarked. "And I'm sure constantly having her in your sight won't factor into her appeasement. Relax, boy."

Tuomas peeled a strip of marrow from the hare's thighbone and lifted it to his mouth.

"How can I relax? Time isn't on my side. I need to help my friend. What if he dies?"

Lilja shook her head. "Don't worry about that. It won't kill him."

"How can you be so sure?"

"Mages have been without their life-souls for weeks at a time, communing with the Spirits, and suffered no ill effects. So long as your friend is fed and watered, as best he can be, he'll be fine."

She spoke flippantly, as though this kind of subject was normal conversation to her. Perhaps it was – based on the level of conversations she seemed to have, there was clearly no mention of small talk or jokes.

But it unnerved Tuomas. Henrik had mentioned that she and her brother – wherever he was – were *too* powerful. Was that why they wandered, rootless, without anybody but themselves? Why she was so strange? What hold did she truly have over the Spirits… or them over her?

"How can *he* survive that long without a life-soul, though?" he asked. "He's not a mage. He's just an idiot."

"You speak highly of him," Lilja said sarcastically. "Is he truly the best company if he thinks it's acceptable to insult Spirits?"

"He just wasn't thinking," Tuomas insisted. "He's the son of one of our leaders, you see."

Lilja raised her brows. "So that gives him a free pass to behave how he wants, does it?"

Tuomas shook his head, suddenly defensive.

"His mother died giving birth to him – the same as my mother, actually. So Sisu – his father – gave him everything. He's used to getting away with things, pulling pranks, having all the attention. And I put up with it because he's my best friend. He's the only other kid in Akerfjorden the same age as me."

He heaved a sigh from the depths of his lungs.

"I know I had my brother, and Mihka had his father, but we grew up together. We had something in common. So, yes, I know he's an idiot, but he's also my best friend. Haven't you ever felt that about anyone?"

Lilja's eyes widened. He'd caught her off guard.

"Yes," she said quietly. "It didn't turn out too well for me, though."

She scratched at her throat, then shook her head, as though chasing away whatever memory had bombarded her. Tuomas felt the shift as though she had thrown out a protective circle.

But he couldn't help himself.

"Why?" he pressed.

Lilja didn't look at him.

He tried again.

"Where's your brother?"

A muscle twitched in Lilja's jaw.

"Gone."

"Gone where?"

Her eyes turned to stone.

"Finish your meal," she said, in a tone which clearly spelled the end of the conversation.

Fighting a frustrated sigh, Tuomas ate the final strip of marrow and placed the bones into a pouch at his belt. They were only small things, but no part of a kill went to waste. It would be disrespectful to the prey to end its life and then only use part of the body. So these he would keep for craft work. He could carve them and then use them to decorate a knife hilt, or bore a hole through them and make beads.

He stretched his legs out, accidentally catching against a blanket in the corner. It fell down and revealed a stack of wood.

Lilja carried on eating, but watched him from under her lashes.

Tuomas stared at the logs, then at her, then at the axe she had given him.

"You sent me out for nothing?"

"One can never have too much wood," replied Lilja.

Tuomas sheathed his knife angrily.

"Or time, so it seems," he snapped.

He got to his feet, snatching his sleeping sack as he rose.

"I've had enough of this. You're not what I was told you would be."

"I'm sorry to disappoint you," Lilja said. "Where are you going?"

"Back to Akerfjorden."

He threw open the flap and strode towards his sleigh, rolling up the sleeping sack in mid-step. He was about to toss it under the tarp when a single loud drumbeat sounded.

His legs locked together as though a lasso had been thrown around them. He grabbed at the sleigh before he could lose his balance, and looked over his shoulder.

Lilja was standing by the tent, drum in hand. The hammer rested gently on the skin, just touching it.

Tuomas remembered the shockwave she had used to defeat the wolves. To be able to do that had told him she was powerful; but now, being on the receiving end of it, he couldn't help but feel the true extent of her *taika*. It was like a physical pressure, as though invisible hands restrained him where he stood. If it had been anywhere other than his legs, she would have crushed the breath from his lungs.

"Let me go," he demanded.

Lilja didn't move.

"Why do you feel the need to go back to Akerfjorden?" she asked.

"Because Henrik said you'd be able to help, and you obviously can't," Tuomas snapped. "So I'm going to see what else we can do to get the Spirit back up there and help Mihka."

"Because you don't like the idea that I'm your only hope," Lilja corrected. "You don't like my manners, my way of doing things, my stubbornness... I've heard all the excuses, boy. Don't flatter yourself by thinking I'm offended by them."

"If you're not offended," Tuomas said, "then why stop me?"

"Because it's the only way you'll stay still for long enough to listen to reason," she replied, not moving the hammer from the drumskin. "Henrik is doing all he can do right now: looking after your friend. Do you really want to go back with no answers and an even angrier Spirit behind you?"

She had a point. He was supposed to be on his mage test – what would it look like if he ran home now, with his tail between his legs, only two days after leaving?

But he wasn't about to let her win that easily.

"He never lied to me."

"Neither did I. I never denied we already had wood. And frankly, there are worse things to get upset about."

"Well, what am I supposed to do? Won't you come back to Akerfjorden with me?"

"No."

"But I was under orders to fetch you!" Tuomas insisted.

"I wager there was no time limit on it though, was there? Anyway, I never was one for following orders," Lilja said. "Akerfjorden can wait. For now, we go further north."

Tuomas stared at her. *North?* That was completely in the wrong direction!

"But Henrik said –"

"Forget Henrik," Lilja cut in. "Henrik's not here. Henrik wouldn't have sent you out here if he could have fixed things. Henrik isn't the one who dug himself into a deeper hole than he knew how to get out of."

She lifted the hammer off the drum and pointed at him with it. The pressure instantly vanished from around Tuomas's legs.

"You say you need to appease the Spirit? She can't be appeased by anyone until she's back in the World Above," said Lilja. "*You* brought her down here; *you* need to put her back, and you don't know how. You need to learn, from ones more powerful than me.

"So I'm going to take you to the Northern Edge of the World. There's an entrance to the World Below there, and you can seek the guidance of the Earth Spirits. I can get you in there, and they'll be able to help you. The Spirit goes back in the sky, your friend's life-soul gets returned, and you can go home like nothing happened. Will that satisfy your *orders* for now?"

Tuomas ground his teeth in agitation, but didn't argue. He knew she was right. But it seemed like Mihka was slipping further and further away on this ridiculous quest he had set upon. Yes, he had only been away from Akerfjorden for two days, but that was two days too many. He should have controlled his anger and never tried to invoke the Lights by himself. Lilja had found him quickly enough – even from the beginning, she had been within distance of the village. How easily he could have tracked her down, sought her help, and fixed everything, had he just left the drum alone!

If Lilja sensed his inner turmoil, she didn't give it away. She just took note of the defeat on his face and, knowing she had won, ducked back into the tent. Tuomas grabbed his sleeping sack and ruefully followed her.

By the time he had stepped through the flap, Lilja was already wriggling into her own sack. She turned her face to the wall.

"Get some sleep. We're leaving early, and you can help me take down the tent."

"I have another question," Tuomas said. "Why were you looking for me? Why am I so important? Because I pulled the Spirit out of the World Above?"

"There are more dangerous things than Spirits roaming about this realm, boy," replied Lilja. "Now go to sleep."

Tuomas stared at her. How was he supposed to sleep when those were her last words to him?

He removed his belt and shoes and laid down. His eyes moved to the fire. The orange tongues had found the new logs and were licking away at them, turning the pale bark black. The heat and dancing flame were hypnotising in the way they moved, never the same twice. It was so much like the Lights.

He reached out a hand, just skimming the top of the fire with his fingers. It reminded him of watching the aurora as a child, unabashed by their sacredness, daring to purse his lips in imitation of a forbidden jest. He wouldn't have dared let any sound out, but the thrill was too tempting. Unlike the other children, he had no parents to stop him. It was only when Paavo had caught him pretending that he had been punished with a slap on the backs of his thighs. Then his brother had threatened to tell Henrik. That had done the trick, and Tuomas had never tried his luck again.

A scornful smile played on his lips. How ironic that the Lights themselves were now his travelling companion.

He threw a glance at the tent flap, half-hoping that she would at least poke her head through, and let him know she was alright. But there was nothing.

Instead, his thoughts turned to Lilja. Who was the person she had cared about so deeply? Was it her brother, Kari? He supposed the two of them must have been close, to wander together as they had for so long.

That raised another question. Where was Kari?

Even as he pondered it, he felt his thoughts becoming groggy. In the end, he gave up, and waited for dreams to take him.

# Chapter Eight

The next morning, Lilja woke Tuomas with a rough shake of the shoulder, and barely waited for him to stand before she started stripping the skin tarp off the tent frame.

The sudden blast of cold instantly snapped him into action. He pulled on his shoes and hurried to help her, gathering the birch twigs laid across the floor which had served as a rough carpet.

Lilja didn't speak or even look at him for too long. Was she still annoyed from him pressing her last night? It was hard to tell if she was or whether this was just her usual way of going about things.

They worked by torchlight, piling everything into the sleighs. Even though he had done this more times than he could count, Tuomas felt a wave of satisfaction. It was amazing to see an entire camp folded down and packed away like this, with such efficiency and care, the only thing left behind was a patch of disturbed snow and the ashes of a fire. Everything of use was taken; even the leftover firewood, stacked under the tarp to keep it dry.

When all was folded and tied down, they retrieved the reindeer. As Lilja tied hers into position, Tuomas ran a rope between the back of her sleigh and the reindeer at the front of his, so they could journey in a single line. It would be easier for the animals that way, to walk in the compacted snow rather than on fresh powder.

Tuomas clambered into the tiny space left in his sleigh. He looked around again for the Spirit. There was no sign of her anywhere, but he sensed she was close. He remembered what Lilja had said the night before, and supposed she would follow at her own distance.

That made him feel a little better – at least she wasn't sitting next to him this time.

He threw a glance at his hands. They had stopped shaking now, but he could still feel the shock from grabbing her wrists. He had never felt power like it. It was beyond the capabilities of any mage, as though it had the strength of all three Worlds behind it.

How had that hit him and yet walked away unharmed? How had he managed to knock Mihka out of it?

He shoved his hands into his mittens. Maybe the Earth Spirits would be able to tell him.

The Northern Edge of the World… he had heard of it in stories, but never thought he would actually see it. The closest village to it was Einfjall, and even that was miles away.

What did it look like? With a name such as that, he imagined a great crevice stretching through the earth; when he looked down into it, there would be no snow or river, such as might carve its way through any normal gorge. No, there would be darkness, like the night had come down below the ground. After all, that was what the World Above looked like. Surely the World Below would be the same?

He sighed. He was letting his imagination run away with him. Soon, he would be a full mage, and he would know all these things. He would visit the other realms just as easily as he would walk into the forest, and he would look back on this quest with the same idle musing as Henrik did of his own youth. The Spirit would be back in the sky where she belonged; Mihka would be awake, sitting beside him, and the two of them would laugh about his stupidity until they were old men.

Lilja set the pace with a snap of reins. The sleighs jolted forward as the reindeer trotted away, leaving the clearing behind. Tuomas settled back in his seat, holding his torch between his knees, and turned his eyes to the stars.

The sky was still dark overhead, and would remain so for several more hours, but Lilja knew where she was going. She angled her reindeer in the direction of the North Star, and after some clever manoeuvring through the trees, the forest began to thin, and they entered onto the plain which marked the beginning of the tundra.

The Sun Spirit slowly crept closer, casting her cool glow across the World. A layer of cloud swept in and blanketed the sky, blurring the line of the horizon, until Tuomas felt like they were moving over a sea of nothingness. Only the occasional sapling or dwarf shrub, bowed under snow, reminded him they were still on solid ground.

He pulled his hat further down until the brim rested just above his eyes. The wind was harsher here. With no trees or other obstacles, it blew hard, with a biting edge which penetrated deep. The skin on his face tightened at its touch. Inside his mittens, he tucked his fingers into his palms. His lips turned numb and his cheeks felt as though they were going to drop off. Soon, his eyelashes and hair would start to freeze.

This was just a taste of why travelling north in the wintertime was foolish. He had been to this part of the Northlands before – it was part of the migration route which the herds followed. But that was later in the year, when it was alive with the colours of hardy plants and mosses. Now, it bore no resemblance to the place he thought he knew. The snow stretched for miles in every direction, the land formless and flat under its thick white coat.

The light passed in the blink of an eye, and the faint faraway glow faded back into darkness. Without breaking pace, Lilja lit her torch again; wedged it against the side of the sleigh with her leg. It was only when the Milky Way appeared that she pulled the reindeer to a stop.

Rummaging in a bag, she dug out some moss and tossed it over for them to eat, before retrieving the tent poles. Tuomas helped her pitch the shelter, wrapping the skin tarp into place. With the two of them, it took much less time, and they were soon sitting around the fire. Lilja plucked the ptarmigan from the day before and Tuomas whittled one of the hare bones with a knife.

He let himself become lost in the activity, shaving the smooth surface away until it started to take shape. The scraping of his blade was the only sound save for the crackling fire.

Lilja worked the ptarmigan with a speed and surety such as he'd never seen, and once again he couldn't help wondering about how she had come to be like this. He knew as well as anyone that nature could be harsh, but at least he'd had a community around him, and they all survived together.

However, even when her brother was here, it would have still only been the two of them. Two people: specks on the huge white World, with only a shelter and two reindeer to their name. There would be no company except each other, no change in faces or conversation.

He pictured them living in a shelter like this one all year round – if they were so nomadic to not even join in the migration routes, they wouldn't have solid summer or winter camps with turf huts. Come blazing summer heat or howling blizzard, it would just be this skeleton of poles with a patchwork of reindeer skin draped over it. Even the tarp itself showed signs of age: the interior was darkened from years of fires. Some areas were newer than others, replaced when they would have inevitably worn thin, but the entire thing spoke of constant use, being raised and struck time after time.

How could they – *she* – get by like this, all alone?

He glanced at the bone and realised the shape he had carved it into. It was crude, limited by size, but two hollowed-out eyes peered from the white surface, framed by a pointed face. A fox.

He hadn't even been thinking of the Spirit, out there in the cold. Unnerved by the carving, he thrust it inside a pouch on his belt.

The evening flew by in a haze of smoke and slumber. Tuomas felt as though he had barely settled and closed his eyes before Lilja was shaking him awake again. The tent was collapsed once more and they continued on their way.

Several miles passed until they reached a huge flat expanse, dipping in the girth of the tundra. Tuomas recognised it as a lake which Akerfjorden folk passed with the herd, now frozen over and dusted with a layer of snow. He felt a small wave of relief at coming across somewhere he knew in the endless tundra.

When they reached the bank, he and Lilja climbed out of the sleighs and, separating them from each other, guided the reindeer across on foot. They walked out into the centre of the lake, then Lilja pulled them to a stop, and began hacking at the ground with her axe to make an ice-fishing hole.

While she widened it, Tuomas fetched a length of antler from his belongings and wound some sinew around one of the points. He attached one of his new fish hooks to the end and baited it. Lilja stuck a flaming torch beside the hole to use as a lure, then tossed down a couple of reindeer skins.

She and Tuomas laid on them and dangled their lines into the hole. Tuomas rested his chin on his wrist as he gently flicked his antler back and forth. The fire threw a flickering orange dance of light and shadows across the ice, and everything beyond its warm circle seemed darker.

Tuomas regarded Lilja in silence. Like her ladle, her antler was carved with intricate designs, some so small, he could hardly make them out. That alone showed her capacity for patience: antler was as hard as stone, and notoriously difficult to work even with the sharpest blade. He couldn't imagine how long it had taken her to complete.

His breath fogged in front of his face.

"Are you cold?" he asked. After just one day of barely speaking, his voice crackled. He cleared his throat, trying to warm it up.

Lilja shrugged. "I've had it a lot colder out here."

"Why are you all by yourself?"

"I'm not a people person," she replied bluntly.

"That doesn't explain not having a village."

"I have everything I need to survive. Who cares if I only have two reindeer instead of a portion of a herd? They suit me just fine, and I can always trade."

Tuomas noted how she had dodged the question. He turned his attention back to the hole.

"I'm sorry if I offended you last night," he said.

"You didn't. I told you, it takes hard work to offend me."

"I don't just mean when I was going to leave. I'm sorry about... the other stuff. I'm just curious, that's all. If I'm going to be travelling with you, I'd like to get to know you."

"So you can remember me fondly when you never see me again?" Lilja quipped.

Tuomas looked at her, then relaxed when he noticed a tiny smile at the corner of her mouth. In the dim light, it was hard to see, but it was there.

"I'm not used to this. Having to make conversation," she admitted. "With my brother, I barely needed to speak at all. We could read each other in silence."

Her eyes changed, staring into the distance at something only she could see. A strange wistfulness appeared on her face, and for a moment Tuomas thought she was going to cry. But then she took a deep sniff, swallowing down the emotion once more.

"How long have you been training to be a mage?" she asked.

Tuomas frowned. She had never questioned him about his own life.

"Uh... just over five months," he said. "Henrik made me his apprentice on my fifteenth birthday. I was born on midsummer – he says that makes me powerful."

"He's right. It's when the Sun Spirit is at the height of her strength."

"How do you know Henrik, anyway?"

"I have been to Akerfjorden before," said Lilja pointedly. "I've been to all the villages. But don't change the subject. How are you managing with your lessons?"

"Not great," he admitted. "Henrik's more likely to send me to sleep than get me communing with Spirits."

"And yet here you are."

Lilja flicked her antler to check if a fish had taken the hook. Feeling none, she returned it to its position.

"Let me guess. You want to be a mage and feel important, but were hoping it would be more fun than whatever your teacher is giving you."

Tuomas went to protest, but Lilja carried on.

"Don't be upset. It's the same story for most mages who thought it was what they wanted."

"Who *wouldn't* want it?" Tuomas said. "If you have the power, why not use it? It's amazing."

Lilja's eyes darkened at his choice of words.

"Amazing can mean many things."

"Well, it is," he insisted. "Henrik just likes to talk. All I've had since we started is theory."

"He's an old man. Of course he likes to talk," Lilja said. "And theory's important, but I'm sure you've heard that enough from him."

She checked her fishing line again. A tirade of emotions chased themselves across her face, as though she was trying to decide whether to say what she was thinking. Eventually, she gave in.

"I struggled too, in the early days."

"Were you bored out of your mind too, never getting anywhere?" Tuomas asked.

"No. I was the complete opposite to you. You want to be a mage. I never did."

Tuomas stared at her, his interest caught.

"Really?"

"Yes. Kari – my brother – was always the one who showed the most potential. Our father is a mage too, you see, in Poro village. That was where we were born, and he taught Kari when he became old enough. But one winter, when I was eleven, I fell sick, and I slept for weeks, caught somewhere between Worlds. And I was met by the Great Bear Spirit.

"It brought me back to life, let me awaken. My father and brother saw the shape of the Bear formed by the mist of my breath. So as soon as I could leave the hut, I started training alongside Kari, to harness my power – a power I never knew I had. I was the youngest mage in generations."

Tuomas's mouth fell open. The Great Bear Spirit was the strongest and most sacred force in nature; the embodiment of all who had gone before and all that would be. Communing with it was the ultimate dream of every mage. To have it come willingly to a dying girl and bring her back from the edge of the abyss... no wonder Lilja's *taika* was so strong.

And, he supposed, no wonder she decided to keep to herself. With that amount of power inside her, and the legacy of being touched by the Bear, could anyone truly feel like they belonged with people anymore?

He recalled Henrik's words about all mages being tested. That illness had been her challenge. Her will to fight it, even at that young age, must have been extraordinary to bring such a Spirit to her.

"Why didn't you want it?" he asked in a small voice.

"Nobody wants to be so ill they're expecting death, boy."

"No, not that. I mean being a mage."

"Not many people do," said Lilja. "Some train hard, others have it thrust on them. Not everyone can bear it. They fail at their test and never recover. But if you make it... you live constantly in two. Not just with the physical and the unseen, but because everyone will come to rely on you and fear you equally. It's certainly a lonely life, if not a fulfilling one. But in any case, it's the path I walk, albeit in my own way."

Tuomas fell silent for a moment. Would he be able to bear his test? If he failed, it wouldn't be just himself who suffered. Mihka would be trapped in his purgatory, and poor Sisu's heart would be destroyed.

His hand lingered over the pouch where the lock of white hair was hidden.

Ever since the summer, Henrik had been trying to tell him what Lilja had gotten across in moments. He realised how little he had truly listened – he hadn't wanted to learn, not really. He'd just wanted to become a mage, with no true thought to everything needed to get there.

"Is that why you never stay in one place?" he asked, desperate for some distraction.

"Nobody stays in one place," Lilja said. "Even you. Everyone leaves their villages for the migrations. And when you all go north, I go south. And vice-versa. It's more peaceful that way."

"But everyone comes back to their villages in the winter," Tuomas pointed out.

"Each to their own," she shrugged. "It's not too fun when you never get a moment's peace. People find out you're linked to the Great Bear Spirit and you can kiss a normal life goodbye. I know wandering like I do isn't too normal either, but it's certainly quieter."

She paused for a moment, contemplating something, then let out a loud sigh.

"The reason why I know Henrik is because I was with the Akerfjorden community fifteen years ago, on the Island of Anaar. The herds had been driven to the coast, and Kari and I were at the migration grounds to trade. That midsummer evening, I helped your mother when she gave birth to you."

Tuomas froze.

"What?"

"She went into labour, and the Akerfjorden midwife had died not long before, so I heard. No midwives from the other villages were close enough. Henrik was sick and couldn't do it himself. I was the only one with the knowledge. So my brother sang the birth protection chants while I delivered you. You were healthy, but your mother didn't make it through. I'm sure you already knew that much."

Tuomas didn't know what to say. His heart felt as though it might burst out of his chest with shock.

"So that's how you knew me?"

"Well, you have changed a little since then," Lilja said dryly. "But even when you were born, I knew you had power. I could sense it in you. I just didn't see you grow into it. Kari and I left Anaar the next day. That was the last time I was even with your village."

"Why didn't you come back?"

Lilja hesitated.

"Because having too much power in one place rarely ends well."

"You mean you and your brother? But you go all over the Northlands together."

"And why do you think he's not with me now?" The way she said it meant she clearly didn't want an answer. "But no. It wasn't a matter of two people. It was three."

As she finished, she turned her eyes pointedly on him.

"Me?" he asked, incredulous. "But... Lilja, if someone like you, with the power of the Great Bear behind you, couldn't put the Spirit back in the sky, then how am *I* supposed to do it?"

Lilja smirked. "Because you have something just as strong, boy."

Tuomas frowned. "What does that mean?"

"It means," she said, "that even when you were born, I knew your *taika* was powerful. When I found you a few days ago, I was on my way to Akerfjorden to fetch you. If Henrik hadn't taken you on as an apprentice, then I would have."

She suddenly reared back with an excited yelp and began reeling in her line. In a matter of seconds, she had pulled a fat grey char onto the ice. It flapped manically in an attempt to get free, but she pinned it down.

"Thank you, Lake Spirits," she muttered. "And to you, fish brother."

She struck it hard on the head with the butt of her antler. The char stilled, and Lilja tenderly laid a hand on its gills before setting it aside.

"We'll eat well tonight," she declared as she lowered her hook back into the water.

Tuomas wanted to ask her more, but one glance at her stony expression told him the conversation was over.

He supposed he should be grateful for the amount of information she had already divulged. But unease and curiosity gnawed at his belly, and his thoughts strayed back to the Spirit, her eyes blazing all the colours of the aurora.

Once again, he looked at his hands. Somehow, he had blocked her, withstood her attacks, and managed to pull her through the skin between Worlds. And now Lilja had admitted to journeying across the Northlands in the middle of winter, just to make sure he was being trained properly.

What was going on?

# Chapter Nine

The next few chars they caught weren't as large as the first, but Lilja rolled them all into a strip of sealskin and bundled it among her belongings to eat later. The fish would last them well out here, where any other prey would become scarcer by the day. Tuomas wasn't even sure how many more opportunities there would be to fish. But Lilja seemed to know the terrain well, and if she was happy with what they had hauled in, he accepted it.

The hole she had hacked into the ice was already starting to freeze when they left. They carried on walking beside their reindeer, unwilling to get into the sleighs until they were on solid ground.

Tuomas had crossed enough frozen lakes to know not to put all the weight together. Spreading out was the best option for the ice to hold them. Moving across was rarely a straight line. There were areas where the ice was thinner, where you could easily fall through. The cold would bring death faster than you could shout for help.

He kept to the white ice, avoiding the grey patches as wide as he could. Those were newer; the freeze would only reach a few feet down. Every now and then, the entire sheet would groan like a huge monster. If Tuomas had still been a child, it might have frightened him. But he set his teeth and carried on, hand tight around the reindeer's harness.

After what felt like an age, they finally reached the far bank. Lilja clambered up first, leaving room for him to follow, and they tied the sleighs back together before settling inside them. Tuomas covered his legs with the blanket and allowed Lilja to take the lead.

As they moved away, his eyes wandered to the blanket, and how the Spirit had hidden beneath it. Where was she now? Had she concealed herself somewhere while she was alone, to keep away from the dim light? Or perhaps she was even getting used to being in this World, and withstanding it more.

That did little to settle his mind. He knew she was probably nearby, tailing them like the spectral fox the ancestors once envisioned her as.

His hand wandered into the layers of hide next to him until he touched Henrik's drum. Even through his mittens, he could feel the power of the painted symbols.

It was a different kind of magic to what he had sensed from the Spirit, or Henrik himself, or even from Lilja. It wasn't as tight in the air; tasted different when he smacked his lips, like lingonberries ripened by the Sun Spirit at the height of summer.

He paused. Was this his power? His *taika*? Was this how it felt without anger driving it?

He hoped so. It was beautiful and warm, joyous to behold.

When the low light had once again given way to darkness, Lilja pulled the reindeer to a halt and they pitched camp for the night. Tuomas stayed outside, tying the animals to one of the tent poles. He made sure to gauge the wind direction, and settled them on the opposite side, so the shelter would block the worst of it. As he worked, the tapping of flint echoed from inside, followed by the slick sound of knife through flesh as Lilja filleted one of the chars.

He pulled a bag of moss out of his sleigh, perched on the rim and threw down a few handfuls. The reindeer approached, knees clicking with every step, and tucked in.

Tuomas's own bull came closest to him, and he scratched between its ears affectionately. It had already shed its antlers before the Long Dark had begun – he made a mental note to find where they had fallen when he returned to Akerfjorden.

Feeling eyes on him, he glanced over his shoulder.

The Spirit was standing there, as calmly as though she had appeared out of thin air. Her bare feet were indistinguishable from the snow, they were so white. Her long pale hair swept back and forth in the wind, and the thin starry garment she wore fluttered around her. It was cut in a way that reminded him of typical clothing, but the material itself could have been spider silk, or woven snowflakes. It defied gravity, floating as though in water.

"How long have you been there?" he asked.

She stayed silent, so he turned back to the reindeer.

"I didn't see you following us," he said. "Didn't the light delay you?"

"It was uncomfortable. But I dare say I am getting used to it."

Tuomas was surprised at himself. He had been right.

"You were concerned about me?" she asked, a note of astonishment in her voice.

"You are my concern," he replied, not looking at her. But the weight of her eyes bore down on him, and his shoulders slumped.

"I know Lilja will say there are no accidents, but it *was* an accident, me trapping you here. I never meant to do this to you."

"You were angry and prideful," said the Spirit, walking closer. "You did not know what you wanted from me."

Tuomas couldn't disguise his shock at her understanding.

"Then you forgive me?"

She pursed her lips. That was too much to ask, and too soon. But her expression was not as stony as he would have expected. She actually looked a little guilty herself.

"I probably would have done something similar in your position," she said in a quiet voice. "The only difference is that you do not understand your own power."

Tuomas pushed himself off the sleigh and took a tentative step closer to her. She watched him cagily, but didn't shy back. Her tail flickered, the tip just brushing the snow behind her.

"Why did you take this form?" he asked. "I thought you were a white fox in your true form."

"Humans cannot comprehend my true form," she replied. "A white fox is the closest you might come to it. But you wanted to speak to me, challenge me; whatever you had in mind. So you forced me to take the shape of something you could comprehend. Something that could talk."

She gestured to her body. "This is what you settled on, whether you knew it or not. Similar to your size and age. And I suppose a little of the old tales were on your mind, too."

To illustrate her point, she swept her tail again,

Her voice was softer than before, and it made Tuomas realise how strange it actually sounded. Despite moving her lips, her speech seemed to be carried not by breath, but by the wind and the cold itself. He could reach out and touch her, physically feel her skin, but it did not contain all she was. The air around her sang with her icy power; he heard the beat of it in his heart.

Yet he sensed she struggled to form words, as though to hear them aloud was a different language. And he supposed it was. Henrik had told him the World Above was a formless place. A place where everything existed alongside its neighbours with no need to announce its presence. Ancient, she might be, but this was completely new to her.

He twisted his fingers together inside his mittens. The Spirit regarded him, then took a step closer.

He immediately backed off.

"You won't harm me?" he asked, unable to keep the panic out of his voice.

"Even if I wanted to, I cannot. You diffused my attack. My powers will not work on you."

"Why?" Tuomas asked. "Lilja mentioned something about my own powers being strong... is that why I managed to stop you from striking her?"

He paused. "Is it why you left Mihka alone when I jumped on top of him?"

The Spirit moved her eyes away, as though she was unsure whether to answer.

"You know, Mihka wasn't trying to insult you, not really," Tuomas insisted. "That's just the way he is, always being silly. He's spoiled and lets it go to his head. You must have seen that from the World Above."

A muscle twitched in the Spirit's jaw.

"Anger does terrible things. You can vouch for that as much as I."

"Are you saying you didn't mean to strike him?" Tuomas asked in disbelief.

"No. I did mean it," she said with the hint of a snarl. "Silliness or none, he was insolent and rude."

"So you attacked him? Aren't there worse things out there than one stupid kid?"

Her eyes swirled red.

"And so now you unleash your tirade: the entire reason you brought me down here, and trapped me in this… *body*," she snapped, spitting out the last word as though it were poison. "Are you happy now? Does it bring back your friend? No, because I am here with you and not up there with him!"

She bared her teeth. Her tail whipped the snow, forming a tiny aurora at her heels. The Lights spun around her like fire.

Tuomas's heart slammed against his ribs. But he stood his ground. He had blocked her twice already – if she tried to attack him again, he hoped he could repeat it a third time.

She looked him up and down. Slowly, her eyes returned to a ghostly green.

"I said I will not harm you," she reminded him. "Are you still afraid of me?"

"Yes," he said immediately.

"Good."

"Why is that good? I'm doing my best. I've apologised; I've tried to explain. Please… can't we just try to work together?"

She regarded him unblinkingly.

"We have both let out our anger now," she said in the end. "You and I are not so different. We shall move forward from this point. And when I am returned in the World Above, I will send your friend's life-soul back, as I said I would. I can… see how much you miss him."

"Thank you," said Tuomas, and he meant it.

They stood in silence for a moment. The reindeer, finished with their meal, let their thin legs fold beneath them, and they pressed against each other to keep warm.

Tuomas spoke up again.

"I wanted to ask you something. You said that my name wasn't Tuomas when I told it to you. Why?"

"You and I are not so different," the Spirit repeated, and her tone was final.

Curiosity and frustration burned inside him, but he decided better than to push his luck.

"If we're working together," he said carefully, "is there a name I can call you?"

There was a long pause before she answered.

"No. Names are a thing of humans."

"So what can I call you?"

"You may… choose a name, if you wish."

Her voice was quieter than before, as though she was resigning herself to something foreign and unsure.

Tuomas looked at her. Her eyes were shining a strange violet colour, tinged at the edges with pale green. He glanced at her ears, and for a moment was tempted to call her Fox or Aurora, or something similar. Something close to what she said her true form was.

But he hesitated. If Spirits had no names, no physical forms, then would a physical name too similar to that do more harm than good?

It struck him that nobody had ever done this before. Spirits were referred to only by their titles. But *Spirit of the Lights* was too much of a mouthful.

What had Lilja called her a few days ago, when they had first met? He couldn't remember – it was something about whiteness?

He was suddenly inspired by the stark whiteness of the body he had given her; how it seemed to sparkle under the faint starlight. If he squinted, he was sure he would lose her against the frosty landscape.

An idea formed in his mind: something which linked both her nature as a winter Spirit and the form she inhabited now.

"You look like the snow," he remarked. "So... maybe the old word for snow? The one our ancestors used, back in the time of the Great Mage."

She looked straight at him. A grin played on her lips.

"I remember that time as if it were yesterday," she said. "I know the word. It was *lumi*."

"Yes. *Lumi*."

"I accept that."

"And... will you please call me Tuomas?"

A wave of discontent flashed across her face, but she nodded.

Tuomas smiled, satisfied that they had formed a truce, however strange and tentative.

The aroma of cooking char wafted through the air. Realising the food was almost ready, Tuomas made his way towards the tent. But he paused outside the flap and looked back at the Spirit.

"Will you join us?" he asked.

"No," she said at once. "It is too hot and too crowded."

"Don't you need to eat?"

"No."

"Alright," he said. "Well, goodnight, Lumi."

He pulled back the flap and disappeared inside. The Spirit watched his shadow on the fire-lit tarp as he settled opposite Lilja.

Once again, the endless night stretched around her.

"Goodnight," she whispered, "my brother."

# Chapter Ten

By Tuomas's count, ten days had passed since he and Lilja fished on the lake, but it was getting harder and harder to keep track of time. The days flew by in short bursts of wintry half-light, growing ever shorter as the Long Dark extended its grip.

The change was even more noticeable as they journeyed further north. Soon, the twilight lessened from a few hours to less than one, the Sun Spirit's power diminishing as quickly as the treeline. Only the hardiest plants continued to grow now, driven to survive solely by their own stubbornness to reach whatever nutrients lingered in the permafrost. The mountains were long gone; the group had bypassed the peaks through a thick neck of tundra, and now they were deeper into the frozen heart of the Northlands than Tuomas had ever been.

The temperature had already dropped. At first it was only an added bite to the air, but then snow hurled itself down on them, with none of the delicate softness which Tuomas knew in Akerfjorden. The wind blew unhindered, through to his bones. He hadn't needed convincing when Lilja suggested they adorn extra layers. Now he was clad in practically every item of clothing he had brought with him, and even lashed a length of leather under his chin to prevent his hat from flying off.

As usual, he was bringing up the rear. Lilja led the way with a sureness which unnerved him slightly. There were no landmarks here, nothing to indicate where they were, or even which direction they were travelling in. But nothing hindered her.

Beside him, Lumi was perched atop the rolls of reindeer hides and tent tarp. The wind didn't appear to bother her at all; she barely even strained against it.

She had agreed to ride with him the day after he had named her. She hadn't said why, but Tuomas couldn't help but feel it was an act of good faith. He had seen how fast she could run – he was sure she didn't have to stay with him and Lilja if she didn't want to.

He pressed himself further down into the sleigh in an attempt to keep warm. A blizzard was on the horizon. A gust of snow swept into his face and tears welled up. He quickly closed his eyes, but immediately wished he hadn't. The water trickled onto his lashes and froze there.

He removed his hands from under his armpits, cupping them over his eyes. It was tempting to rub them, but that would only make the icy hairs snap off. The only thing to do was let his own body heat thaw them.

Lilja pulled her reindeer to a halt, and Tuomas's almost ran into the back of her sleigh. He eased his eyes open, cringing at the feeling of tugging skin.

"Let's get the tents!" Lilja said, struggling to be heard over the wind. "Put yours up too; the animals need to shelter! Hurry, before it gets any worse!"

Tuomas wasted no time. Lumi jumped down from her perch so he could wrestle the poles free. Lilja helped him stick them into the ground, but the butts skidded as they hit a thick layer of ice under the snow. Tuomas retrieved his axe and began hacking a series of notches, to give the poles something to grip onto.

The whiteout was encroaching on them. It was like the swarms of mosquitoes in the summer months: their clouds so thick that Tuomas could hardly bear to open his mouth for fear of swallowing them. He batted flakes away from his nose, the skin cracked with cold.

Lilja crouched on all fours and he clambered onto her back, using the added height to tie the poles together at the top. He was just about to fetch the tarps when Lumi put a hand on his shoulder. He strained to see her – the swirling snow almost made her invisible.

"Tuomas, look," she said. Her voice barely rose above the wind, yet he heard her.

He peered in the direction she was pointing. His lashes were completely white, like thick feathers; he could hardly make out anything. But then he noticed what had caught her attention: a figure, approaching on skis.

Before he could say a word, Lumi ran behind him and vanished into the snow. He went to call after her, but realised she didn't want to be seen. It was best to leave her.

"What is it?" Lilja asked.

"Someone's coming," he answered.

Lilja staggered forward and faced the figure. It gradually came into view, body wrapped up from head to toe. Even its eyes were covered with thin discs carved from bone, slits cut into them to guard against the snow. With them, it looked like a strange owl-creature.

When it saw them, it stuck its ski poles into the snow and raised a bow.

"Stop!" Tuomas shouted. "We don't mean any harm!"

The figure immediately lowered the weapon. It moved closer, holding out a hand in a sign of friendship.

"My name is Sigurd, from Einfjall," it announced in a deep voice, slightly muffled by furs. "What are you doing out here?"

"Pitching camp," replied Lilja, rather tersely.

"Not in this weather!" exclaimed Sigurd. "Come back with me, shelter at my village!"

Tuomas threw a sideways glance at Lilja. She didn't seem happy about the idea of going among people.

"Come on," he pressed. "By the time we get the tents up, we'll be frostbitten."

"The boy's right," said Sigurd. "Have your reindeer follow me – leave the tent poles, we can come back for them when the storm's passed."

He didn't wait for protests, and approached Lilja's reindeer, looping a length of rope through the closest one's harness. Then he tied the other end around his waist, so he could walk in front of them and not be separated.

Tuomas climbed into his sleigh and drew the blanket tightly around himself. It took a few more moments before Lilja agreed, and she threw herself in beside her belongings with a frustrated sigh. As soon as she was inside, Sigurd set off. He grasped his ski poles as he passed them, leading the way into the howling wind.

Tuomas looked for Lumi, but there was no sign of her. He supposed that even had she been standing right in front of him, he might have missed her in these conditions.

Knowing there was nothing else he could do, he bent his head and completely covered himself with the blanket. His reindeer let out a snort of discomfort. Hopefully there would be some lichen at Sigurd's village which he could give the animals. Einfjall couldn't be too far, if their rescuer had set out to find them on foot.

Soon, they slowed down. Tuomas peeked out of his scarf. The faint outlines of turfed huts loomed from the snow like ghosts, and his heart leapt with relief. Even in the storm, he could just catch the scent of woodsmoke, of cooking meat and fresh herbal tea. It smelled like home.

When they reached the huts, Sigurd untied himself and helped Lilja out of her sleigh. He removed his skis, wedged them against the wall of the nearest shelter. Then he dug around in a large bag at his belt and drew out a handful of moss. Tuomas smiled in thanks as he threw it down for their reindeer, then proceeded to help unhitch them so they could eat.

Lilja and Tuomas hastily covered their sleighs with a sheet to keep out the worst of the snow. Tuomas snatched their sleeping sacks, but noticed that Lilja took only her drum. Out of all her belongings, that was the one she couldn't part with, even for a single night.

"You can sleep with my family," Sigurd offered. "We have room, and food for you."

Tuomas smiled at his hospitality. It had long been a custom among their people that if someone was in need, or came seeking shelter, they would not be turned away. Neighbours were simply extended family, and back in Akerfjorden, nobody would bat an eyelid if someone made themselves at home in your hut for the evening. It touched him to know that no matter how deep into the abyss he travelled, there would always be good people to offer help.

Sigurd held open the door of the hut, inviting them inside. After a small pause, Lilja ducked under his arm. If Sigurd was offended by her hesitation, he didn't show it; only hastened for Tuomas to follow.

Tuomas threw one last glance over his shoulder, in case Lumi was lingering nearby, but there was no sign of her. So he crawled into the hut, and Sigurd shut the door behind them.

Two faces looked up as he entered: a woman and a girl, side by side at the far edge of the hearth. A pot was in the flames in front of them, the delicious smell of sautéed reindeer drifting from under the lid. Tuomas gave them both a grateful smile, then crawled to the reindeer skin where Lilja had seated herself.

Sigurd busied himself removing his layers and eye-discs. As he shed his furs, a bright tunic was revealed; the woven details different yet again from what Lilja wore. Tuomas regarded them with interest. Every village had their own way of decorating clothing and tools; it was a way to identify where someone came from without even having to ask.

Sigurd pulled off his hat and ruffled his hair with one hand. It was as black as night, and cut short into a fringe across his brow. Then he hung his bow beside two others which were strung up on the turfed wall – Tuomas presumed those belonged to the woman and girl. They were made from a single limb of pale ash wood, obviously gathered from the south of the Northlands – there was no way that tree would grow here in the tundra. Each one was strung with a stretched reindeer tendon; beside them were quivers made from sealskin and adorned with beads. The arrows inside were fletched with snowy owl feathers for silent flight. Efficient, yet beautiful.

"Please forgive me for earlier," Sigurd said, noticing where Tuomas was looking. "I was tending to our herd and thought I heard the bells of another's reindeer go by, so I came to see if anyone needed help. But there's been talk of something bad wandering about."

Lilja frowned. "What do you mean, something bad?"

"I don't know for sure. But something unnatural-looking, at any rate, or so I've heard. Some people are saying it's a troll, come down from the mountains. I'm not sure I believe them, but you can't be too careful!"

He patted his bow as though it was a trusted pet, then settled beside his family and kissed them both on the tops of their heads.

"Where are my manners?" he muttered. "This is my wife, Alda, and my daughter, Elin. Welcome."

"Thank you," Tuomas smiled. "I don't know what we'd have done if you hadn't found us."

Lilja glowered at that, but didn't contradict him. She just stared intently into the fire. One finger slipped under her scarf and traced the line of her scar.

Sigurd's eyes lingered on her for a moment. Then he gasped.

"By the Spirits! Lilja, is that you?"

Lilja stiffened, but she didn't answer.

Alda leaned forward, peering at her face from across the fire.

"It is!" she cried. "We thought you were dead!"

"It takes more than cold to kill me," Lilja muttered. "It's nice to see you. I have chars in my sleigh – you're welcome to the largest one as thanks."

Sigurd waved a hand dismissively. "Never mind that, we'll sort it out after the storm. How long's it been, ten years? How are you?"

"Fine," Lilja said. She turned her eyes to Alda. "How's the leg?"

"Practically like new, after that poultice you gave me," smiled Alda. She laid a hand over her calf and gave it a rub, as though nursing the old injury. "I just wish I'd had more to pay you with than some bone needles."

Sigurd smiled. "I would ask what you're doing, travelling by yourselves so far north – in winter, of all seasons.

But seeing you, Lilja, it makes perfect sense. Never one to settle, were you?"

Lilja didn't move.

"Where's Kari, anyway? I'd have thought he'd be with you?"

A shadow passed across Lilja's face. One hand strayed to her drum and lingered over the bloody smear on the skin.

"He's elsewhere. I really don't want to talk about it."

Tuomas watched the exchange carefully, trying to figure out if the family knew something more about Lilja's brother than she was letting on. But he couldn't read their reactions – Alda went about checking the meal and Sigurd simply offered a reassuring smile. Elin looked just as clueless as Tuomas himself. There was nothing to suggest a death; if that had been the case, Alda and Sigurd would have made the sign of the hand to wish souls well on their journey.

Realising that conversation wasn't going anywhere, Tuomas instead looked at Elin. He vaguely recognised her from the journeys to the coast, but didn't recall ever speaking to her. Each village had their summer camps on different islands, so they only came together for a few days to trade and share stories before moving on again.

She had the same raven black hair as her father, extending down her back in a braid which made it look like a sting. Hers was also cut into a fringe – he recalled that was a customary style for the people of Einfjall. She was small and toned, her face round and her nose turned up like a button. Her large eyes, the colour of ripe nuts, held a peculiar fusion of warmth and sharpness in their depths.

"Weren't there three of you?" Sigurd asked. "I was sure I saw another person."

Tuomas hesitated, but quickly decided not to mention Lumi. If she had kept her distance, it was obvious she didn't want to be brought up. And he was glad to finally be forging some kind of friendship with her, he didn't want to tear it down so soon.

"No," he said.

"Probably the snow playing tricks on your eyes," smiled Alda.

"Probably," Sigurd agreed, then sniffed the air. "When will that food be ready? I'm starving! And I'm sure our guests are, as well!"

Elin peered over the rim of the cooking pot to check the contents.

"It won't be long," she said, then gave Tuomas a toothy grin. "So, what's your name? I don't know whether I've seen you on the migration route. To speak to, at least."

He smiled back sheepishly. She'd obviously been thinking the same thing as him.

"I'm Tuomas," he replied.

"How old are you?"

"Fifteen."

"The same as me."

There was no more talk while Alda hoisted the pot away from the flames. Elin held out a supply of carved wooden bowls as her mother served the portions with a bone ladle. Just the sight of it made Tuomas's mouth water. The sautéed meat was mixed with red lingonberries: a simple dish, but so hearty and filling that it never failed to satisfy.

The bowls were handed out, and everyone took a moment to thank the Spirits and the reindeer for its sacrifice, before they dug in. Tuomas withdrew his small knife and heaped the blade with food, taking care not to spill any down his chin.

"So, Lilja," said Sigurd, "I'd imagine even a wandering mage has common sense. Why are you this far north? You'll get cut off from going back if you're not careful."

Lilja swallowed her mouthful of reindeer before replying.

"We're going to the Northern Edge of the World."

Elin's eyes widened at that. "Really?"

"Why not during the thaw?" Sigurd pressed. "It would be a lot easier for you!"

"No, it must be now," said Lilja. "We need to speak with the Earth Spirits. Anyway, at least at this time of year, it will be summer in the World Below."

Tuomas frowned. "Summer? What are you talking about?"

"The World Below is said to be the opposite of whatever it is here," explained Elin, rather wistfully. "When it's winter here, it's summer there. Night here, day there. That's what the mages say, anyway. They're the only ones who can ever get down there."

"I've never heard of that," Tuomas said, surprised Henrik hadn't mentioned it.

"Well, our village is the closest one to the Northern Edge of the World," said Sigurd. "It's common knowledge here. Down in the south, not so much."

"Anyway, what's all this 'we' stuff?" asked Alda, eyeing Tuomas. "Are you Lilja's son?"

"No!" both of them said in unison. Then they glanced at each other awkwardly, and Tuomas noticed Elin stifling a giggle.

"No," he said. "I'm not. I'm just..."

"My apprentice," Lilja cut in.

Tuomas shot her a questioning look, but decided to go along with it. No matter that Lilja obviously had a past with Sigurd's family, it was clear she didn't want to go into details. And, he realised, neither did he.

He turned back to his meal scraped the bottom of the bowl with his knife to ensure no morsel was left behind. Everyone else did the same, until all the dishes were set down. Elin gathered them and put them by the wall, to be washed later when the blizzard had ended. Then she dragged her sleeping sack aside to make more room closer to the fire. The overlapping birch twigs on the floor snagged on the fur as she moved it.

"You can sleep here," she said, motioning at the space she had uncovered. "We'll get your belongings from your sleighs later."

Tuomas smiled at her. "Thank you."

Sigurd wiped his knife on a strip of cloth and placed it back into its sheath.

"That was delicious, Alda."

"You'd say that if there was mould growing on it," she threw back with a wry smile, and he pulled a face at her.

"Anyway, I'm in the mood for a tale. Let's do something with the evening – it's not as though we can go ice fishing tonight," he said.

"Father, tell the one about the mage who wore human skins like a coat!" Elin piped up.

"That's a gruesome one," Sigurd remarked. "Do either of our guests have any stories to tell? Anything exciting from south of the tundra?"

Tuomas paled. Hardly anything of interest happened in Akerfjorden, and recent events were out of the question. He threw a glance at Lilja, hoping she would be able to think of something.

To his faint surprise, given her reserved nature, she nodded.

"I suppose it would be good to get my voice used to speaking properly again."

Sigurd looked at her curiously. "It's really been that long without Kari?"

Lilja glared, but spoke no more on that subject. Instead she said, "I'm afraid I haven't come by any new stories. But there is one which I never get tired of."

She turned her eyes on Tuomas for a moment longer than necessary, and began.

"At the dawn of time, the Sun and the Moon Spirits lived together as sisters, together in the World Above. And they both gave birth to a child: the Golden One bore a son, and the Silver One a daughter. The Sun Spirit's boy was as bright as day; talented, smiling, perfect in every way – and the Moon grew jealous, because her own daughter was cool and confined to the darkness. So, one day when the Sun wasn't looking, she switched the children, kidnapping the boy and leaving the girl in his place.

"But the Golden One was too kind to turn the Moon's daughter away. So she raised her as her own, showing her all the love she had given to her own son. And the Son of the Sun grew up in the Silver One's shadow, until the day he learned about his true parentage, and how he had been stolen from his mother.

"He tried to return to her, but was unable. So he leapt from the sky in the form of a red fox, and landed in the World Between, choosing this place over the lie he had been raised on. He determined to become the greatest mage the realms had ever known, and find a way to go home to his mother: the Sun Spirit."

Tuomas couldn't suppress a grin. It was one of his favourites from childhood. He hadn't heard it in years.

He rocked forward on his knees and watched Lilja closely, hanging onto her every word. Every now and then, she coughed and cleared her throat, but didn't let it hinder her. She seemed wrapped up in the story herself – it reminded him of when she had fallen into a trance and chanted, as naturally as breathing. For someone who often spoke rarely and sharply, this flowed like music.

Lilja glanced at her listeners in turn, the glow of the fire reflecting in her eyes.

"To help him on his journey, the Earth Spirits from the World Below gifted him a pair of their own magical white reindeer, which he used to build himself a magnificent herd: the herd from which all herds are descended. He ate their meat and drank their milk, and it gave him an immortal life. He walked through centuries, mastered chants and powerful *taika*, nurtured the humans who flocked to him. They became his new family, but every Midsummer, when the Golden One is at her most powerful, he would turn his eyes to the sky and whisper his love, of how he would someday return to the World Above.

"And all the while, the Sun and the Moon watched him, each longing to have him back. One midwinter night, the Silver One appeared to him, begging for him to return to her instead of her sister. But he became frightened, and gathered his people, telling them that he intended to travel south to where the Long Dark's grip was not as strong, where the endless night would be broken by small hours of his mother's glow. Some decided to stay in the north, and formed the villages of Poro and Einfjall. A small band of others chose to go with him.

"They walked for weeks and weeks, growing hungry and tired, crossing tundra and forest and fjord. His people became weak, and so, forsaking his own health, the Great Mage gave them the otherworldly meat and milk. His life began to wane, yet he led them on, until they reached the edge of the ice, and made a new home on the shore.

"But his body was mortal now, and struggled to survive. His life-soul was the Spirit he had been in his previous life, and it could no longer sustain him. The cold entered his bones, until he fell down through the ice and died. The people named the place where he fell the Black Water, in memory of his sacrifice."

Tuomas's eyes widened. This was a part of the story he hadn't heard before. The Black Water was the Mustafjord, on the border of Akerfjorden. He knew about the Great Mage who had died leading the way across it, but had always assumed him to be a man, albeit an extremely competent one.

Was Lilja honestly saying that those two stories were connected? That he'd had a Spirit as his life-soul? The Son of the Sun? Was that even possible?

She paused for a moment, swallowing to moisten her throat.

"High in the World Above, the Sun and Moon Spirits watched it all. The Golden One was heartbroken that her son would never come back to her, but she was determined to make some light out of all the darkness. So she bid her adoptive daughter care for all the souls who pass into the World Above, to be the guardian of her son, to ensure he never came to harm again.

"The Daughter of the Moon accepted, and now she leads the ancestors in their dances through the sky, sweeping up the snow with her tail. Some claim to have seen her running in the form of a white fox."

Tuomas's heart skipped a beat.

"Lumi," he muttered.

"What did you say, boy?" Sigurd asked.

Tuomas looked around. The spell of the story was broken. He shook his head.

"Nothing."

It only took a moment for Sigurd to shrug it off, and he grinned widely at Lilja, congratulating her on telling the tale so masterfully.

But she didn't meet his gaze. She only glanced quickly at Tuomas before turning her eyes back to the fire.

# Chapter Eleven

Tuomas slept fitfully. He had slept on harder ground than this, but something writhed in his stomach and refused to let him settle. And all the while, the storm raged outside. Dirt fell from the turf encasing the hut and the wooden beams trembled. The sound penetrated his dreams and he imagined the entire structure collapsing on them, burying them beneath a mound of soil and snow.

He opened his eyes and lay staring at the fire. It was well-stocked to last the night, and the flames burned gently with a hypnotising flicker. As they reached hidden residues within the logs, they transformed into brief tongues of blue and violet. It was like a miniature aurora, right there in the tent.

He didn't bother wondering how long he stayed like that, hoping he might drop off back to sleep. The terrible winds slowly stilled, and from his sleeping sack, he could see the faint pinpricks of stars appearing through the smoke hole. Across from him, Sigurd snored softly. The sound reminded him of Paavo.

His heart grew heavy. He missed his big brother so much. In his memory, he could picture Paavo's face clearly; then it morphed into Henrik's, then Sisu's, then Mihka's, with his shock of white hair. And then, finally, the whiteness spread, until Lumi was looking out at him.

He heaved a sigh and sat up, glancing around at his companions. Alda had her nose buried in Sigurd's neck, snuggled close to him to stay warm. Elin lay beside Tuomas, but at a respectful distance. Her face was half-covered by her hair, fringe sticking up at odd angles.

Lilja, however, was nowhere to be seen.

Tuomas eased himself free of his sack and crawled to the exit, quietly pulling on his coat and hat. Then he slipped his feet into his shoes and stepped outside.

As he shut the door, he knocked against Sigurd's skis. He caught them before they could make any noise and set them back against the wall. Then he stood still for a moment, listening, in case he'd woken someone. Hearing nothing, he relaxed and walked away.

The blizzard was over, and a fresh blanket of snow stretched as far as the eye could see. It melted seamlessly into the sky, so he had to strain to place the horizon line. It was only broken here and there by the silhouettes of storage houses, propped several feet off the ground atop a set of sheared tree trunks. His and Lilja's sleighs were practically hidden under several inches of white powder. Tuomas was glad they had covered them with the tarp, otherwise there would be no way of fetching anything from inside.

Now the storm had cleared, he could see the village properly for the first time. It was a little smaller than Akerfjorden, the huts built lower to the ground to withstand the stronger winds blowing over the tundra. Snow had banked up against them on one side, several feet deep in places.

Behind the settlement reared the imposing face of a mountain, its summit lost in the low cloud, the flanks caked white with snow and ice. It seemed to glow in the strange directionless light, every flake reflecting what little there was. It immediately struck him as a place of importance, and knew it must be the Einfjall shrine.

He felt power radiating out of it like heat from a hearth. Anywhere else, the mountain might not have been unusual, but out here, all by itself, completely different from all that surrounded it, it was special. The forces of nature had put it here, and now it served as a way to connect with the other Worlds: a place where the barriers separating them from the people were thinner.

Akerfjorden's winter camp had its own natural shrine: a gnarly tree stump in the forest, which had grown into a twisted shape during its lifetime. Poro would have one too; perhaps a cairn, a formation in the land, or even a simple engraved post. The one at Akerfjorden was quite small, but size didn't really matter. There wasn't much left of it, yet its strangeness showed how magical it was. All the other trees grew tall and straight; all different, but still of the same design. To be unique spoke of power.

Henrik would often go to the stump, as his predecessors had before him, to lay offerings to the Spirits, asking for favours and good fortune. Likewise, Tuomas could picture the Einfjall mage drumming up there on the mountain, halfway between the World Between and World Above. Lilja passed through here ten years ago – had she been up there too, once?

Lilja… He remembered she hadn't been in her sleeping sack.

He looked at Sigurd's hut, squinting to see in the low silvery light. He noticed something he hadn't before: a line of footprints, curling away around the back. He followed them, taking care to place his feet carefully so as not to crunch the snow. The tracks led around the edge of the village, to the base of the mountain.

Then he heard something. For a moment, his heart raced. But as he listened, he recognised the sound.

It was sobbing.

He reached the last hut and peered around it. Sure enough, Lilja was sitting on a rock several feet away, face buried in her hands. Her entire body was shaking – from the cold or her crying, Tuomas couldn't tell. She didn't even have a torch with her.

He hesitated, unsure what to do. His first thought was to comfort her, but why would she have come out here, in the freezing night, if she didn't want to be alone?

Deciding to leave her, he took a step backwards. But under the snow, his shoe hit a patch of ice, and he fell onto his side with a grunt.

Lilja's eyes snapped in his direction. She hadn't seen him, but Tuomas knew his cover was blown, so he stepped into the open.

It was too dark to see any of Lilja's features, but she quickly wiped at her cheeks.

"What are you doing out here?" she barked. Her voice was tight from weeping

"I couldn't sleep," Tuomas replied as he brushed snow off his trousers. "What's wrong?"

"Nothing."

She said it too fast.

"Lilja," Tuomas tried again, "it's alright. Do you need anything?"

"No," she said. She was still on the defensive, but her tone softened a little. "I'm fine. Memories are hard, that's all."

"You mean, being back in a village?" Tuomas asked.

She looked at him for a moment, then shrugged.

"You could say that."

She wiped her face one more time and trudged over to him.

"I'm going back to bed. Are you coming?"

"In a moment. I just wanted to get some air," Tuomas said. "Are you sure you're alright?"

Lilja threw him a glance as she passed. "I'm fine."

Without another word, she disappeared around the side of the hut. Her footsteps grew fainter, then Tuomas heard her opening the door to Sigurd's shelter. Moments later, silence fell once more.

The cold began to bite at him, so he walked back in the same direction. Keeping moving was the best way to stay warm. He wiggled his toes inside his shoes to get the blood flowing; circled his shoulders and bounced up and down for a few moments. A small fire pit was behind him, but it was empty and covered in snow; even if it had been lit, no flame could have survived the blizzard.

Soon, he arrived back to where his and Lilja's sleighs were parked. What memories could have affected her so badly? It was alarming to see her cry – he'd never imagined her as having any expression except one of stone and glaring eyes.

He knew it was best not to pry. For as alone as she'd been since childhood, he had to remember she also had a life before meeting him. He had no right to judge or assume what she might have gone through – though he secretly hoped he might find out one day.

And when she was feeling better, he would ask her where she had heard that version of the Great Mage story.

Letting his thoughts drift, he looked out towards the tundra. He felt as though he was by himself in an empty world. Not a breath of wind blew, nor a single cry sounded from some faraway animal. Even the Spirits in the air around him seemed strangely distant. Yet he still strained to catch the faintest movement: a flash of white hair or the flick of a fox tail.

"Lumi?" he whispered. "Are you out here?"

There was no answer.

He remembered his drum, still packed into the sleigh with his other belongings. He pulled back the tarp, straining against the weight of the snow on top of it, and fished around with one hand until he found the instrument and its hammer. He pulled them out and walked away again, slowly beating the skin. Maybe that would help him summon her.

He had to talk to her. That much he knew. He needed to make sure she was unharmed after the storm.

After a few minutes of nothing, he sank to his knees, resting the drum on his lap. He closed his eyes. His bare knuckles went white on the hammer, and he struck it with faster motions, a chant coming together in his throat.

He didn't even need to think; it was as though the sound was already fully formed in his chest. All he had to do was open his mouth and let it flow out like water.

This time, however, he managed to keep control. His souls didn't loosen, he kept his feet firmly on the ground. He let himself feel that hot summery *taika*, allowed it to consume him. It tasted sweet on his tongue; deliciously warm. He felt as though he was lying in a meadow under the Sun Spirit's shining face. It was almost enough to shrug out of his coat, but he forced himself not to do that.

He basked in his own uncovered power, rolling in it like a child would play in the sea. He could do this. Both Henrik and Lilja had said he was strong. Now, he could do some real mage work, prove to them he was capable of that title. This quest was supposed to be his test – surely a little practise wouldn't hurt.

Instead of wishing himself outward, as he had done in the past, he pulled in. He breathed deeply and icy air flooded his lungs.

"Lumi…" he whispered.

A growl echoed in the distance.

His eyes flew open. She wasn't there – and neither was anyone else. He was still alone. But he felt a presence, all around him, as though something was trying to press through from another realm.

Then the growl came again: deep, guttural. The air took on a horrid rancid taste that almost made him retch.

He stopped drumming.

"Who is with me?" he asked carefully.

There was no answer. He got to his feet, unease writhing in the pit of his stomach.

What kind of animal made a noise like that?

The humans' settlement was barely visible in the distance, but the Spirit could spot the hut which her companions had taken shelter in. She kept her eyes on it while she waited out the blizzard, sensing the Storm Spirits sprinting across the tundra.

*Stay strong, White Fox One,* they whispered before whirling away into the sky.

She watched them go with an air of melancholy. The snow tore around her, whipping her hair over her face. She flattened her ears to stop the wind howling down them.

It was wonderful to feel the blissful cold seep through her earthly flesh. After an age spent in weightlessness, it was still difficult to bear the closeness of everything, but she was slowly getting used to it.

The storm passed, and she looked back at the village, dusted white against the massive flank of the mountain. She refused to go closer. She couldn't let the humans see her like this… at least, no more humans, not yet. The mage woman was enough, and that had been a choice forced on her.

But the boy… Tuomas… he was a different matter.

So many humans only became familiar to her when they joined her dance through the skies. While in the World Between, they were as far away as the furthest stars. She couldn't distinguish one face or voice from the other. And that was the way it had always been.

But then Tuomas had come along.

Even from the beginning, she had sensed his souls, followed him whenever she could. When he had been born, she had been sleeping away the hot summer, but as soon as her Lights began to shine that winter, she had never truly looked away.

That evening when the foolish Mihka had dared to insult her display, she would have struck down any other who came to his defence. But of all the people watching, it was *Tuomas* who had leapt on top of him and shielded his eyes.

It was strange to call him Tuomas. It felt just as wrong as being in this physical body; so constrictive and pale compared to her true form. She had even mentioned it, back when he first pulled her down here.

But he didn't remember her. And she wasn't sure whether it would be best to tell him or not.

She stayed still, falling into her own trance, and felt herself just brush the edge of how things were in the World Above. There was no sense of time or urgency. No need to do anything except exist, to dance the silent dance, to throw her ever-changing Lights across the inky sky.

A smile traced her lips. Soon. Soon, she would be back there, back home.

And alone again.

A sudden pain ripped through her chest and she flinched. It disappeared as quickly as it had come, but left a curious ache, spreading through her whole body. It was like a fire had been lit inside her.

She gasped in agony, but she had no sooner clutched at her breast when something trickled down her face.

She wiped her forehead and looked at her fingers. A drop of water shone in the waning light.

For the first time since being pulled from the sky, she felt a jolt of genuine fear.

Then she heard the slow, steady sound of a drum.

The beats tugged at her, calling to her Spirit essence, but she stayed still. It was him, Tuomas, trying to summon her – to check she was unharmed by the storm, no doubt.

She allowed herself a small smile. Forget that he had to put her back in the World Above in order to save his friend – he was so concerned about *her*, about her safety. He didn't need to do that.

Could he sense their connection too? Was it starting to come back to him? Did she dare hope he would realise on his own, and spare her further pain?

Suddenly, the air changed.

It would have been unnoticeable to a human, but for a Spirit, it was like being submerged in water. It tasted bad, smelled bad. It was something not quite physical – something evil.

She leapt to her feet and spun around, and came face to face with a demon.

Horror paralysed her. It was an effigy: a creature made by a wicked mage. She couldn't see any human control in its hollow eyes, but that didn't mean a life-soul wasn't inside it, driving it, urging it to do some foul bidding.

*Life-soul…*

She could take souls. She could rip it out.

She raised her hands, summoning her magic, but before she could strike, the demon swung at her. Its bony arm slammed into her stomach and sent her flying backwards.

She landed with a thud, but was on her feet in moments, flinging her power at the creature. It growled and came towards her again, long claws protruding from its fingers. They cut through the air like knives. She wasn't sure if they could truly harm her, but didn't stay close enough to find out.

She kept to the defensive, hurling magic, her hands and arms glowing with the aurora. The demon shuddered upon each impact, but she kept going. Blasts like this would have struck down a human instantly – it was the same power she had tried to use on Lilja… and which Tuomas had stopped.

*Tuomas…*

That brief lapse in her concentration was enough. The demon took one huge stride forward and shoved her so hard, she fell straight through the snow and hit the icy ground beneath.

The demon bolted in the direction of the village. She scrambled up, swaying from the impact. But then she gritted her teeth and gave chase.

No matter that the humans would see her. There was no choice now. She could sense, with horrid certainty, who the creature was running towards, and she had to stop it.

# Chapter Twelve

The silence exploded. There was a bloodcurdling shriek, and a figure bounded towards Tuomas.

He fell back, too alarmed to even scream. The thing was upon him in moments, pressing him down. The drum flew from his grasp.

The creature was massive: at least two heads taller than Sisu; naked, skin dry and pale, torn into ragged fleshy scraps that stroked his cheek as it leaned over him. A stench like carrion filled his nose and made him gag. Its face was skeletal and oversized in all the wrong places, like something a child might have drawn in the snow. A large red gash had been sliced across its cheek.

Tuomas stared into the thing's hollow demonic eyes. There was no life in them.

Then he did scream. He tried to fight it off, but it grabbed his wrist in one bony hand and slammed it down. The other hand trailed down his front, pressing over his heart.

Frantic, he snatched at his belt, finding the hilt of his largest knife. He tore it free and slashed upwards.

The flint blade made contact and a second wound opened on the creature's face. The demon growled, but it was a sound of anger, not pain. Without warning, it gripped his throat with its free hand and lifted him clean off his feet.

Tuomas clutched at its fingers, gasping for air, feet pedalling as he tried to kick. His knife dropped to the ground and was instantly lost in the snow.

"Help…" he tried to choke out, but the hand tightened around his throat and cut him off. Darkness swam at the edges of his vision.

Something shot past his head.

The demon wailed and dropped him. He landed heavily on his side and looked up to see what had happened.

The shaft of an arrow was protruding from the creature's skeletal shoulder. But it still hadn't gone down. It looked more enraged than ever.

Tuomas clumsily scrambled away from it, his movements hindered by the fresh snow. But then relief filled his body. His scream had been heard. A crowd was running towards them from the village.

At the head were Sigurd and Elin, who was already drawing a second arrow. More people poured from the huts, all armed with knives, bows and even ice fishing harpoons. Some were on skis, bellowing incoherently as they rushed forward.

"What is that thing?" Elin shouted.

"Never mind, just get it away from him!" replied a woman in a skirt of white reindeer fur: the mage.

The villagers quickly surrounded the demon and jabbed at it with their blades and poles, shooting arrows into its body. It swung madly at them, letting out roars which made Tuomas shudder. The air was so heavy – it churned his stomach and he struggled not to vomit.

A flash of green suddenly lit up the night. Shocked gasped filled the air.

Tuomas looked up, straight at Lumi.

She was standing behind the demon, her arms raised, throwing spectral Lights straight into its back. She spun her hands as though dancing and the aurora surrounded the creature, tightening like a lasso around a reindeer. It jolted back and forward, bellowing in fury.

Sigurd's mouth fell open.

"What is this?"

His words broke the spell which had fallen over the crowd.

"It's a Spirit!"

"It's her! The Spirit of the Lights!"

"What's she doing here?"

With a roar, the demon spun on the spot and broke free of Lumi's grasp. The mutterings of the villagers turned once more to battle cries. Lumi struck out again, the aurora flying from her like lightning. With every strike, a red trace rose around the swirling greens as her anger grew. It seemed to be hurting the creature, but it still stayed on its feet.

Tuomas stared at it in horror. Would nothing bring it down?

He noticed his knife at the demon's feet. He snatched it and staggered upright, but before he could start fighting, someone grabbed him by the back of his coat. He fought free and turned to see Lilja, her drum in one hand.

She didn't look at him. Her eyes, still bloodshot from crying, locked onto the demon with an intensity he had never seen before.

Without a word, she pushed him behind her. She removed one of her own knives and went to advance on the demon.

But she wasn't quick enough. It barrelled through the villagers and came straight for Tuomas.

Lilja took a swipe at it, but it elbowed her aside and grabbed him, bundling him over its shoulder. He pounded at it with his fists, but to no avail, and the creature ran.

The villagers gave chase, but they were growing smaller and smaller by the moment. Lumi broke into a sprint, still flinging Lights at the demon. Tuomas flinched as one landed inches from his chest.

Lilja tied her drum onto her belt.

"Give me those!" she snapped, shoving a nearby man out of his skis. She thrust her feet into them and powered after the demon. When she got close enough, she dropped the poles, pulled her drum up, and struck it so hard, Tuomas was surprised she didn't break the skin.

A shockwave ploughed into them like a blast of icy air, and the demon's knees gave out, sending it sprawling onto its front.

Tuomas scrambled free. The demon tried to catch his legs again, but he leapt over its fingers and ran to Lilja.

As soon as Elin was within range, she raised her bow, and let fly. With incredible aim, the arrow plunged into the demon's eye.

That finally dealt some damage. The creature's howls transformed into agony, and blood stained the snow a brilliant red.

The villagers approached, Sigurd in the lead, knife raised. But they had no sooner gotten within reach when the demon fled, melting into the snow as though it were made from nothing more than air.

Tuomas stared after it, rooted to the spot. Then he looked around for Lumi. But she was gone too. There was only a faint green glow in the distance as she ran to take cover.

Lilja reached him and grasped his shoulders.

"Are you hurt?" she asked.

"No," he said. "What was that? Why was it here?"

Lilja cut him off, pulling him close so nobody else would hear.

"You were drumming for her, weren't you?"

Tuomas swallowed guiltily.

"Yes... I wanted to make sure she was alright after the storm..."

"Stupid boy! Forget that she's in a physical form; she's still a Spirit! Nothing can harm her, the winter least of all! Did you even bother to warm the drum over a fire to get it ready? Did you cast a protective circle before starting a chant?"

Tuomas felt the blood draining from his face. He had forgotten!

His words fell over each other.

"I... I thought that, since I knew exactly who I wanted to speak to..."

"What, that you didn't need to protect yourself, in case anything else came to say hello?" Lilja bared her teeth. "Some teacher Henrik is! Stupid idiot boy, get back to the shelter and stay there!"

She threw him away and turned to the villagers.

A middle-aged couple was approaching. One was the mage woman in the white skirt. She wasn't as old as Henrik, but her blonde hair was streaked with grey, cascading down her back in thick ponytail. The man beside her was adorned with the same antler and bone beads as Sisu, Maiken and Anssi back in Akerfjorden; so Tuomas immediately knew he was a leader. The only difference was that while Akerfjorden's beads were sewn in an undulating pattern to mimic the Mustafjord's waves, this man's formed a large point, practically identical to the mountain behind the village.

Lilja nursed her scar with one hand as they reached her.

"Birkir, Aino," she greeted. "Is anyone hurt?"

"Not that I can see," the man replied. "What are you even doing here, Lilja?"

"Just passing through," she answered.

Another man ran up to Birkir and grasped his sleeve.

"That was the Spirit of the Lights!" he hissed. "Why was she here?"

"Don't worry, we'll figure it all out," said the mage woman, Aino. Her voice was softer than a reindeer calf's fur. "First of all, we need to secure the village, make sure that thing can't come back. Will you help me, Lilja?"

Lilja nodded, then noticed Tuomas, still standing behind her.

"I told you to go to the shelter!"

Tuomas stepped forward to argue, but Elin took him by the elbow.

"Come on, she's mad enough already," she said quietly.

Growling in defeat, Tuomas allowed her to lead him away from Lilja, snatching up his knife and drum as he passed them. He looked at the instrument, trying to let the anger settle, but it only boiled higher.

How could he have been so stupid and naïve to not even remember the basics of the craft?

All of a sudden, he hated the drum. Without it, he never would have trapped Lumi, or alerted that demon. He had a mind to throw it as far as he could and never pick it up again.

But then the fury twisted inside him and bit at a place it never had before. Henrik wouldn't have passed the drum to him, or insisted he be the one to go out and right Mihka's wrong, if he hadn't trusted him. It wasn't just any drum he had given; it was his own, older than Tuomas himself.

With a jolt, Tuomas saw how he had broken that trust; had broken it from the very beginning. He broke it by not listening when he had the chance, by not taking the old mage seriously, by getting a taste of the sacred power and thinking it made him special. And now, because of his arrogance, it had brought nothing but misery. This was supposed to be his test, and he was failing at every turn.

He glanced back at Lilja. She and Aino were walking in a circle, beating their drums, chanting a protective spell. He could sense their *taika*, forming a giant invisible shell around the entire village. It made the air heady; he caught the smell of flowers and freshly-dried earthy tang of angelica, chasing away the rotten stench the demon had left behind.

It was so much greater than his: refined, controlled. True, he had somehow been able to block Lumi's Lights, but what use was that when he couldn't even cast a circle?

He lowered his head in shame, biting his lip so no angry tears could escape.

They arrived back at the hut and Elin held the door open. The orange glow of the fire inside spilled across the churned snow.

"Come on," she said. "Leave them be."

Tuomas ducked under her arm and fell upon his sleeping sack. He didn't bother taking off his coat. After an event like this, the leaders were sure to summon everyone once the village was secure.

Alda looked up from the opposite side of the hearth, her eyes wide with alarm.

"What happened? Did you manage to fight it off?"

"Yes," Elin replied.

"What was it?"

"I don't know. But it won't come back – the mages are putting up a circle."

Elin paused, fidgeting with unease.

"The Spirit of the Lights was there as well."

Aino turned pale. "What?"

"But she was in human form, Mother. She wasn't in the sky."

"That's impossible…"

Tuomas closed his eyes, as though doing so would shut off his sense of hearing as much as his sight. Elin regarded him as she hung her bow back up on the wall.

"Are you alright, Tuomas?" she asked softly.

"I'm fine."

Tuomas took one last look at Henrik's drum before he threw it into the corner.

# Chapter Thirteen

As soon as Lilja and Aino had finished casting the circle, Sigurd poked his head into the shelter.

"Come on, the leaders are ready for us," he said. "Everyone needs to go," he added, throwing a glance at Tuomas.

Elin sprang into action. Alda pulled on her coat and jammed her hat down over her hair. When she was ready, the three of them stepped outside, Elin leading the way between the huts towards the centre of the village.

The layout reminded Tuomas of the main communal area at Akerfjorden, with several tree trunks laid in a circle to serve as benches, and a large fire pit in the middle. Many of the villagers were already there, a couple of men kicking snow out of the pit. When it was clear, fresh logs were placed atop each other, and the empty space beneath them stuffed with thin peels of birch bark. Once a flint was struck, it didn't take long for a flame to catch, and soon everyone sat around it, whispering among each other in concern.

"That was no troll, was it?"

"I thought trolls carried blades as long as an arm…"

"But the Spirit of the Lights was here as well!"

"And she looked like a girl…"

"Never mind that. Why did that… *thing* go after that boy? Something's not right."

Feeling eyes on him, Tuomas kept his face down and stared into the fire. A log fell and spat sparks into the night.

Elin and Alda went to sit with Sigurd, who put a protective arm around each of them. Then Lilja perched at Tuomas's side, keeping a notable distance between them.

He could tell she was still furious with him. The anger radiated off her like she had set another fire right next to him.

On the other side, Birkir, the leader, cleared his throat. The hum of muttered voices instantly faded.

"Everyone is accounted for and unharmed," he started. "I don't need to tell you that we've been lucky. Thank you all for coming and helping to drive that creature away. But something like that coming into our village is no small matter. We need to get to the bottom of this."

"What was it?" a man asked. "A troll?"

"We never knew for sure whether it was a troll to begin with," Birkir said. "That was just a rumour. Aino, do you know what it was?"

"Not a troll," the mage woman confirmed. Her words were heavy and serious. "I think it was a demon."

Seeing she had everyone's attention, she got to her feet and addressed them all. The fire bounced off her ruddy face and highlighted all the strange angles of her skin.

"Never have I seen one, but I know of their kind. They are created by... well, I wouldn't even give the honour of calling them mages. Whoever makes one is a wicked person; powerful, dangerous. They distort the very nature of what we are."

Lilja pressed her lips together, not looking at Aino.

"The demons are made by building an effigy, out of snow or earth," Aino continued. "The mage chants life into it by giving it his life-soul and half of his blood. Then the two of them can walk independently, but he can see through its eyes, make it do his bidding."

Tuomas shuddered. He'd heard of those things in old stories used to frighten children, but never had he imagined how they were actually created. His stomach turned over at the thought.

"If a life-soul is inside the demon, does that mean that the mage who controls it is surviving only with his body-soul?" he asked, barely masking his horror.

"Yes, but they aren't truly separated," explained Aino. "It would be, in a twisted way, similar to when a mage goes into trance: the body-soul stays behind and the life-soul wanders to commune with the Spirits. But instead of travelling, the life-soul stays inside the demon's form, to bind it."

"But how can anyone survive with half their blood missing? And half their souls?" a woman asked, her voice shrill with revulsion.

"As long as the demon lives, he will suffer no ill effect," Lilja said suddenly, making everyone turn to look at her. "If the demon is vanquished, he will be drastically weakened. But should the two be separated in any way – a great distance put between them – the demon will go rogue. It will roam until it carries out the last task set to it."

Aino's brows lowered. "What do you know of this?"

"No more than you," Lilja countered. "But, wandering as I do, I've heard tales of them. Of how they can be killed. The only way is to strike them in the heart – that's where the life-soul and *taika* is held. Hit there, and it will lose the blood and life-soul given to it, and fade away."

She got to her feet, twisting her hands together anxiously. Tuomas couldn't hold back a frown. He knew she wasn't used to being around people, but now she seemed like a scared little girl.

"I know a few of you will probably remember me from the last time I was here. I'm so sorry for that thing coming here. I can't believe I didn't sense it coming."

"It wasn't your fault," said one of the men seated close to Birkir – Tuomas could tell by the similar decoration on his clothes that he was also a leader. "Nobody was hurt, and when we heard your boy shouting for help, we all came because we chose to."

Everyone nodded in agreement, but Tuomas blushed. It wasn't Lilja's fault, it was his. Tears threatened to spill and he quickly lowered his face so nobody would see.

"What are you doing in Einfjall, Lilja?" a woman asked. Then she turned her eyes on Tuomas. "And who's he?"

"My apprentice," said Lilja, not missing a beat.

"I thought he didn't look like you," Birkir remarked.

"He's not my son," Lilja snapped. "I took him on when I was passing through Akerfjorden."

"And you didn't think to stay there with him?" Aino inquired, genuinely curious. "It's difficult enough to learn our craft, let alone being on the move all the time."

"I don't stay," said Lilja pointedly.

Across the fire, Sigurd shifted his weight on the log, then spoke up.

"That demon went after Tuomas. Why? And... what was the Spirit of the Lights doing down here in a body like that?"

His last question brought forth a fresh wave of mutterings. Some people even made the sign of the hand to ward off evil. Aino noticed and shook her head.

"Now, there's no need for that," she assured, as though talking to children. "The Spirit of the Lights may be frightening, but she's not wicked."

*That's one way to put it*, Tuomas thought drily, his hand going to the pouch containing Mihka's hair.

But despite his cynicism, he found himself warming to Lumi a little. Their truce had to mean something. She had even exposed herself in order to defend him, even though she'd made it clear she didn't want to be seen.

"But… she won't be able to get in, will she?" Birkir asked anxiously.

"No. The circle will keep out everything not human," replied Aino.

Everyone relaxed at that, but Tuomas cocked an eyebrow. So even though Lumi had been labelled as not wicked, the protective circle would still bar her from accessing the village? She was trapped out there with the real wicked thing?

Lilja seemed to have the same thought, because she threw him a sideways glance. Her eyes were still firm, but she gave the tiniest of nods; too small for anyone else to notice.

Tuomas understood. Lumi was strong enough to take care of herself. And the demon might not be dead, but it was seriously hurt. Elin's arrow had dealt more damage than anything else which had been hurled at it, even Lumi's Lights.

"That still doesn't explain why the demon went after him," another woman said, nodding her head in Tuomas's direction.

Tuomas squirmed. To make such a beginner's error as he had was embarrassing enough, but now he had to admit it in front of all of Einfjall?

He threw a pleading look at Lilja, hoping she might step in and help him, but she didn't move a muscle.

"You want to be a mage?" she whispered. "Then own your mistakes."

All the villagers turned their gazes to Tuomas. The moment dragged into an eternity as he stood up. He felt like a ptarmigan standing out in the middle of the tundra, surrounded by archers, just waiting to be shot.

"It was my fault," he said in a small voice. "I was... trying to practise my drumming. I didn't prepare properly. I'm so sorry. I put you all in danger."

He ran his tongue nervously over his chapped lips.

"Please forgive me."

Beside him, Lilja nodded and turned her attention back to the fire. She stroked her throat with one hand.

Birkir looked at Tuomas for a long time, then offered a gentle smile.

"Thank you for being honest," he said. "Luckily nobody was hurt, including you."

"No-one is without error," Aino added. "Sit down, boy. You are our guests here, and as long as you are here, we'll offer protection and shelter."

"Hear, hear," Alda said. "They slept in our hut, Birkir. They're more than welcome to stay. We have the room. It's hardly the time of year to be travelling, Lilja, even you must admit that."

"I agree," Lilja replied tightly, "and thank you for your hospitality. But we can't stay."

"We insist," said the other leader. "You'll be safe here, especially now the protective circle is in place."

Lilja shook her head.

"I appreciate the offer, but no. Tuomas and I have come north for a reason. We need to seek help from the Earth Spirits in the World Below. The easiest way to get there is at the Northern Edge of the World."

A fresh wave of mutterings started. Several people looked curiously at Tuomas again, and he did his best to smile back.

It was clear the villagers were interested as to why they needed to cross into one of the Spirit realms, but they respected Lilja enough to not press her. So she hunched her shoulders forward, as though it was a physical strain to have all those eyes on her.

Birkir noticed her discomfort and spoke once more.

"Well, as thanks for helping Aino to protect the village, we'll give you anything you need to assist you on your journey. And, of course, you're welcome to stay here with us as long as you like, whenever you like."

The others nodded, and there was an immediate flood of offerings of food, clothes, furs, and tools. Tuomas's head swam with the generosity.

Even though it was the way of the Northlands, once again, he was humbled by how kind their people could be. No matter that he'd confessed to endangering every one of them. To survive out here, where the Spirits took just as much as they gave, discord and war had no place.

"Thank you," Lilja said. "But honestly, we don't need anything more. Our sleighs are almost full as it is. All I might ask is for someone to come to the Northern Edge with us, to look after our animals until we return. With the distance, I'd rather go by sleigh than by skis."

Sigurd was on his feet in moments.

"I volunteer. You stayed a night under my roof. Let me help you again."

Lilja smiled, though it was still strained.

"Thank you."

"I'll come as well," said Elin.

Remembering her impressive shot at the creature, Tuomas nodded at Lilja.

"At least we won't have to worry about that demon again if the two of them come with us." he whispered.

"We shouldn't have to worry about it *at all*," she hissed.

Tuomas's eyes hardened.

"I apologised! Isn't that what you wanted?"

Lilja glared back at him, keeping her voice low.

"I'm glad you owned up to it, boy, but don't push your luck with me just yet. I'm probably the only one here who knows just how dangerous that thing is. So be happy you're still alive and leave me be."

Tuomas fell silent. For as much as he wanted to press her, this wasn't the time or place. She would forgive him in her own time, in her own way.

"There's nothing more to be said or done tonight, then," said Birkir. "Let's all go to bed. When were you planning to leave, Lilja?"

"As soon as the blizzard was over," she replied. "I didn't want to overstay our welcome."

"Nonsense. I told you, you are welcome here. But there's no point setting off when you've had hardly any sleep. The Northern Edge of the World is a day's ride away. You'll need your rest."

Tuomas half-expected Lilja to refuse, to want to get away from Einfjall as quickly as she could. But he was relieved when she nodded in agreement. She had only managed a few hours' slumber, and he none at all. Now the fright of the attack was over, he was fading fast, eyelids becoming heavier by the moment.

With a few more hearty words, the meeting was dismissed, and everyone retired back to their huts. Tuomas went to speak to Lilja, but she stormed ahead, not even pausing to look at him.

Elin came to his side.

"Is she always like that?"

"Pretty much," he replied. "She isn't really used to being with people."

"So I see." Elin glanced at him. "Are you alright? You're whiter than the snow."

Tuomas swallowed. "It's nothing. I just… got a shock, that's all."

"That's all?" She ducked a little to catch his eye. "She looked really angry with you."

He shrugged. "She'll come around. I hope."

"I'm sure she will. Nobody can stay angry forever. And no-one was hurt, that's the important thing," said Elin. "Stop beating yourself up. Come on, let's get back to sleep. We've got a long day tomorrow."

She walked off, so he could follow in his own time. As he watched her, a wave of relief washed over him. It had been horrible standing in front of the village and admitting his own stupidity, but now it was done, he felt a little better.

He made his way back, following the routes of trodden snow between the huts. However, as he walked, a new thought came into his mind.

The creature had only come because he had drummed without a circle. It hadn't tried to kill anyone. It had just tried to capture him.

*Only him.*

Somewhere out there, in the endless Northlands, somebody wanted him.

# Chapter Fourteen

The next morning, Tuomas was woken by a sharp shove.

His eyes flew open to see Lilja. She was already dressed and her long hair hung loose, twisted into waves from the tight braids she always wore it in. She looked different without it tied back: younger, almost childlike.

"I let you sleep for as long as I could," she said. "Now get up. We've got to go."

Her tone was definitely softer than the night before, but Tuomas could tell she was still annoyed.

He clambered out of his sleeping sack and rolled it up, tying it shut with two strips of leather. Alda was by the hearth, cooking some more sautéed reindeer – from the smell of it, it was almost done. Sigurd and Elin were nowhere to be seen.

Tuomas was surprised at himself. He must have slept very deeply to not have been woken by the scent of food, or even by others moving around. Paavo could barely sit up and get his shoes on without stirring him.

Paavo.

His heart wrenched. He'd never been away from his brother for this long.

Lilja grabbed her coat from a beam and pulled it on. Her empty mittens dangled loosely from the cuffs, their red and blue trim vivid against the white fur of her sleeves. She bound the coat shut with her belt, laden with various pouches and blades concealed inside leather sheaths. Finally, she took her drum and tied it to the buckle with a thong.

The bloodstain on it caught Tuomas's eye again. How had that happened?

It was yet another question he'd have to ask her when the time was right. He got the feeling that if he tried now, she might completely blank him for the rest of the journey.

She combed her hair with her fingers, then began weaving it into braids with practised speed. When she was done, she strode outside; Tuomas heard her hitching the reindeer up to the sleighs.

Alda gave him a warm smile.

"How are you feeling?"

"Fine," he replied, but a hand still crept to his throat, where the demon had snatched him. He could still feel its bony fingers, smell its rancid breath.

"Are you in pain?" Alda asked.

Tuomas quickly lowered his hand.

"No. Just thinking."

Alda read him easily.

"Try not to worry about that demon. It won't get through the protection circle. And soon you'll be in the World Below, you'll be safe there. If the Earth Spirits aren't protecting you, Lilja will."

Tuomas noted how Alda hadn't mentioned safety on the journey itself, but mused that she probably wouldn't be so calm about her husband and daughter joining them if she didn't trust Lilja. Her power as a mage truly preceded her wherever she went.

His eyes strayed to Alda's trousers. Lilja had mentioned she had treated Alda for a leg complaint the last time she was in Einfjall. He hadn't noticed Alda walking with a limp, so whatever Lilja had done must have worked well.

No matter that Lilja had nothing – wherever she set foot, she lent her help and expertise. Here, she had healed Alda. In the Akerfjorden community, she had delivered him. Despite her demeanour, she was a good woman, and he had to admit his growing respect for her.

Alda lifted the pot out of the flames and spooned out helpings. She called for everybody to come inside, and they all ducked one by one into the hut. Elin and Sigurd were completely ready; they didn't even take off their hats to eat.

Unease grew in Tuomas's stomach, almost putting him off the meal, but he forced himself to keep going until his bowl was empty. He needed the strength. However, he couldn't ignore how much he wished he could just be back in Akerfjorden, with Mihka and Paavo. He would even take Henrik's boring company and bitter tea if it meant an end to all this madness.

Who had sent that demon? Even when surrounded by the villagers, why had it completely ignored them and gone after him?

His hand went to his belt, and found the little pouch holding the lock of Mihka's hair. No matter that this was his test. It had never been for him.

He felt something else inside the pouch: small and hard. He pressed at it through the sealskin, exploring it with his fingers. Then he remembered: it was the little fox he had whittled out of the hare bone.

Lumi's spectral eyes swam into his mind.

Yes, this was for Mihka. But there would be no saving Mihka unless he sent her back first. That was the priority now.

He stayed silent as they left the hut and prepared to depart. It was still dark, with not even a hint of the shadowy half-light yet. The Moon Spirit's face was almost completely gone: only a sliver remained hovering in the endless night. The lone light source came from torches stuck into the ground near the sleighs.

Tuomas and Lilja removed all their unnecessary belongings, leaving only what was needed for a return journey. Birkir appeared, along with his two fellow leaders, to help. Then they offered a few handfuls of moss to the reindeer, which the animals set upon with vigour.

When everything was done, Lilja took Tuomas's arm.

"Stay close," she said in an undertone.

Tuomas read her meaning at once.

"Do you think that demon will come back?" he asked.

"I don't know," she admitted. "But be on your guard. It knows where you are now."

So he had been right. The creature had come only for him last night.

Tuomas faced her directly.

"You're not telling me something," he said.

The light of the torches reflected in Lilja's eyes.

"It's best left for somewhere less exposed."

She gave a subtle nod towards the villagers, then climbed into her sleigh without another word. Tuomas heaved a frustrated sigh as he took a seat in his own and rested Henrik's drum on his lap.

Elin and Sigurd approached, their arms laden with reindeer moss and firewood, which they deposited in the backs of the sleighs. Alda watched from the door of the hut, hands tucked under her armpits to keep them warm.

Elin and Sigurd approached her and each gave her a huge bear hug, planting kisses on her cheeks.

"We'll be back soon, Mother," Elin promised.

"I know," Alda smiled, her mouth drawn tight with cold.

163

She laid a hand on Sigurd's face. The two of them gazed at each other lovingly, then Sigurd climbed into the front sleigh beside Lilja. She shuffled away when he got too close, leading to an uncomfortable cough from Sigurd.

Elin leapt into Tuomas's sleigh and threw her bow down at her feet so she could hold a torch.

"Have you got everything?" he asked.

Elin nodded. "You?"

Tuomas tapped the drum. "Yes. But this is the most important thing."

Elin gazed at it in wonder.

"I've never seen one of these up close before," she murmured. "Can I touch it?"

Tuomas angled it towards her. Her eyes widened and she pulled off a mitten to tentatively run her fingers over the skin.

"It's smoother than I thought," she said. Her thumb hovered over the face of the Great Bear Spirit in the centre. "It's beautiful."

Tuomas nodded. It truly was beautiful. Even in the darkness, the symbols seemed just as vivid as ever. He couldn't believe he had thrown it into the corner like a child discarding a broken toy. This was a sacred thing, so much more than a mere musical instrument.

Henrik was right. He needed to control himself. Not just his power, but his temper as well. It had already led to enough problems.

But first of all, he needed to have a long talk with Lilja.

Birkir came forward, a hand on his heart.

"Go in peace," he said warmly.

"Stay in peace," Tuomas replied. "Thank you."

A dark cloud settled over him at saying the familiar farewell. The last time he had shared an exchange like this was with Sisu.

Lilja gave a curt nod of gratitude, then snapped the rope attached to her reindeers' harnesses. Tuomas urged his own animal to follow, and the sleighs jolted forward. Einfjall fell behind them, its houses and people growing ever smaller in the shadow of the mountain.

Tuomas felt a sharp pressure in the air as they passed through the protective circle.

He glanced around. Would the demon sense they were outside it now? His eyes scanned the black horizon, trying to pick it out.

But there was nothing. Not even a breath of wind.

*It's injured,* he reminded himself. *It won't come back.*

Even as he thought it, he clenched his fists inside his mittens. He never wanted to see that disgusting thing again.

They headed back the way they had come when Sigurd had found them, and easily located the spot where they had tried to pitch a shelter. The poles were still sticking up in a skeletal cone, white from frost. With a few blows of an axe, the ends were free. After loading them into the sleighs, the group set off again, turning right to align themselves with the North Star.

As the sleighs moved further into the darkness, Tuomas looked out at the flat landscape. He understood how many people could see it as bleak and treacherous, but he couldn't deny how captivating it was in its simple beauty. Nothing existed here save the snow, sky, and winter Spirits. He could feel them, just out of sight and reach, observing from their hidden overlapping realms. Any humans who came here were just passing through, never to stay or leave their mark.

He threw a quick glance at Elin. She didn't seem to have sensed the Spirits around them – or if she had, not as strongly as what he felt. Her eyes were also wandering, but without any kind of intent. He was sure, however, that in the sleigh up ahead, Lilja was feeling the exact same thing as him.

He bowed his head, acknowledging the Spirits' presence. And then, so fleeting that he thought he imagined it, he saw a flash running over the distant snow. There was a streak of white hair, and the flicker of a tail, trailing a faint green glow in its wake.

He smiled. So Lumi was fine, after all.

For the first time since the demon's attack, his heart warmed in relief.

The already short day seemed even shorter the further north they journeyed. What would have been an hour of bluish glow in Akerfjorden was now a tiny line across the horizon, so cold and far away, it barely seemed to belong to the same World. The only way to truly keep time was by the spinning stars overhead.

The snow shone a faint turquoise, completely undisturbed, and the sleighs cut through it like a knife. This was a place where the Sun Spirit refused to cast even a fraction of her warmth. Tuomas knew that in summer, it would never set here, but the idea of summer was so distant that it wasn't worth thinking about. Never had he been anywhere so cold, so desolate.

And it was a constant monotony. Nothing changed. The convoy just kept going in a straight line. No more animal tracks crossed the land. No more shrubs grew. No mountains reared in the distance. It was mind-numbing.

"I haven't been here in ages," Elin said, her words slightly muffled by the scarf wrapped around her face. "You know, when I was little, I used to think that eventually you would reach the end of the World and fall off."

Tuomas looked at her from beneath lashes turned white with ice.

"When was the last time you were here?"

"About three years ago. I didn't really like it. Too cold."

"So why did you come this time?"

"I've always wanted to see the Northern Edge of the World. I've never been that far north."

Despite the freezing temperatures, a little colour rose to her cheeks. "And I wanted to help."

Tuomas smiled, even though she couldn't see it under his scarf.

"Well, I'm glad you're here," he admitted. "I've never seen anyone shoot an arrow so well."

"I've had a lot of practise," Elin said, all sheepishness gone. "Mother wanted me to stay home and learn women's stuff, but I preferred going out hunting. She gave in once I promised to help her cook whatever I brought back in the evenings."

Tuomas nodded. Barely an hour since setting out from Einfjall, Elin had spotted a hare. Everyone else had missed it, but she'd managed to pick out its white coat from the expanse of snow, and put an arrow clean through its eye, killing it instantly. It was big and fat, and would give them a fantastic meal on the journey home. Lilja had skinned and gutted it there and then, before packing down the meat and pocketing the bones to make needles. But, in her own silent gratitude for Elin's skill, Lilja had presented the fur to her, to make a new pair of mittens when they returned.

Elin gave a gentle tug on her hat to pull it further down over her ears.

"So… what are your parents' names?" she asked. "Lilja was quite keen to mention you weren't her son."

Tuomas hesitated before answering.

"Their names were Erik and Veera. But they're dead. Both of them."

She held a hand to her mouth. "I'm so sorry."

"It's alright."

"I've never lost anybody. I can't imagine what that would be like."

"I don't remember them, really. My big brother Paavo raised me," said Tuomas. "My mother died giving birth to me, and my father was killed by greylegs when I was two."

He sighed. "Paavo remembers them better. It still hurts him to think about them. But I've got him, so I guess it doesn't matter, so long as there are still people who care about you."

"True." Elin lowered her eyes. Then she smiled, jostling him. "And I did notice you were just as quick to say you weren't Lilja's, either! Is she really that annoying?"

Tuomas couldn't hold back a grin.

"She's alright. She's just used to keeping to herself. I think having me around has thrown her a little."

"You say that as though it wasn't a choice," Elin noted.

He stiffened, suddenly defensive. He understood why she was asking questions, but he still didn't want to divulge everything, at least not yet. So he fell silent, and turned away.

Elin blinked, his dodge not lost on her. But she seemed to take the hint, because she didn't press the matter.

The ground dipped slightly, and out of the whiteness there appeared a lake: an icy expanse in the middle of the infinite tundra, covered with a layer of snow. It was almost perfectly circular, as though some ancient hand had carved it out of the landscape and time hadn't touched it since.

The reindeer slowed as they moved onto it, wary of the new surface, but quickly found their feet and carried on. Tuomas clambered out of the sleigh and took hold of his animal's harness, muttering in a low voice to comfort it.

A figure emerged in the distance.

Elin frowned, trying to focus on it.

"What is that? A person? Out here?"

Tuomas didn't answer, too busy attempting to see it himself. He supposed it must be one of the Earth Spirits, perhaps guarding the entrance. He had never heard of that being done at openings to the other Worlds.

But then he noticed pointed ears and a sweeping tail.

Lumi.

When they were closer, he tugged on the rope to make the reindeer stop. He let go of the harness and approached her. She had her back to him, staring up at the sky.

"How did you get here before us?" he asked.

Lumi turned around.

"Are you underestimating me again?"

Tuomas swallowed nervously, not sure if she was angry. But then she relaxed, and let her thin lips curl into the smallest of smiles.

"I am glad you are safe," she said.

"Me too. Otherwise, who else will put you back in the sky?" Tuomas replied with a grin. He lowered his voice. "Did you see the demon on your way here?"

"No. I ran ahead to look for it, but there was no sign."

Tuomas wasn't sure if that made him feel better or worse. He supposed it would be hiding somewhere, licking its wounds – or perhaps even returned to the wicked mage who had sent it in the first place. But it was like Lumi: it left no footprints or tracks of any kind. If she couldn't find it, nobody could. It could be anywhere, and that chilled him to the bone.

A gasp from behind him made realise he wasn't alone with her anymore. Elin and Sigurd were staring at Lumi, their eyes wide with shock.

Sigurd fell to his knees.

"By the Spirits... it *is* her!" Elin breathed.

"Don't be afraid of her," Tuomas encouraged. "She won't hurt you. I promise."

Lumi shot him a pointed look, thinly veiling her displeasure of him assuming anything, but she kept silent.

Sigurd lowered his head in respect.

"It's an honour to meet you."

At the show of reverence, Lumi instantly mellowed.

"Thank you," she said."

The sound of Lumi's voice seemed to snap Elin out of staring. She clasped her hands together and bowed like her father, until the brim of her hat was almost touching the snow.

"Alright, get up, you'll freeze," muttered Lilja.

She had retrieved some of the moss from her sleigh and tossed it to the three reindeer, who wasted no time in diving on it. She scratched behind one of the reindeer's ears, then approached Lumi with a polite nod.

"Glad to see you here, White Fox One," she said.

Lumi didn't reply, but her irises turned a warm shade of pink, and that seemed to be enough.

Sigurd and Elin got to their feet, both still too stunned to even brush the snow off their trousers. Sigurd's eyes were almost as wide as the bone discs he had worn when Tuomas had first met him. Elin kept glancing between him and Lumi, stunned at how at ease he seemed with the Spirit.

Wanting to break the awkward silence, Tuomas turned to Lilja.

"So... uh, how much further until we get to the Northern Edge of the World?"

"A few feet," she replied, and pointed to a spot behind Lumi.

Tuomas followed her finger. A hole was gaping open in the ice, wide enough for a fully-grown man to float in lengthways. He had been so relieved to see Lumi, he had somehow completely missed it.

There were none of the rough edges of an ice-fishing hole – it didn't even look as though it had been made with a tool at all. Instead it seemed to be formed naturally, frozen in a perfect circle, the dark waters clear and open to the air.

"That's it?" Elin asked incredulously.

"That's it," Lilja said. "I haven't been here for a while, but it looks exactly the same."

Despite not knowing what to expect, Tuomas couldn't hide his surprise. He had thought the Northern Edge might be a literal edge. Like the river of night which he had imagined: something so obvious, it would be impossible to mistake it for anything else. Or perhaps the faraway sea ice, beyond the summer islands. Not something as simple and unassuming as a lake. If he squinted, he could almost be on the frozen Mustafjord.

He stared at the hole. At first, he was stunned by how the water inside was still liquid, but then a more pressing question came to him.

"Are we supposed to swim down? We'll freeze!"

In answer, Lilja knelt at the edge of the hole and pulled her drum onto her lap.

"Get yours, boy," she said to Tuomas. "And you two, get a fire going. We need to open the gateway."

# Chapter Fifteen

Sigurd and Elin set about building the fire, and Tuomas fetched his drum from the pile in his sleigh. Lilja pointed to the other side of the hole, and he sat there, sinking a little into the snow until his knees came to rest on the ice beneath.

A shiver ran through his body. Usually he would lay a reindeer skin down to keep the worst of the cold coming through. But Lilja hadn't done that, so he supposed they wouldn't be here for long.

She looked at him. Her face was as stoic as ever, but her blue eyes shone, and Tuomas's heart swelled. Even after everything he had done, she was actually trusting him to help her open the gateway.

Sigurd struck a flint over the tinder and Lumi instantly stepped back, away from the heat. The movement startled Elin, who was still stealing wide-eyed glances at the Spirit. But Lumi stared back each time, with her unbroken icy composure, and Elin would gulp and find something else to occupy herself. As the fire slowly spread over the wood, Tuomas noticed that her hands were shaking.

He managed to catch her eye.

"Are you alright?" he mouthed.

Elin nodded, but it was a jarred movement, stiff with nerves.

He couldn't help feeling a little guilty for not telling her and Sigurd what – *who* – might be joining them on the journey. They had already seen Lumi, but not like this, not up close.

As though reading his thoughts, Lumi turned her eyes on him. Just a week ago, he wouldn't have been able to read her face, but now, he thought he recognised a flash of relief.

But for what? That they were finally going to get help for sending her home? Or that they were unharmed by the demon?

Tuomas remembered the way she had fought it the night before. Despite being bound in human form, she had still moved like a Spirit; her body held no weight. Even though her Lights hadn't been what eventually injured the creature, she hadn't stopped attacking.

She took a step closer. Tuomas gulped, telling himself not to be afraid. Then he bowed his head.

"Thank you," he whispered.

Lumi didn't blink. Her eyes fluttered with green fire.

"You are welcome," she said, in a voice softer than falling snow.

A drop of water appeared at her hairline and ran down her face.

Tuomas frowned. Her skin looked different. There was a sheen over it, like liquid – not as firm as it had been when he first brought her out of the sky.

He went to ask her about it, but Lilja cleared her throat and the contact was broken. Lumi walked away, her ears slanting back at the sound. Tuomas turned his attention back to Lilja.

He noticed Elin and Sigurd watching from the side, and his stomach flipped. He'd never drummed in front of anyone before.

But there was no going back now. If he wanted to be a mage, and do this in front of an entire village, he had to start somewhere.

He closed his eyes and prayed to any Spirit who might hear him.

*Please don't let me mess this up again.*

The fire was going strong now, and Lilja held her drum over it, motioning with a flick of her chin for him to do the same. He carefully clutched the instrument by the back beam and let it hover atop the flames. The heat radiated through into his fingers, and made the symbols dance in the warm light.

He withdrew the drum, resting it in his lap. Lilja cast the protective circle, and gave him a single nod.

Tuomas nodded back. He was as ready as he would ever be.

They began a rhythm, with Lilja leading, letting the beats echo out into the darkness. Tuomas immediately felt his souls loosening. His head swam and instinct took over. A strange warmth grew in the pit of his stomach, and then Lilja began to chant. It was both guttural and soaring, ululating and harmonious, with hardly pause for breath.

Caught up in her sweeping sound, Tuomas opened his mouth, letting his own chant spill out like a river. There were no words, but there didn't need to be. He knew exactly what he wanted, and the song became that thing: to open the gateway, to cross into the World Below. Distantly, as though hearing it from the other side of the horizon, Lilja's chant spoke of the same goal. Their drumbeats and voices intertwined, dancing into the sky with the smoke. The air pulsed with *taika*.

He didn't care anymore that he had an audience. Elin and Sigurd could have been a million miles away. All that mattered were the drums and the shifting power all around. It felt like the Sun Spirit at midsummer; sounded like a little child playing gleefully at a lakeside; tasted of ripe berries and air so fresh it stung the lungs.

Then there was a sound like a rushing stream, and Tuomas opened his eyes.

The hole was glowing – not from under the water, but even deeper. Lilja stared at him, urging him to continue, not breaking her chant for a moment.

Tuomas carried on, holding onto the *taika* as he brought the hammer down again and again. The light grew, filling the hole. It bounced off the ice and reflecting off in a million rays.

It reached the surface, and a herd of ghostly white reindeer spilled out. They galloped across the lake in all directions, without a sound or hoofprint in their wake. Elin and Sigurd fell back in alarm, the animals running straight through them and vanishing into the distance.

Lilja stopped drumming, and Tuomas hurriedly put his instrument down too. The reindeer bounded past him. He could almost feel their soft fur, hear their bells and the clicking of the tendons in their legs.

He stared after them, mouth agape, but then Lilja's hand appeared on his shoulder.

"We need to cross over now, before it closes," she said.

Tuomas looked at the hole. The last of the spectral reindeer were still pouring out, but the glow had already started to fade.

Lumi leapt in without hesitation. She instantly disappeared, and Lilja followed, her drum tucked under one arm.

Tuomas turned a glance towards Sigurd and Elin.

"Will you be alright?" he called.

"We'll be fine!" replied Sigurd. "Go on, hurry!"

Tuomas turned to Elin. "I'll see you soon."

She managed to return a smile, but he didn't see it. Clutching the drum to his chest, he screwed his eyes closed, and dropped into the hole.

He half-expected to hit the water, but its icy shock never came. He just fell, the light burning through his eyelids. He didn't dare open them, worried that it would blind him.

Suddenly, the air transformed into something sweet and light. The coldness vanished and he felt heat on his face. When he breathed in, he smelled pollen and moist earth.

He crashed onto something hard. The thing rocked with his weight and he almost lost grip on the drum.

Then he heard Lilja's voice beside him.

"It's alright. We're here."

Tuomas slowly opened his eyes, squinting in the light. It was coming from above him, in a brilliant blue sky. But he knew it wasn't the true sky, where Lumi's Lights danced or the Moon Spirit turned her pockmarked face. This was the World Below: an entire other realm lay between here and the World Above. Instead, the light was coming from where the hole had been, now glowing so brightly, it almost looked like the Sun Spirit.

He sat up, nursing his shoulder. The thing they had landed on was a wooden boat, sitting in the middle of an identical circular lake as the one they had just stood on. However, instead of being frozen, it was thawed and clear, the water rippling in a soft breeze. Distant banks were edged with green shrubs and the crowns of silver birch trees, their colours so saturated, it almost hurt to look at them.

"It's summer," Tuomas blurted in wonder.

Then he remembered what Elin had said back in Einfjall: this place was the opposite of the World Between. At the height of winter up there, it would be summer down here.

He wriggled out of his coat and mittens. Sweat was already beginning to run down his back. The change in temperatures made his head spin and he took a few deep breaths. Lilja seemed to be struggling too: she stripped down to her tunic and fanned herself with her hands.

But Lumi looked the worst of all. She sat at the prow of the boat, knees drawn up to her chest. The wet sheen on her skin was more pronounced than ever now. She squirmed in discomfort, ears flat, bending her head down in an attempt to shade her face.

Tuomas's heart jolted. If she had struggled in the faraway winter light, and kept clear of any fires, this place would be draining for her. No matter that it was a Spirit realm; there was no hiding the pain she was in.

He noticed some oars in the bottom of the boat. He and Lilja took one each and they began to row, aiming for the nearest bank. Before long, they approached the blissful shade of a willow tree, its long branches trailing in the water.

A figure stepped out from behind the trunk. Tuomas was so taken aback, he almost dropped the oar.

He could immediately tell it was one of the Earth Spirits. Like Lumi, she took the form of a human woman; her movements so light, she appeared to be floating above the ground. She also had the same features as Lumi: petite yet sharp in places, with large striking eyes that pierced all they looked upon.

But that was where all similarities ended, for the Spirit was made entirely from leaves and petals. Tuomas wasn't sure if she was even solid, or whether behind the flora was nothing but empty air. Blades of grass fell about her face like hair, dotted with sprigs of fragrant heather. Birch leaves, both green and silver, lay over each other in the form of a face. She was dressed in a rich tunic of yellow saxifrage, embroidered with what looked like starlight and patches of white reindeer fur.

Lumi jumped out of the boat and landed hard on the ground. She hurried under the shade of the willow; arms thrown up around her face. Her hair turned damp and stuck to her snowy skin.

Without a word, the Earth Spirit touched her on the forehead.

There was a small flash, and Lumi let out a gasp of relief. The wetness vanished from her flesh, and her eyes momentarily flashed pink before melting back to their usual iridescent green.

"What was that?" Tuoms asked under his breath.

"Our friend has graciously protected her from the heat of this World," Lilja said.

The two of them climbed out of the boat and Lilja lowered her head in respect. When Tuomas stayed still, she slapped him on the arm. He muttered an apology and followed suit.

"Lilja Bear-Mage and Tuomas Sun-Soul," said the Earth Spirit. "Welcome to the World Below."

Tuomas frowned. *Sun-Soul?* He had never been called that before.

"Earth One," Lilja replied. "Thank you for allowing us entry to your realm."

The Spirit smiled. The leaves on her cheeks rustled with the movement.

"Come with me. You may shelter in a place less exposed."

The Earth Spirit headed away from the lake. Her steps hardly disturbed the grass underfoot. With every movement, Tuomas caught the scent of flowers.

He dragged the boat onto the shore so it wouldn't float away, then picked up the two drums, handing one to Lilja.

She took it, but grasped his wrist with her other hand.

"Don't wander off," she said.

"I won't," Tuomas replied. "The demon can't follow us down here, can it?"

There was a dark warning to Lilja's expression.

"Our host is generous, boy, but there is danger here too."

Tuomas nodded to show he understood. He would ask her later, when they were alone.

He let Lilja go first and fell behind to walk with Lumi. She glanced at him as he came close, but didn't move away.

The glow behind her eyes was dimmer than normal. Another drop of water ran down from her hairline.

"Are you alright?" he asked quietly.

Lumi shook her head. "This is the furthest I have ever been from the sky."

Tuomas gave her a small smile of comfort. He wanted to say something – anything – about how he appreciated her patience, how sorry he was, how grateful he'd been when she defended him from the demon. He wanted to tell her that, despite the circumstances, he didn't hate her; even his fear of her was slowly transforming into genuine respect.

But when he opened his mouth, nothing came out. Words would simply dilute the meaning behind whatever tangle of emotions he wanted to voice.

Lumi looked straight ahead, her mouth set in a line, ears erect. Sensing she wasn't gong to say anything else, Tuomas turned his attention to the surroundings.

It didn't take long for him to be captivated. The bushes and heathers around the lake had given way to clusters of birch, pine and aspen. Their branches disappeared into a dense green canopy; the trunks were carved with spirals and circles, similar to what might have been painted on a drum. The bright sky shone through from above, transforming the leaves and needles into a mosaic of light which danced on the spongy ground.

Here and there, more of the white reindeer grazed, their heads crowned with the most impressive antlers Tuomas had ever seen. The animals were still a little transparent, but more solid than they had been above in the snow. They were all grazing on bountiful amounts of lichen, yet paused to lower their heads in respect as the group passed by. Tuomas supposed it must be because they sensed the Earth Spirit and Lumi.

He was reminded of the story of the first reindeer. After the Great Mage had died, the reindeer he had been gifted from this place multiplied and populated the Northlands with their descendants. But time in the World Between made them heavier, and the Sun Spirit tanned their thick coats from snow white to a mirage of brown.

There was more to this place than just what he could see. He almost had to pinch himself as a reminder that it wasn't a dream. This was the World Below: a place of magic and power, which could usually only be reached by a mage's life-soul in trance.

But yet here he was, physically walking in another realm. It was unheard of.

He looked at Lilja, her two pigtails trailing down her back. Once again, he remembered how she had been touched by the Great Bear. The strength of her *taika* was truly unbelievable, to be able to open a gateway like this. No wonder Henrik had been wary of her.

But he knew Lilja now, knew that there was nothing at all to worry about. Henrik was probably just jealous; unnerved by her abrupt manner or the rootless way she lived. And there had never been a female mage in Akerfjorden. She would have been easy for him to victimise.

Women mages were not unheard of – Aino in Einfjall was a perfect example. But Henrik was old and set in his ways. And if the reputation of the Great Bear Spirit had somehow preceded Lilja, there was a perfect opportunity for prejudice.

*I'll soon fix that*, Tuomas decided.

When Lumi was back in the sky and Mihka's life-soul returned, he would convince Lilja to come back with him. She could move in with him and Paavo if she wanted, and the three of them could sit around the fire with a bowl of Paavo's stew.

It was the least he could do to repay her for all she had done. And then, perhaps, she could finally have a home again.

# Chapter Sixteen

The trees became denser and Tuomas spotted two fires in the distance. They were torches, set into a sheer rock wall, either side of a large cave. From a distance, it looked like a gaping maw flanked by burning eyes.

A wave of unease washed through him. The cave made him think of a giant monster lying in wait to swallow them.

Lilja's had mentioned there was danger down here, and she was right: this place was where trolls were supposed to have come from. The old stories said they lay in the ground, away from the Sun Spirit's reach, sleeping away the centuries until hunger called them to rise. Then they would force their way into the World Between, taking reindeer and people alike.

But this wasn't a troll. It was just a cave. Nothing in there could harm them.

As soon as they walked inside, the air became cooler and damper. More torches lined the walls, throwing strange flickering shadows everywhere. They travelled deeper, the earth pressing in around them, along a path which twisted and wound in all directions like the root of a huge tree. Then they turned a corner and emerged into a wide cavern.

An array of fires cast a warm and welcoming light all around. Other tunnels and caverns were visible, honeycombing through the rock. Stalactites protruded from the dark ceiling like teeth, dripping water down into clear pools which had collected beneath them across centuries. Some of the pools had even broken free and trailed away in tiny streams.

But it was the walls that took Tuomas's breath away.

All of them were beautifully decorated with paintings and carvings, in colours he had never seen in pigment before. From floor to ceiling, they showcased Spirits, landmarks and stories. There were the Sun and Moon Spirits side by side, their celestial children hovering beneath them; the Great Mage walking across the Mustafjord; herders driving the reindeer through the mountains; the Spirit of Passage guiding the recently deceased away from their graves. And on the wall straight ahead, the Great Bear Spirit filled the entire space, its form outlined in a million white dots.

His head swam with the details. It was far too much to take in at once. He could have stood and looked at the artworks all day.

But the Earth Spirit didn't stop and led them to the largest fire in the centre of the cavern. Hearth stones had been arranged around it, each covered with bowls of food. There was sautéed reindeer, salmon cakes, mashed lingonberries, dishes of cloudberries and roots, and spits of roasted ptarmigan.

"You are welcome to help yourselves," said the Spirit. "I must converse with my kin, and find the best way forward with your predicament."

"You have not asked them what the predicament is," Lumi noted.

The Earth Spirit glanced at her with a smile. "I heard it in the chanting, White Fox One. You must be returned to the World Above. We can assist you with this, but it is best to discuss. To not be impulsive."

Lumi's eyes narrowed at that last remark, but she didn't say anything.

Lilja bowed her head.

"We thank you for your generosity, Earth One," she said, then she approached the Spirit and whispered something. Tuomas couldn't make out what they were saying.

He walked over to Lumi. She was standing close to the wall, as far away from the fires as she could get. For the first time, she didn't glare at him or try to avoid him as he came close.

"I do not feel sure about this," she muttered. "There is some kind of corruption in the air."

Now she mentioned it, Tuomas noticed it too. Despite the wondrous sights, the air didn't seem right. And it wasn't just because they were in a cave – he had explored caves in the World Above and they didn't feel like this. Not heavy, like it was pressing on his lungs. When he breathed in, there was a metallic taste in his mouth.

"How are you feeling?" he asked, hoping to change the subject. "You're not too hot?"

"No."

"I wanted to ask, I thought you didn't want people to see you. Why did you come so close to Einfjall?"

"Because I could not stop the demon before it reached you," she said. "I tried to pull the life-soul out of it, but it got away. I had no choice but to follow."

Tuomas gathered his nerves.

"Yes, you did."

Her eyes locked onto him.

"You didn't have to defend me like that," he carried on.

"You sound surprised," she said.

"I am," he admitted. "Is it just because I need to send you back to the World Above?"

Lumi didn't blink.

"You mean, just because you need to appease me."

Her tone was like ice. Tuomas worried he had gone too far and lowered his head.

"I'm sorry. I honestly never meant to pull you out of the sky."

"And yet you did."

Lumi looked past him to the wall behind. Tuomas followed her gaze. On the red rock, a painting depicted the Sun and the Moon, the faint details of faces visible in their gold and silver discs. Underneath them ran two foxes, outlined in white and red.

"You are more powerful than you know," she said.

"You and Lilja like saying that," Tuomas muttered.

"Because it is true."

"How? I couldn't stop that demon. I brought it to Einfjall. And I trapped you. I'm not powerful, I'm just stupid."

Lumi raised her eyebrows a little, as though she agreed. But then she shook her head.

"All that shows your power. You must simply learn to control it."

Tuomas swallowed. Henrik had said the same thing.

"Lumi, listen," he said. "Aino – the mage at Einfjall – said a demon like that is controlled by a wicked mage. It tried to run off with me. Do you know why?"

Her ears twitched.

"If you are asking me who sent it, then no, I do not know."

Tuomas sighed.

"I'll ask Lilja. I know she's not telling me something."

He turned around. Lilja and the Earth Spirit were still speaking in hushed voices. Then the Spirit gave a gentle nod.

"He is contained," she assured. "All is well."

At that, Lilja visibly relaxed. "Thank you."

The Spirit turned on her heel and vanished into the air, as though she was nothing but smoke. The leaves and flowers which had made her fell to the floor in a pile.

Tuomas's eyes grew wide.

"Where did she go?" he asked.

"You heard her: to speak with the other Earth Spirits," Lilja replied abruptly. Her voice sounded tighter than normal, as though her throat was swollen.

She kept her back to him and settled by the hearth. In one smooth motion, she laid her drum beside her and picked up a bowl of the cloudberries, flicking them into her mouth.

Then she buried her face in her hands.

Tuomas and Lumi glanced at each other in alarm. Lilja sniffed loudly, breathing hard as she struggled to get herself under control.

Tuomas took a tentative step towards her.

"Lilja?" he asked.

"I'm fine," she said, the words strangled by a sob.

"You're not. What's wrong?"

She wiped her cheeks with her sleeve. Tuomas knelt next to her and laid a hand on her arm, but she jerked away as though burned.

"Sorry," he muttered, backing away from her.

He twisted his hands together nervously. His eyes moved to the food and he considered taking some, but the unease came back and turned his stomach over.

Lilja coughed, wiping her face one last time. She looked over her shoulder at him.

"I told you I was fine," she said, softer now. Her tears had gone, but her eyes were still bloodshot.

Tuomas bit his lip. It was now or never.

"Lilja, I need to talk to you."

She went still. He half-expected her to shrug it off or ignore him, but then she gave a tiny nod and motioned to the space on the other side of the fire.

"I know. Sit down," she said.

Tuomas did as he was told. He looked at her expectantly through the flames. Lilja didn't meet his eyes straightaway; instead she laid a hand on her drum, as though drawing strength from the symbols. Her thumb rested over the bloodstain.

She opened her mouth, then closed it again. Tuomas could tell she was struggling to find where to begin. But he sat still, forcing himself to be patient.

"I knew about the demon before I met you," she said in the end.

Tuomas nodded. "I gathered that. Did you know it was coming after me?"

"Yes. I hoped it wouldn't find you, but it's drawn to power. When I saw the Spirit of the Lights ripped out of the sky, I knew it wasn't natural – that you had done it. So I headed out to Akerfjorden. To protect you, to take you away; I didn't really have a plan. I just knew I needed to get to you first."

She put another cloudberry in her mouth and sucked on it.

"I knew about it… because I saw it made," she said, her words heavier than stone. "Kari made it."

Tuomas's blood froze.

Kari? Her brother?

"I tried to stop him," Lilja continued. "He intended to send it after you so he could steal your *taika*. He was with me when you were born; we both knew how powerful you were. When I refused to help, he set it on me. But I managed to get my drum and I summoned the Great Bear Spirit. It said it couldn't kill him, because he had split his souls, but would take him to a place where he wouldn't be able to do harm."

She motioned to the cave around them and Tuomas's mouth fell open.

"He's *here?*" he gasped.

"I don't know where," Lilja said. "I don't want to know."

Tuomas stared at her, and then at Lumi, who looked just as alarmed.

Lilja watched him closely, gauging his reaction. The fire reflected in her eyes and lit up her face at strange angles. There was a desperation to her that Tuomas had never seen before – it was obvious how difficult this was for her to talk about. He supposed this was the first time she ever had.

"What the Earth Spirit said just now, that *he is contained*," Tuomas ventured. "She meant Kari?"

A muscle twitched in Lilja's jaw. "That was a private conversation."

"I'm sorry, I overheard," he said.

Lilja heaved a sigh. "Yes. She meant Kari."

"I don't know what to say," Tuomas admitted. "What happens now? You said in Einfjall that the demon can be killed?"

"Yes. Your friend injured it, didn't she?" replied Lilja. "I did as well. When it attacked me, I sliced it with a knife. But I was hurt myself; I didn't go for the heart. That's the only way to kill it."

She sighed and rubbed her face again as more tears threatened to spill over.

"When I summoned the Great Bear Spirit, and it brought Kari down here, the demon got away. I knew it would obey the last order Kari gave it: to find you and keep you for him. The

Bear said it was up to me to make sure that didn't happen. So as soon as I'd recovered, I started on my way to Akerfjorden."

Tuomas took a shaky breath.

"Why didn't you tell me sooner?"

"I didn't want to frighten you. And when I saw the Spirit of the Lights with you... well, that complicated things."

Lilja glanced at Lumi. "With all due respect, White Fox One."

Lumi nodded, but remained silent. Her tail swept softly back and forth.

The shadows seemed to close in around them, until even the fires appeared dimmed. Tuomas breathed deeply, trying to take it all in.

He finally understood why Lilja had been so quiet and abrupt when it came to her brother. How could anyone reckon with such a dark burden, all alone, out there in the frozen night?

"Thank you for telling me," he said.

Lilja sniffed back a sob, determined to not let him see it. "You're welcome."

Quietness descended on the cavern, broken only by the crackling of burning logs. The two of them picked at the food without speaking. Then tiredness overcame Tuomas, and he barely recalled lying down before slumber swept him away.

# Chapter Seventeen

He wasn't sure how long he slept. When he awoke, the fires were still burning strong. He couldn't tell if new logs had been added to them or if the old ones had somehow not come apart yet. The darkness was unchanged; no holes in the walls or ceiling allowed any daylight to seep through. But he supposed he wouldn't have been able to tell either way. If this place was the opposite of the World Between, which was currently in the middle of the Long Night, then it would be the Long Day here.

He sat up carefully. His neck was stiff from lying on the hard floor. He massaged it with one hand and looked around, letting his eyes readjust.

Lilja was still on the other side of the fire, also asleep, curled into a foetal position. Tucked up like she was, with her plaits tumbling about her face, she almost looked like a child rather than the woman she was. Her cheeks were still flushed from crying, and her eyes twitched in the grip of a dream. One hand was thrown out before her, resting on her drum.

Lumi, however, was nowhere to be seen. Tuomas wasn't sure whether he was expecting to see her asleep too. Did Spirits even need to sleep?

He got to his feet and walked towards the wall where she had been standing, in case he had somehow missed her in the shadows. But there was nothing except the stunning murals.

In the flickering firelight, they almost seemed to be moving, like the Lights might dance across the sky. He ran his fingers over the nearest one, of horrid-looking creatures emerging from a lake.

Some of these stories, he'd never even heard of before. Would Henrik know about them? He would have to ask when he got back to Akerfjorden.

Just thinking of home tugged at his heart. It was almost easy to forget he'd hadn't even been away for a month yet. And he was still no closer to saving Mihka. What must poor Sisu be thinking? Tuomas could imagine the leader bent over his son: the only family he had left, never taking his eyes off him for fear he might slip away.

Tuomas opened the pouch at his belt and drew out the lock of hair. Its whiteness shone. Even the roots were bleached; all of Mihka's natural black had disappeared like grass under snow. He would never get it back, Tuomas was sure of that. This was who he would always be: touched by the fox fires.

"Don't worry," Tuomas muttered, closing his fist around the hair. He put it back in the pouch and pulled the drawstring closed so not a single strand could escape.

The food was still around the hearth. He pulled a leg from one of the roasted ptarmigans and bit off a mouthful. The meat was tender, seasoned with lingonberries. Before long, he had devoured it down to the bone, which he dropped into one of his pouches for later.

He tasted metal on his tongue. He frowned, wondering if he'd bitten his cheek and drawn blood, but when he inspected his mouth, there was nothing. Then he caught a whiff of that strange heavy scent from before.

He wrinkled his nose in disgust. Had something died in here?

Nerves gnawed at his belly. Where had Lumi gone?

His hand went to his belt, running over his knives until he reached the drum. Should he try to summon her back?

*No*, he thought. The memory of his last attempt was still fresh in his mind. And Lilja was sleeping more soundly than he'd seen in days. He didn't want to annoy her again by waking her.

"Lumi?" he called, as loudly as he dared.

Lilja stirred.

Tuomas hurried towards the entrance to the caves. He watched her for a moment, worried he had disturbed her, but she just let out a groggy moan and curled even tighter into herself.

A soft breeze whistled through the tunnel beside him and swept his hair into his face. He tasted the strangeness again, filling his mouth; piercingly cold.

Something told him she had gone down here. Maybe she'd left in search of the corruption she had sensed when they arrived. That had to be the same thing he was smelling, and it was coming from this direction.

He glanced back at Lilja. She had told him to stay close.

But if there was danger in this World too, surely it was best for Lumi to stay with them. For as beautiful as it was, he wanted to learn what he needed from the Earth Spirits and then get out.

It had been hard to pinpoint out in the open, but down here in the depths of the earth, he sensed something dark lingering at the edge of each shadow. Something purely of the Spirit realms, where no human had ever set foot before.

He turned back to the cave entrance. He didn't want to be alone here.

"Lumi?" he hissed into the darkness. The cave swallowed his voice; not even the tiniest echo answered him.

He gritted his teeth and hurried down the tunnel.

Despite the torches along the walls, the gloom immediately enveloped him. The temperature plummeted, and his breath misted in front of his face.

Wasn't it summer here? Was he going to walk back into winter?

He shook his head and told himself not to think stupid things. It had been awkward just getting into the World Below, getting out was likely the same.

"Lumi?" he called.

Her name bounced back and echoed around him.

There was no answer. He cursed her light feet.

"Lumi, where are you?"

Still nothing.

He pressed on, sucking in his stomach as the passageway became narrower. He pulled his drum around so it was off his waist, and held it close to protect the delicate skin from the sharp rocks.

He groaned in dismay when he noticed the path branching off into two openings. Only the one on the left was lit by torches.

He didn't remember this from earlier. And which route had she taken? Did she even know where she was going?

"Lumi!" he called again, louder this time.

A voice came back, but it wasn't hers.

"Tuomas, is that you?"

He froze. That was a cry he recognised, and it turned his blood cold.

"*Paavo?*"

"Yes, I'm here! I'm stuck! Help me!"

The voice was coming from the right-hand tunnel. Tuomas didn't waste a second and bounded down it.

"Keep talking, help me find you!" he yelled.

He ran for what seemed like forever, following the contours of the passageway with his hands. Every now and then, he hit a piece of rock jutting out from the wall, but didn't feel any blood, so he kept going. With every step, Paavo's voice became louder.

His heart pounded in his ears. How did his brother get into this place? How long had he been here? Ever since the morning Tuomas had set out from Akerfjorden, when nobody had seen him?

"Where are you?" Paavo cried desperately. "Help me!"

"I'm coming! I'm almost there!" Tuomas called.

He was close. The voice sounded as though it was just on the other side of the wall.

He bounded forwards blindly and his foot caught a shallow step, sending him stumbling onto all fours. Then he looked up, and noticed the tunnel curving around a bend, faint light just visible on the walls.

He bound his drum back onto his belt and walked towards it, one hand held before his eyes to shield them. After so long in the darkness, even the soft glow was blinding. The horrid smell was stronger here and his stomach rolled with nausea.

He crept around the corner, and his breath caught in his throat.

He was in another cavern, much smaller than the last, with only a single fire which threw out a pitiful amount of heat. Beside it stood a large cairn of rocks, all balanced atop each other until they formed a hollow dome. And inside, just visible through the gaps, was Paavo.

Tuomas ran over. Paavo was horribly pale, bones protruding under his skin. He looked ill – almost dead.

"Are you alright?" Tuomas asked breathlessly. "What are you doing down here? How did you even get here?"

"They took me. The Earth Spirits," Paavo whimpered, his cheeks streaked with tears. "I offended them – I went to kill a reindeer for you, for a new sleeping sack. I was in such a hurry, I forgot to honour them."

Tuomas's heart pounded. Was this what he had sensed was wrong? The Earth Spirits had never intended to help them after all?

"When was this?" he asked. "The morning I left?"

Paavo nodded. "Yes, I went to the herd, but the Spirits were waiting for me."

Tuomas stared at him. He had never heard of anything like this happening before. If someone was disrespectful to the Spirits, they usually suffered misfortune in a more subtle way. Their animals might sicken, or their hunt fail. They might be struck down with illness themselves. They wouldn't be taken into a Spirit realm like this.

But then he remembered Lumi's retaliation on Mihka; how shocking and seemingly impossible that was. Nothing was impossible anymore.

"How are *you* here?" Paavo asked. "Are you by yourself?"

"No, I'm here with one of the wandering mages," Tuomas explained quickly. "Her name's Lilja. She'll be able to help you."

"Can *you* help me get out? I can't break through from the inside. There's some kind of magic holding this thing together."

He pushed at the rocks to demonstrate, and sure enough, they stayed exactly where they were.

Tuomas inspected the cairn. There was nothing obvious keeping it in place, but when he extended a hand, he could feel power radiating off it. It was strong; no kind of physical effort would break the rocks apart. The smell was stronger around it too – he couldn't tell if it was coming off the structure or from within it. The Earth Spirits obviously hadn't wanted Paavo to go anywhere.

Was this really fitting of forgetting to utter thanks? How long were they planning to keep him down here?

"Try drumming," Paavo suggested, noticing the instrument at his belt. "You should be good enough at it by now!"

Tuomas smirked.

"There's only one way to find out."

He untied the drum, warming it over the tiny fire with one hand and drawing his circle with his other. Then he raised the hammer and began a beat, letting his own summery power build in the same quick crest as he had used to summon Lumi.

But this time, he kept control of it, forcing it towards the cairn, directing its heat deep into the rocks. He took up a chant, pouring more energy into it with every breath, until the drumming became erratic and goosebumps rose on his arms.

Then, with an almighty crash, the stones blew apart.

Startled, Tuomas broke off the chant. A wave of exhaustion slammed into his chest and he fell to the ground.

The cavern swam before his eyes. His hands twitched uncontrollably; the drum rolled away on its edge. It passed through the circle, breaking its spell, before clattering down.

*So this is why you aren't supposed to come out of a trance too early*, Tuomas thought weakly.

His life-soul was loose. He could feel it floating somewhere above his body, still attached but not yet settled. It was like being drunk. He tried to command himself to sit up, but his arms and legs seemed miles away.

Paavo stepped out of the pile of fallen rocks. He glanced around, stretched, testing his freedom. He smiled broadly.

"Thank you," he said, words tinged with a relieved laugh. "It feels so good to finally be out of there!"

Tuomas went to smile back, but then he paused.

Paavo's mouth was higher on his face than it should be. When he was inside the cairn, it had been hard to notice, but now it was clear as day.

Paavo turned to him, and Tuomas let out a gasp of horror. His eyes were as hollow as a dead tree. One was milky white: completely blind.

Paavo placed both hands on the back of his head and pulled. The skin broke apart, peeling away like a piece of clothing, and revealed a sallow-skinned man, a long scar across his throat, the flesh puckered and bloodshot as though it had lain in water. His hair was sandy blonde, stringy with dried sweat, hanging over his empty eyes.

"You're just as gullible as I hoped you'd be," he grinned, and regarded Paavo's skin with an air of amusement.

Tuomas shuddered. He should have realised that wasn't his brother – Paavo would never have been so vague with his questions. This man had simply played on the answers which Tuomas himself had given.

"Who are you?" he demanded. But deep down, he knew.

He flinched as the man drew close.

"Can't you see the resemblance? I'm the *other* wandering mage."

*Kari.*

He snatched the drum with one hand. He regarded it idly, then tied it onto his own belt. Tuomas tried to get up, but he was still too weak. Kari knelt beside him and pulled him across his lap. Tuomas tried to wrench himself free, but Kari held him down, tearing at his tunic with his free hand until two long strips fell to the floor.

Tuomas opened his mouth to cry out, only for Kari to tie one of the strips across his lips. Then he flipped him over and bound his hands behind his back.

"Let's go and do some wandering," he smiled.

Without another word, he dragged Tuomas to his feet and bundled him down the tunnel, into the shadows.

She stared up at the sky, hiding just inside the cave mouth where the light couldn't touch her. It was still bright, as she knew it would be, but she had needed to get out of that cavern. It was so difficult to be surrounded by all the history on the walls; her Spirit brethren captured in ancient paint, weaving their stories like she wove her Lights.

One of the white reindeer ambled up to her and sniffed at her face. She laid a hand on its neck and ran her fingers through the thick fur. It was so dense; she couldn't penetrate it to feel the skin beneath.

It hurt to be so far from the World Above. At least in the World Between, she could still look up and see it; the only thing separating her from home was a barrier thinner and clearer than ice. Here, there was solid earth too: a false sky like a dome, where the Sun Spirit never truly shone and the Moon Spirit's face never turned.

And while she didn't lament the lack of her mother's presence, it continued to serve as a reminder of where she was: deeper than she should ever be.

She wiped water from her forehead. It dripped onto the grass at her feet, glittering in the light.

Then she heard something though the trees.

The reindeer's ears pricked up. At first, she thought it was another one, but the noise was too clumsy to be one of these graceful animals.

As though in confirmation, the reindeer beside her leapt away and disappeared into the forest.

She frowned, listening hard. It sounded like feet – human feet – hurrying through the undergrowth.

There was a muffled scream.

Then she saw them in the distance: two figures emerging from a second cave mouth, heading for the lake. The first one dragged the other behind him; he was struggling, but his movements slurred, as though he was drained of energy. She caught a glimpse of pale blonde hair.

She gasped.

*Tuomas.*

She sprinted towards them, hardly feeling the light as it seared her delicate skin. Water streamed down her arms.

She recoiled at the sight of the man pulling Tuomas, at the hollow eyes rolling in his face. She knew, without a doubt, this was the mage who had bound that demon. She could feel the power coming off him in sickly waves. But it was different to any other mage she had ever sensed. It was dense, raging, wicked.

Tuomas noticed her. His eyes were wide with terror.

"Lumi!" he managed to yell through the gag.

The man drew a knife from Tuomas's belt, twisted it, and slammed the butt into his temple. Tuomas tumbled onto his side, knocked out cold. Then the mage pulled him close, withdrew his drum from under his arm, and struck it.

There was a flash of white and she was blown backwards, tumbling though the ferns like a leaf.

Indignation flared within her – no mage would dare mistreat a Spirit like this! But as quickly as it came, it was replaced by fear. Not for herself, but for Tuomas. Whatever the mage wanted him for, it could not be good.

She jumped up, but Tuomas and the man were gone. There was a thundering sound in the distance as a thousand reindeer stampeded away in alarm.

Her eyes went to the hole in the sky. The mage must have taken him back into the World Between.

She considered running back to fetch Lilja, but stopped herself. There was no time.

Hoping with all her might that Sigurd and Elin were still waiting above ground, she closed her eyes, summoning all her power, more than she had ever dared to use outside of her own realm. Its wintry chill filled her and her body became lighter, until her feet lifted off the ground. She hovered, hair sweeping around her, like a flurry of snowflakes caught in an updraft.

She thought of the World Between, pictured it, and held it close until she could see every detail. The vast tundra, the clear open sky…

Then she let go. Air flew past her; it became cold and crisp once more. She broke through the thin skin which divided the realms; the barrier which only Spirits could cross unaided. Her feet touched down, and came to rest atop powdery snow. Blissful cold darkness surrounded her.

She was back on the frozen lake. In the distance, she could just make out one of the sleighs which had brought her companions to the Northern Edge.

She set her eyes on it. Tuomas was in there, and she had to catch him.

Somehow, she had to save him.

# Chapter Eighteen

Tuomas woke with a start.

His head rang; when he moved, he felt the stickiness of dried blood on his temple where the knife butt had struck him. There were stars all around, and for a moment he panicked. Where was he? Dead?

*No.*

As his senses returned, he realised he was lying down, on his back. His arms were raised above his head, still bound at the wrists, hooked over a pointed rock. His ankles were tied together too, with the scrap which had previously been around his mouth. The smell of woodsmoke was on the air from a nearby fire, whipped in all directions by the wind. Cold bit down to his bones the pressure of *taika* bore down on him. It was so concentrated, he could physically feel it on his skin.

He looked about. He was bound to a boulder, its surface polished smooth by the elements. All around it were antlers, colourful braids, loops of hair tied to logs so they wouldn't blow away.

To the side was a sleigh – his own, still piled with supplies of logs and pelts. His reindeer was tethered at the front, bent down against the biting wind. The bull looked at him with its huge black eyes, as though it wanted to help him.

He frowned. Why was it winter again? Had they come back to the World Between?

Then he heard the crunching sound of feet sinking into snow. He strained to look up, and saw Kari approaching, his figure backlit by the fire's glow. He wasn't wearing mittens or a hat, but his torso was covered by a mage's coat of white reindeer fur, matted with old dried blood. He had smeared his thin face with ash, the same way Henrik did at major ceremonies. The open gash on his throat was dark in the flickering light, like a horrid second mouth.

"So you're awake," he remarked.

In an instant, Tuomas remembered what had happened. He thrashed about, trying to get free.

"Don't waste your energy," Kari said. He touched the wound on Tuomas's head, then the fabric around his wrists. "I'm sorry about all this. I know it's very impolite. But it was the only way to make sure you didn't run off."

Tuomas fought to stay calm.

"Where am I?"

"The shrine on Einfjall mountain: the highest point I could find in the middle of all this flatness," said Kari. "The closer we can be to the World Above, the better."

So that was the reason for all the antlers and objects. They were offerings, left by generations of mages over countless years.

Tuomas thought quickly. If they were back at Einfjall, that would mean he had been out cold for a full day – it was difficult to tell from the constant lack of light.

He wondered if it was worth screaming to alert the villagers, but the idea fell apart just as quickly. The summit was too far away for anyone to hear him.

Kari tugged at the buckle of his belt. Once it was free, he pulled it out from under Tuomas's back and tossed it aside.

"You won't be needing this," he said.

Tuomas watched in dismay. All his knives and axe were attached to the belt.

A growl made him look around, and he yelped in fright.

The demon was standing there, its one remaining eye as hollow and dead as Kari's. Now they were together, he realised Kari's blinded eye was on the same side.

How had it crept up on them so quietly? It hadn't even left footprints.

Just like Lumi.

His heart leapt when he thought of her. Kari had left her behind, but was she safe?

"Admiring my handiwork?" Kari asked. He approached the demon and held a hand to its ragged cheek, as though caressing a child.

"It's amazing, isn't it?" he continued. "It was painful at first, and strange, having your life-soul in another body… but better than being locked in that Earth Spirit prison. Thank you for letting me out, by the way."

Tuomas trembled. It was terribly exposed up here, and the wind stabbed straight through him. The cold was too painful to describe.

"You sent that thing after me," he said.

"And even when I was trapped down there, it still obeyed the last order I gave it: to find you and bring you to me." Kari smiled at the monster. "Too bad you got loose – this would have all been over with so much faster if it had managed to keep hold of you."

He turned back to Tuomas. "I really am sorry for how crude this all is. But it's for the greater good."

"You're a mage!" Tuomas cried. "You're not supposed to hurt anyone!"

"There are always exceptional circumstances."

"Why? You did all this to get to me? What's so important about me?"

Kari regarded him with a look of genuine surprise.

"You don't know?"

"Know what?"

Tuomas struggled against his bonds, but it was no use. They were tied too tightly.

Kari let out a sharp laugh. All his previous gentleness disappeared in an instant.

"Oh, this is precious! You were travelling with Lilja and she never even told you?"

He ran a finger along Tuomas's jaw. Tuomas shuddered – he could feel the power, how warped it was, the complete opposite to what a mage's *taika* should be. The smell of it filled his mouth and he coughed violently, trying to get it out of his lungs.

Kari's hand trailed down until it was resting over his heart.

"You're the Son of the Sun," he said.

Tuomas froze. He remembered Lilja's story, of the Spirit which came to the World Between as the Great Mage, led the people south to Akerfjorden, died when he fell through the ice…

"No, I'm not!" he snapped. "He's been dead for generations!"

"Life-souls always return. You know that. Even a life-soul which was once a Spirit."

"I'm not a Spirit! I'm a boy! My parents were –"

"Yes, yes, humans, I know." Kari waved a hand impatiently. "Erik and Veera. I remember them. Your parents *here*, in the World Between. But your life-soul is not of this realm. It comes from the World Above. It is of the boy the Moon Spirit stole away, who leapt willingly into this World, and became the most powerful human who ever lived."

Tuomas's eyes widened. "You're insane."

"Oh, no, I know exactly what I'm talking about," said Kari insistently. He touched his torn throat. "Do you think I would have done something like this for just anyone? I'm not going to lie about how much it hurt."

He drew closer, until Tuomas could smell his rancid breath.

"You work it out. How many times did Henrik tell you how powerful you are, how you must control your *taika*? And how wondrous it is that you were born on midsummer, when the Golden One is at her strongest?"

Tuomas shook his head. "That doesn't prove anything!"

"I was there that day, I know it's true," said Kari. "So does Henrik, and all your Akerfjorden leaders."

He gripped Tuomas's face in his bony fingers.

"You're lying to yourself," he hissed, "Red Fox One."

Tuomas's mind raced. Henrik knew about this? It was impossible! He couldn't be the Son of the Sun!

But then he recalled Lilja telling the story, and how she had expanded on the ending. She had revealed that the Daughter of the Moon was none other than Lumi herself. And Tuomas was the only one who had managed to block her Lights, to pull Mihka out of her grasp.

Lumi had said, when he ripped her from the sky, that his name was not Tuomas. She had yelled at him that he should know his power. In the cave, not long ago, she had looked at the painting of the Sun and Moon Spirits, with their children beneath their faces.

Two foxes. One white… and one red.

His breath snatched in his throat.

Lumi was his sister. Not by blood, but by something more. They were both Spirits.

All along, she had known it was true.

His face must have changed, because Kari drew away with a satisfied smile. He headed for the sleigh and the reindeer snorted as he came close.

"Leave it alone!" Tuomas snapped, fighting back a shiver as the cold swept through him.

"I'm not after your animal," Kari replied.

When he returned, he held Henrik's drum and hammer under one arm. In his other hand was one of Tuomas's knives.

Tuomas eyed the blade in terror. Why did he have that?

"I'm surprised Lilja didn't tell you," Kari carried on. "I'm guessing you've been with her a while? It's a long way from Akerfjorden to the Northern Edge of the World."

"She might not have known," Tuomas shot back.

"Of course she knows!" laughed Kari. "She delivered you – she sensed that life-soul come into you as sure as I did! And through all our wanderings, we stayed away from Akerfjorden, to give you space to grow. But I looked in on you from time to time. I went into a trance and travelled there to check on you. Just for fun at first. But then... I admit, I became a little jealous."

His tone grew darker and he adjusted his grip on the knife. In the firelight, the flint looked even sharper. Tuomas tried not to panic.

"Look at you. Little more than a child, with all that raw otherworldly *taika* inside you! I worked and studied so hard, struggled through my test with hardly anything to show for it. And then Lilja came along, touched by the Great Bear Spirit... No matter how much effort I put into my power, it will never be enough. I've been a mage for longer than you've even drawn breath, and yet here you are. Just a boy! I should be able to break you between my finger and thumb! But you are so much more!"

He composed himself, taking a few deep breaths before continuing.

"And I will make it so much more. This is for the good of everyone. All the people I'll be able to help; all the songs which will be sung of me. It's the best outcome."

Behind him, the demon growled. Tuomas caught a whiff of its stinking breath and recoiled.

"The Spirits will punish you for this!" he cried.

"The Spirits don't care," Kari snarled.

He held up the knife. Tuomas flinched, but instead of bringing it down into his flesh, Kari cut the cords holding his coat together. He pulled the fur aside, then began slicing the blade up Tuomas's tunic, cutting it open. His skin crawled as the edge slid along his chest.

"It was best to leave this part until you woke up," Kari said. "Otherwise you would have frozen solid."

When Tuomas spoke, his voice was hoarse with fear.

"What are you going to do?"

Kari smiled. It was so soft; in any other circumstances it would have seemed friendly.

"I'm going to put that life-soul of yours to better use," he replied. "My little demon will be its new home. And then Lilja and I will share out that beautiful *taika*… but I will get the larger share, of course."

Tuomas's breathing quickened.

"Lilja's my friend."

"She's my sister," Kari pointed out. "And, quite frankly, if you honestly thought she was your friend, you don't know her at all."

By this point, he had finished cutting through Tuomas's tunic, and held the material apart to look down at his bare chest. Tuomas shivered as the cold seeped into his flesh.

"She… got that demon away from me!" he argued, his teeth chattering.

"So she could get you to trust her!" Kari chuckled triumphantly.

Tuomas shook his head. "I don't believe it."

"Then I suppose you also won't believe that she has a little stake in that demon too?"

"*What?*"

"Did you ever see a mark like this on her?" Kari motioned to the scar on his throat.

Tuomas went to snarl a reply, but then he realised – it was exactly the same as Lilja's scar.

He hadn't been sure how she might have gotten it, and had known better not to press her for answers. Yet now, the final piece fell into the puzzle, and his heart sank.

She had been in league with her brother all along.

"No!" he gasped.

"She didn't want anything to do with it at first," said Kari. "So I got the demon to give her a little slash. Once my intent got into her blood, she came around to my way of thinking. But then the Earth Spirits came and dragged me down into that prison. Not Lilja though. The demon got away, and so did she."

"That's not what she told me!"

"Another ruse? Smart girl. Let me guess, she said she had nothing to do with me?"

"You're lying!"

"I told you the truth about who you are, which is more than she did, boy. Why would I lie about her?"

Tuomas choked back an angry sob. He couldn't feel his fingers anymore.

"It mustn't have taken her long to go after you, though," Kari added nonchalantly. "She wouldn't have sent me the skin of your big brother otherwise."

Tuomas shrieked. His memory flashed with Kari peeling off Paavo's face, throwing it to the floor, stepping over it like a dirty lifeless rag...

"No... she couldn't have..."

It was enough to finally bring tears to his eyes. He blinked them away, but they trickled onto his cheeks and froze there.

Kari placed a hand on his chest to feel the temperature. Tuomas's skin crawled beneath his touch.

"Nice and cold," he muttered. "Don't worry, you won't feel a thing now. I'll make it quick."

Tuomas pulled madly at his bonds with all the strength he had left.

"Help me!" he screamed. "Somebody, please!"

The wind whipped his voice away into the night.

Kari laid a finger across his lips.

"Hush, now. Let's get that lovely golden life-soul into its new home. Time to give it over to someone who knows how to use it."

He beckoned the demon closer until it was leaning over Tuomas, with all the rapt attention of a curious child.

Then Kari raised the knife.

"Time to see what the *taika* in that beating heart tastes like."

# Chapter Nineteen

A flash of green hit Kari's hand and the knife flew over the side of the mountain.

He howled in pain, clutching at his wrist. Another flash slammed into him, knocking him down and sending Henrik's drum into a snowdrift. The demon roared and went to run, but a third wave sent it tumbling back towards its master.

Tuomas strained his neck to see his rescuer.

Lumi was standing there, ears flattened against her skull, eyes blazing a furious red. Her hands and arms glowed with the light of the aurora.

She ran to him and began tugging at the bonds around his wrists.

"What are you... doing here?" he managed to mutter through lips rapidly turning blue with cold.

She didn't reply; just gave the fabric a final tug. It loosened and he hissed as blood flooded back into his hands. She turned her attention to the ties at his ankles, but then the demon leapt to its feet and came at her.

"Lumi, look out!" Tuomas cried.

She dived away, narrowly avoiding its claws and thrust her palms against its chest. More of her Lights shot out and blew it backwards. The demon's growls became shrieks of pain; behind it, Kari screamed as each blow landed.

The sound spurred Lumi on and she drove the demon towards the edge of the mountain. The air became thick with her magic. Her tail whipped at the snow and flung up another aurora, which circled her in the howling winds. She didn't stop, shooting Light after Light into the monster with a fury Tuomas had never seen.

Kari thrust his hand into the snowdrift after the drum.

Lumi held her arms high, gathering all her power, ready to deal the finishing blow.

A shockwave hit her and she fell across Tuomas, pinned down. Kari was on his feet again, the drum in his hand. The hammer rested lightly on the skin.

He regarded Lumi with excitement.

"I can't believe it!" he cried. "Daughter of the Moon! How are you here like this?"

Lumi tried to get up, but Kari struck the drum again and restrained her. He approached and grasped her chin to regard her pale face. She glared at him, her tail thrashing furiously.

"How dare you!" she snarled. "I will tear that life-soul out of your demon before this is over!"

"I'm not afraid of you, White Fox One," Kari said.

He pushed her off Tuomas so she was kneeling beside him. He hit the drum once more for good measure, and she stayed there.

Tuomas's heart sank. Lumi had come here to help him, and now she was trapped as well.

That gave him a strength he didn't realise he had left. Gritting his teeth, he forced himself to sit up. The surroundings spun with the movement and he saw double. The scent of Kari's *taika* wormed into him and he fought the urge to retch.

He focused on the drum in Kari's hand. He tried to make a grab for it, but missed and toppled into the snow.

He started trembling again, more violently than before. His chest was still bare, and the ends of his hair were beginning to freeze, blonde strands turning pure white. He couldn't feel his hands; he hadn't worn mittens since emerging in the summery World Below.

He was too weak. Never mind what Kari had in store for him – if he stayed exposed for much longer, he would die from the cold.

"Let her go!" he managed to shout. "Please!"

Kari ignored him.

"Brother and sister, side by side again," he remarked. "This is poetic. Why not let you stay together even now?"

He smirked at Lumi. "You'll withstand the cold much better than he will. You can wait. I'm just sorry that you'll have to watch this."

He placed the drum at his feet, leaving the hammer over it to keep Lumi restrained. Then he turned to the demon, beckoning it with one hand. It limped closer, injured from the beating it had taken, but still strong enough to do what was commanded.

With a low growl, it wrapped its bony fingers around Tuomas and lifted him up, forced his arms behind his back. Kari fetched the discarded belt and removed another knife.

Tuomas did his best to kick out at the mage, but his feet were still bound, and he only succeeded in losing his balance. The demon held him fast, not letting him fall.

"Help!" he cried again. "Lumi!"

She snarled, trying to get free. Kari grabbed Tuomas's torn tunic and held it aside. He brought the point of the knife to his chest, directly over his heart.

Tuomas barely had a chance to catch his breath before the blade pierced his skin. Blood left a hot line down his front.

He screamed.

Lumi shouted, but he didn't hear her words. There was only the knife, almost at his breastbone, slowly working deeper and deeper...

Something whistled past his ear.

The demon suddenly let go of him. Tuomas collapsed in a heap, a hand over his wound. He hazily noticed an arrow sticking straight through the demon's neck.

Then another arrow shot past him and struck it in the chest.

In the heart.

A torrent of blood spilled out of its mouth and Kari shrieked. He clutched at his own throat; eyes huge with panic.

The demon went berserk, thrashing about, flaps of skin flying in all directions. It kicked the fire and sent sparks shooting into the night. One of its feet hit the drum and dislodged the hammer, freeing Lumi.

Kari looked on as his monster grew smaller, shrivelling like a leaf in autumn, as half his own life-force disappeared before his eyes. Then a small sparkling orb drifted out of its mouth.

Kari tried to grab it, but it slipped through his fingers like smoke. Tuomas could almost sense the Spirit of Passage holding it, carrying it out of reach.

A third arrow embedded in Kari's leg. He howled, barely managing to stay upright.

Tuomas began dragging himself away, leaving a bloody trail on the snow as he moved. The knife hadn't gone too deep, but the gash was enough to sap any energy he had left.

Hands appeared on his arms and pulled him the rest of the way. He groggily looked up and found a rounded face, framed by black hair.

"Elin?" he breathed in amazement.

"Yes, it's me. We're both here," she replied. "Hang in there. We're going to get you out of here."

Sigurd appeared over her shoulder. "He's freezing. We need to leave. Now."

Tuomas's heart swelled with relief. Sigurd bundled a spare coat around him, then picked him up and carried him to the nearest sleigh. Once inside, he was wrapped in a blanket and furs laid across him. Elin slipped in too and pressed herself against him to share her body heat, her hand over his chest to stem the blood.

Some warmth began to come back, but the chill had gone deep into his bones. And he still couldn't feel his hands. That was never good. He had been cold before, but not like this. It could be the beginnings of frostbite.

Then he saw Lumi on her feet.

She strode over to the mage, crouched by the remains of his demonic servant. His face was already thinner, his skin paler than death. He was only half-alive now; only one soul remained in his body. He was a shell, clinging on with his fingertips.

Lumi looked at him icily, her tail twitching in anger. Her hands glowed: a swirling mixture of green and red. Then she raised one and plunged it into his chest.

Kari let out a scream like nothing Tuomas had heard before. Beside him, Elin jumped with horror.

Lumi brought her face close to Kari.

"Are you afraid of me, now, little man?"

Her eyes turned red. She twisted her wrist and Kari cried out.

"I have your other soul in my grasp right now," she hissed. "I should rip it out of you."

Tuomas held his breath.

Lumi pulled her hand free.

But there was no soul in it. Instead, she stood up and kicked Kari squarely in the chest. He tumbled onto his back, trembling fingers over his heart.

"But I will not do that," Lumi said.

Kari let out a shaky gasp.

"Because you can't. You can take a soul, but not a life." She glared at him.

"You are not worth it. All life and death are equal, but you are below even that."

Droplets of water appeared on her skin. Kari managed a small smirk.

"You're letting warm emotions touch you, White Fox One," he said. "Be careful. They're not meant to be felt by Spirits like you."

Lumi narrowed her eyes, and for a moment, Tuomas thought she would go back on her hesitation. But she simply picked up the drum and his belt and strode away, her head held high, wiping the water away with her wrist. Her gaze met Tuomas's briefly before she jumped onto the back of the sleigh.

Sigurd didn't waste a moment. He snapped the rope, and the reindeer set off down the mountain, leaving the dying mage alone with his lonely fire, surrounded by darkness and bloodstained snow.

# Chapter Twenty

The Sun Spirit was high overhead: bright with the fullness of summer. The air filled with the thundering of hundreds of hooves. The reindeer were in the corral on the migration island, antlers knocking together as they tried to avoid the ring of herders closing in on them. The calves had only been born a couple of months ago, and now it was time to mark them, so everyone knew which animal belonged to whom.

Tuomas threw a lasso and caught one. It struggled to run after its mother, but he reeled it in and restrained it under one arm. He almost lost his grip on it, so Mihka ran over, grabbing the calf around the neck.

"You never were great at this, were you?" he teased.

"Shut up," Tuomas muttered through a laugh.

He whipped out his knife and quickly cut his mark into the animal's ear. Then the two boys let it go, and it hurried away with an indignant snort.

Mihka took off his cap and ruffled his hair, the black strands shining. The hard work had made it sweaty, and plastered it to his skull. Tuomas stood behind him, lasso at the ready, his eyes combing the herd as it rampaged around them. There were a couple more calves which had been born to his females, he knew it. He just needed to spot them.

"Tuomas?"

He looked around. The voice was distant, directionless. Mihka hadn't heard it.

"Tuomas! Can you hear me?"

His body jolted. He opened his eyes and saw the curved beams of a turf hut.

He was lying on his back, wrapped in layers of fur and cloth; so tight that he couldn't move his arms. His vision swam in and out of focus. The scent of roasting meat wormed up his nose.

He sighed. It had only been a dream.

Then everything came flooding back to him: the journey north, the sight of Kari, the ordeal on the mountaintop…

He sat bolt upright, and immediately wished he hadn't. His head spun and pain coursed through his muscles. But the worst of it was in his hands – it was enough to make him cry out.

"Careful!"

Someone eased him back down. He squinted at the face, trying to make out who it was.

"Alda?"

"Yes," she replied. "You were kicking. I thought you might be waking up at last."

"How long have I been asleep?" he asked groggily.

"Two days. You took quite a beating." Alda smoothed his hair off his forehead and felt his temperature. "You were frozen stiff when Sigurd and Elin brought you back here. Now, let's see."

She carefully began to unwind the blankets from around his body until she got down to the sleeping sack. Then she pulled that aside and lifted his tunic to check the wound on his chest. Tuomas noticed it had a poultice across it. He moved a little, and with a relief, felt no stitches tugging at his flesh.

"Where are they?" he asked.

"Hunting," said Alda.

She eased his arms out of the sack and held his hands in her own. Tuomas winced as she touched them. Then he looked at them properly and yelped in horror. His skin was swollen and purple, bulging around the nails, which still had a tinge of blue to them.

He instantly realised why they were hurting so much. Up on the mountain, he had stopped being able to feel them – when Kari had kidnapped him, he'd been out in the freezing cold for a full day with no mittens. Now the ice crystals in his flesh were beginning to thaw, and his body was discovering the newfound damage.

"Frostbite?" he said, more a statement than a question.

Alda's grimace confirmed it.

"Aino rubbed them with snow and herbs as soon as you got back here, but it hasn't helped. Nothing to do but keep you warm and rested."

She placed his hands back inside the sack and covered him up again. Tuomas was glad he couldn't see them anymore. He knew what would come next: the blisters, then the skin would peel off in strips.

He had seen it before. Several years ago, an old woman went out in a blizzard to get water and lost her way in the swirling snow. Sisu and the other leaders found her the next morning at the edge of the forest, her feet numb and unresponsive. A few weeks later, flesh and bone had rotted away, and she never walked again.

He screwed his eyes shut. What would happen if he lost his hands? The thought was terrible. He held his breath and prayed to every Spirit he could think of.

Despite the layers, he was still freezing. It felt like his bones had turned to ice. Another worry crossed his mind – what if hypothermia set in? Now his body had gotten a taste of air outside the sleeping sack, he could feel clammy sweat on his skin.

He supposed even a toddler would be stronger than him in that moment. If illness struck, could he recover?

Alda poured some herbal tea into a cup, placed one hand around the back of his neck and held the rim to his lips. It was so strong, Tuomas almost gagged – it reminded him of the stuff Henrik would brew after every arduous lesson. But he kept it down. He knew how important it was to stay warm and hydrated in a state like this.

A wave of exhaustion overcame him, and before he could resist, he sank into sleep. It was deep and dark, raging with intense imagery. The slumber brought no rest. Each time he awoke, he was more tired than before.

Dreams merged with the smoky interior of the hut. Faces peered out of the knots in the beams; before turning into clouds and rivers which defied gravity.

He was looking at his reflection in a clear sheet of ice, a pair of pointy red fox ears rising out of his hair… caught the milky scent of new-born calves… saw the demon coming towards him, Kari's knife raised high as the drum beats thrummed as fast as his heart…

Then Kari was standing in front of him, face still smeared with ash and hair blowing crazily in the mountain wind. Blood flowed freely down his arms. A heart was in his hands, and he leaned forward to take a huge bite out of it…

Tuomas's chest burned. That was *his* heart… Kari was here and he would *eat his heart*…

He screamed. He couldn't move his fingers. He felt them oozing something, sticking to his sides.

Elin drew back the covers and helped Alda clean his hands. Skin came away with each dab of the cloth. He spun in the sleeping sack, exhaustion dragging him from his body. His souls trembled inside him.

After what felt like forever, he managed to ease his eyes open again.

His hands were bandaged to the wrists. He wiggled one of them free and tentatively rubbed his head. The fox ears were gone. It had only been a dream.

Sigurd, Alda and Elin sat around the hearth, eating salmon cakes. As soon as Elin noticed he was awake, she threw down her bowl and crawled over.

"How are you?" she asked.

Tuomas grimaced. "Sore."

"I'm not surprised," Sigurd remarked. But then he smiled and gently patted Tuomas on the shoulder. "You're a tough one, boy."

"How did you know where I was?"

Elin glanced at her father.

"The Spirit of the Lights. We'd made camp at the edge of the lake. She ran into the tent and said you'd been kidnapped; that one of the sleighs had been taken. So we took the other one and went after you. But she ran ahead – that's how she got to you first."

She shuffled closer to him.

"Tuomas, I know you've got something to do with her. Why is she in human form?"

Before he could answer, there was a knock on the door.

"Aino?" Sigurd called.

"No," came the reply. "It's Lilja."

Tuomas's blood ran cold.

The door opened and she stepped through. She took one look at him and knelt at his side.

"I told you not to wander off," she chided, but then her voice softened. "I left the World Below as soon as I saw you were both gone; I followed back here on skis. I'm glad to see you're alright, boy. What happened?"

She reached towards him.

Tuomas jerked away.

"Don't touch me!" he snarled.

Lilja frowned.

"What's the matter?" Alda asked.

"I know about you!" Tuomas blurted. "Kari told me everything… you're in league with him! You murdered my brother!"

Lilja recoiled as though he had slapped her. Around the hearth, Alda and Sigurd stared, their faces white with shock.

"I… I never did!" Lilja insisted. "I am a mage! Mages do not rule and we do not kill! I said that to Kari, back when he made that demon!"

"You knew he was the one who made it?" demanded Sigurd. "You knew, and you didn't say anything?"

"I hardly say much at the best of times," Lilja snapped.

"You were protecting him," Tuomas hissed. "You didn't take me to the World Below to help Lumi. It was so I could set him free! And you gave him Paavo's skin so he could trick me!"

"It must have been an illusion. You know mages can do that. I never laid a finger on your brother – I haven't seen the boy since you were born! Whatever he said to you on that mountain, they were lies! He wanted to weaken your resolve, so you wouldn't try to fight back!"

"I don't think he was the liar," Tuomas said coldly.

He swung a hand at her, caught her collar and pulled it down. The scar shone in the firelight.

"Kari had one just like it," he said. "He wasn't the only one controlling that demon."

"That's not true!"

Lilja smacked his hand away, causing him to yelp in pain. She quickly tried to apologise, but Sigurd was on his feet in moments, his face a dark cloud of anger.

"I think you'd better leave," he said, tone dangerously low.

Lilja looked between him and Elin.

"It's not true. I swear! I was protecting him!"

Sigurd advanced on her.

"Get out. Now."

Realising she was beaten, Lilja lowered her head and backed out of the door. She threw one last glance at Tuomas, biting her lip to stop herself from crying. But he refused to acknowledge her, and she didn't say another word.

With a final sigh, she disappeared into the night.

# Chapter Twenty-One

Time flew, with hardly any way to mark it. The final dregs of midday twilight finally faded and cast the Northlands into true polar night. Midwinter was almost upon them. The wind blew like a ferocious creature, bringing storms and blizzards, and villagers were forced to venture out and shovel the snow away from their doors.

To Tuomas, it all passed in a haze. He struggled through fever dreams, the pain of his hands spreading like fire. The worst was when Elin and Alda cleaned them and the skin came away, on some occasions accompanied by a nail. The tips of two of his fingers blackened and dissolved, until he was left with only misshapen stumps.

He distantly heard Elin telling him of things going on, even though it sounded a million miles away. Lilja had taken her belongings and sleigh and left when they were all asleep. Birkir and the other leaders put men to work patrolling the outskirts of Einfjall in case she or Kari tried to come back.

There had been no sightings. Tuomas wondered if the raging snowstorms had killed them both.

Two weeks after Sigurd evicted Lilja, Tuomas found the strength to wriggle out of the sleeping sack. The fever had finally broken and he had managed to fight off the last of the ice in his bones.

Alda turned away to give him some privacy as he pulled on a fresh set of clothes.

"You seem a lot better," she remarked.

"Too bad I wasn't on my feet last night. I could have gone on the hunt with Elin and Sigurd," said Tuomas.

"Don't push your luck."

Tuomas slid the tunic to his waist and picked up his belt. Aside from the missing knives, everything was still there. The greatest relief was seeing the little pouch with Mihka's hair inside.

It was difficult to fasten the buckle with his damaged hands, but he managed it, and let his fingers linger on the pouch. Then he felt the harder outline of the bone carving. He recalled whittling it, back in Lilja's tent, into the face of a white fox.

Two talismans: one for his friend, and one for his... sister.

*Sister Spirit.*

His heart raced. He needed to speak with her.

He cleared his throat to tell Alda he was decent, and slipped his feet into his shoes.

"I'll fetch us some water," he offered. "I need to have some fresh air."

"Wear your mittens," Alda said.

"As if I need reminding," Tuomas replied, but he smiled as he said it.

He pulled on his coat and hat, and she helped him get into his mittens. Then he picked up the pail and stepped through the door, immediately sinking into several inches of snow.

He took in a huge breath of air. It was freezing, and chilled his lungs, but he didn't care. After two weeks of being stuck inside, it was wonderful. He let it out slowly, watching a cloud form in front of his lips.

He walked away from the huts, out to where nobody had trodden, and laid the pail on its side to kick snow into it. It was the fastest and easiest way to get water in the dead of winter – afterwards, it was only a matter of melting the snow down.

He scooped a handful from the ground and sucked it into his mouth. The cold stung his teeth, but he held it there until it thawed, and swallowed the sweet water.

His eyes wandered to the huge bulk of the mountain over the village. Its shadow loomed against the sky, slopes caked with ice.

An uncomfortable chill shot through him. Up on that desolate summit, he had almost died. He wondered if Kari was still there, huddled around the remains of his fire, frozen stiff…

Henrik had said that some mages were tested through illness. In any other circumstances, what he had just been through might have been enough. But not now. This was all so much bigger than he'd ever thought.

"Tuomas."

He spun around, and came face to face with Lumi.

She reached out a hand, but stopped. Tuomas realised the protective circle was still in place – it had been cast to keep out everything not human, not just demons. Her palm pressed against it like a sheet of clear ice.

"I'll come to you," he said, and stepped forward, through the barrier.

It was a strange feeling: a sharp tug against his face. Usually circles evaporated as soon as they were touched, but Lilja and Aino must have cast this one particularly strong.

Lumi lowered her hand. Her eyes glowed a soft turquoise.

"I am glad to see you are feeling better," she said.

"Thanks. How are you?" he asked.

"I am fine." She glanced up and down his body. "You have lost weight."

"It happens when you're sick," said Tuomas. "Lumi, listen... I need to talk to you."

She stood still, waiting for him to continue.

"You knew who I was, didn't you?" he asked. "The... Son of the Sun."

Lumi hesitated for a moment.

"Yes."

"Why didn't you tell me?"

"Because I was not sure it would be best for you. You had a life, a mission you needed to accomplish. I simply became ensnared in it when you summoned me."

Tuomas frowned.

"You kept quiet because you didn't want to confuse me? You knew it would hurt me to know?"

Lumi's ears twitched.

"But how is it possible?" he muttered. "Kari said that it's my life-soul... that it came down here."

"That is correct," she said. "I knew it was you from the moment you put me in this body. When you left the World Above, your life-soul was reborn into the form of a human child. That is what enabled that child – that man – to become the greatest mage ever known. And then he led the way south to form a new village, but died on the way. Because he sacrificed his immortality to help the people."

"I know. The village was Akerfjorden," Tuomas finished. "But wait... in the legend, you were there, too. It's why everyone is so scared of you: you ripped out his life-soul."

Lumi's eyes narrowed.

"Yes, I did. But not for the reasons you are thinking. You... *he*... was drowning. I had to make sure the life-soul would be safe. Pulling it out was the only way."

Tuomas blinked. "So... you didn't... kill him? That's not why he drowned?"

Lumi recoiled in horror.

"Of course not! I never would! And I cannot kill. I can take a soul, but one soul only. The Carrying One – the Spirit of Passage – is the only Spirit who may take both."

Tuomas looked at her. Even the story, so branded onto everyone's consciousness that it could have been a living memory, was wrong? Would anything be simple anymore?

"It makes sense that you should have been born at that same village in this life," Lumi carried on. "And at midsummer, too."

"But... that story is older than the oldest man in Akerfjorden," said Tuomas. "That life-soul had to have gone into others before me."

"Not necessarily," Lumi replied. "Life-souls and body-souls do not come back in a new form the moment their old one dies. And the life-soul of a Spirit responds to power. Do you honestly think I would have let you pull me out of the sky if I could not fight back?"

She had a point.

"It was Lilja and Kari," he realised. "They were in Akerfjorden when I was born. Lilja said that too much power in one place rarely ends well – that was why they left afterwards."

"*Taika* to *taika*," agreed Lumi.

"Wait... they couldn't have arranged for me to have that life-soul, could they?"

"Of course not. Even they are not that strong. But Lilja carries the touch of the Great Bear Spirit, the most powerful of us all. That alone would have been enough to bring that life-soul into your body."

Tuomas sighed. "Lilja betrayed me. Sigurd sent her away."

"I know."

Lumi's tail twitched behind her back.

"You and I were together in the World Above, before the first herders walked here," she said. "We knew each other. You thought the Silver One was your mother, and I thought the Golden One was mine. But then the Sun told me the truth, and I told you. And you jumped out of the sky to get away. I tried to pull you back but it was too late.

"Not long after, I first danced my Lights through the sky. I looked down on you – your life-soul – whenever I could. I saw your death and rebirth. I watched you grow. Every single time you turned your eyes to the aurora, I was looking back at you.

"I am the White Fox One, and you are the Red Fox One. In another story, we might have swept up the Lights together, side by side. We are opposites, yet the same. No matter what forms we take, we are bound."

She sighed. "I would give anything to take you back there. Back home, with me."

Tuomas looked into her eyes, and noticed the emotion she was barely holding back. It seemed she was trying to not burst into tears.

But Lumi didn't cry. She *couldn't* cry.

"Please, be honest with me," he said. "Why didn't you tell me before?"

Lumi pressed her lips together. For a moment Tuomas thought she wasn't going to reply. But then she smiled, and it was the widest, most genuine expression he had ever seen on her face.

"Because I care about you," she said. "No matter the circumstances of me being here… it was all worth it, to see you again. My brother."

She reached out and grasped his hands, gently so as to not hurt him.

Tuomas froze. She had never willingly come this close to him.

She was like holding light itself: cold and smooth, no weight at all. Her very touch made him shiver. It reminded him starkly that she was not of this realm; that only the body he had bound her in kept her from lifting into the air.

It struck him how even now, she was formless. Although he could see her face, her flesh, even individual strands of white hair, it was nothing. She reminded him of how water would take the shape of the cup or kettle which held it. Under her pristine skin, he faintly noticed the same shifting colours which danced behind her eyes, like the subtle sheen of pearl within a shell.

Then he felt something wet seeping through his mittens. He pulled himself free and held Lumi at arm's length.

She was soaked from head to toe. The water was coming out of her, running over her skin like a summer rain… or a melting icicle.

Horror rattled him.

"What's happening to you?" he gasped.

Lumi's expression transformed from joy to unease.

"Stay there," he snapped, fighting to keep panic under control. Then he ran back towards the village, leaving the pail behind.

When he reached the mage's hut, he pounded on the door.

"Aino!" he cried.

She peered out in alarm, rubbing her eyes.

"What's wrong?" she asked through a yawn. "Why aren't you in bed?"

"Aino, please come here," Tuomas said. "Quickly!"

Aino disappeared for a moment to put her shoes on, then stepped outside, tying her coat shut in mid-step. Not wanting anyone else to overhear the conversation, Tuomas beckoned for her to follow, and the two of them hurried back to the outskirts of the village.

"What's wrong?" Aino asked again. "Tuomas, I barely got back from the shrine an hour ago. I had to purify it after everything that happened; I'm drained."

"I'm sorry, but it's an emergency," said Tuomas.

Then Aino saw Lumi.

She gasped and almost fell over, her eyes so wide, Tuomas thought they might fall out of their sockets. Lumi gave her one of her unblinking stares and Aino lowered her head in respect.

"It is an honour to receive you," she said nervously. Then she glanced at Tuomas. "How do you know the Spirit of the Lights?"

"It's my fault she's here," he said. "I pulled her out of the World Above, and I need to send her back."

In an instant, Aino's face changed.

"So that's why you were on your way to the Northern Edge of the World."

"Yes. But Lilja and I kept quiet because we didn't want to scare anyone. And she stayed away – we respected that she wouldn't want anybody to know."

"I understand," said Aino, her eyes constantly moving back to Lumi. She shook her head in wonder.

"How did you even manage to get her into this form? You're just a boy."

Lumi pressed her lips together, but didn't respond. Tuomas hurriedly changed the subject.

"Something's wrong with her," he said. "She was as cold and crisp as snow at first. But now… I think she's *melting*."

Aino's brows rose. She regarded Lumi with a new level of interest, tentatively reaching out towards her face as though afraid she would bite.

"May I?" she asked.

Lumi kept eye contact with her, but gave the slightest nod.

Aino slipped her hand out of her mitten and pushed through the circle to feel Lumi's forehead. When she drew away, her fingers were slick with water.

Tuomas's breathing quickened. He had first noticed the wetness on Lumi's skin when they reached the Northern Edge of the World. Back then, it had just been a sheen. Now, it looked as though she had jumped into a lake. Even her starry dress seemed duller.

Aino lowered her hand. Tuomas noticed it was shaking a little.

"You have been in this realm too long, Spirit," she said. "You have begun to feel, to recognise human emotions. And they are too warm, too human, for the World you come from."

Tuomas froze with realisation.

The bond between them, which she had mentioned only moments ago, was slowly destroying her from the inside out.

"So what do we do?" he asked, his mouth dry.

Aino pulled her mitten back on.

"I don't need to tell you. She needs to go back into the World Above. The sooner, the better. But I'm afraid I can't help you."

Tuomas had expected as much.

"Lilja couldn't, either. It has to be me."

"I won't be much help to you at all," said Aino. "I am a mage, yes, but I deal with healing the sick, communing with the Spirits for good fortune... my *taika* is not as strong as Lilja's. Or even yours, boy. I can sense it coming off you."

"Could you sense it before?" he asked. "When we first arrived, I mean?"

"Yes. But not like now. Before, it was like the gentle trickle of a river. Now, the current has risen. Your power feels warmer, more alive, since you returned from the mountain."

Tuomas and Lumi shared a glance. They didn't speak, but the same thought passed between them. Up on the mountain, Kari had told Tuomas the truth.

Tuomas laid a hand over his chest. He still couldn't quite believe it – let alone think of Kari without panic flaring. But that revelation must have done something to his *taika*, whether he'd recognised it or not.

Aino didn't seem to notice his unease, because she continued talking.

"You need to keep a hold on that power, Tuomas. Especially now your apprenticeship with Lilja... has come to an end. But since she's left us, I think I do know someone who can assist you."

Tuomas suppressed a groan. How many people and places would they have to go to in the name of so-called help? Mihka seemed further away than ever. He began to wonder if he would ever pass his test and undo everything, or if he would be roaming the Northlands forever in this never-ending quest.

He looked at the sky. The Sun Spirit was truly gone now; this should be when the aurora was at its strongest. Yet Lumi was melting away before him like ice in a spring thaw. And the constant darkness wouldn't last for much longer. Soon the light would return, and spell the end of the Long Night for another year.

Lumi struggled enough in the faint twilight, and refused to go near any kind of heat. If she wasn't back in the World Above before the darkness ended, she would surely disappear. And so would any chance of Mihka's survival.

There was no other option.

"Who is it?" he asked.

"His name is Enska," said Aino. "He's the mage of Poro village. It's not far from here: a day's journey to the east."

She paused. "He's Lilja and Kari's father."

Tuomas gritted his teeth. His chest still burned from where the knife had gone in.

Could they truly trust the father of those two? The man who had trained them both and nurtured their incredible power?

Aino noticed his uncertainty.

"I've met Enska several times on the migrations, before Kari and Lilja were even born," she assured. "He's a good man. He's not like them."

"I thought Lilja was good," Tuomas pointed out.

"He's the only one I can suggest," Aino said. "I understand your reservations, but there isn't much choice. *I* can't do anything to help."

She looked to Lumi. "If nothing else, Spirit, he may be able to slow your... condition."

Lumi flicked her tail, then swept it back and forth thoughtfully. After several long moments, she glanced at Tuomas. A bead of water ran over her temple as she moved.

"We should go," she said.

Tuomas looked straight back, not bothering to hide his concern.

"What if it turns out to be another trap?"

"Then we shall work our way out of it again."

As she spoke, more water escaped her hairline. Then she swayed where she stood, so Tuomas grabbed her shoulders.

She seemed so different from the creature he had first seen that night when he summoned her. The unshakable pride was still there, but now she held herself more loosely. Her eyes had lost some of their iridescent shine. She almost looked translucent; he could swear he could see the line of the horizon behind her.

Lumi didn't say anything. She simply reached up and placed her own hands on his shoulders.

That hurt Tuomas even more than if she had tried to attack him. The gentleness was too human for him to bear.

"Alright," he said. "We'll go."

Aino laid a comforting arm around his back.

"Don't be afraid," she said. "The worst is over now. Kari is gone. Nobody could survive being up on a mountain for that long, especially with only half his blood and souls."

"Did you see him up there? Is he dead?"

"I didn't, but it's snowed since you were there. He's buried under it. And Lilja is probably far away from here. I doubt you will ever see her again. I know *I* never expected to."

A sudden thought passed through Tuomas's mind.

"Aino, have I passed my test yet?" he asked. "If you can sense my *taika* more, am I a true mage now?"

Aino shook her head slowly. "That's not for me to answer. Or your teacher, for that matter. Only you know when you're ready. Do you feel ready?"

Tuomas paused.

"I don't know."

"Then you aren't there yet. You'll feel it when you are. There's no mistaking it."

She knelt in front of the two of them.

"Thank you for trusting me with your secrets. You are always welcome in Einfjall. Now, come on, Tuomas. You need to be careful with your hands."

As they walked back to the huts, Tuomas glanced over his shoulder to see Lumi disappearing into the shadows. He only paused for long enough to fetch the pail of snow.

# Chapter Twenty-Two

When Tuomas got back to the hut, Elin and Sigurd had returned from their hunt. Elin looked up from the hearth, where she was busy gutting a hare.

"Where did you go?" Alda asked. "I was getting worried!"

"I'm fine," Tuomas replied. "I went to see Aino. And Lumi."

That got Sigurd's attention.

"The Spirit?"

Tuomas hauled the pail to the fireside and set it down so the snow could melt. Then he sat next to Elin. He hesitated for a moment, thinking how best to approach the subject.

"I have to put her back," he said. "But I need help – help that Aino can't give me. So she's told me to speak to the Poro mage."

Elin's eyes widened.

"You're leaving?"

"Don't be ridiculous," Alda said firmly. "You can't go anywhere while your frostbite is still healing!"

"That's why I was wondering if you might come with me," said Tuomas. "I know it's a lot to ask. You've done so much for me already. But this isn't something which can wait. It's important."

"Nothing is worth your health," Alda argued.

"It isn't about me," he said. "It's Lumi – the Spirit. She can't stay here much longer. And as long as she's here, my best friend back home is stuck between life and death. I need to go."

Alda's face was white with angst, but she didn't say anything else. Tuomas worried he had upset her.

"I don't mean to sound ungrateful," he said softly. "I wish I didn't have to leave."

Elin wiped her bloodied hands on a rag.

"I'll come with you," she said. Then she looked at Sigurd. "Will you, Father?"

Sigurd glanced at Alda, not wanting to meet Tuomas's eyes. He shook his head.

"Not this time. I can't leave your mother alone at midwinter," he said. "I'm sorry, Tuomas."

Tuomas gave him a small smile. "There's nothing to be sorry about. I'm thankful for everything you've done; I feel awful having to ask for more."

"Stop beating yourself up," Elin snapped. "I'm coming. It's not the first time I've been away; I can manage. You two will be fine without me for a while, won't you?"

Sigurd didn't look happy about it, but Elin didn't look away from him, and eventually he relented with a loud sigh.

"Just make sure you don't get hurt," he said.

Alda finally turned back to Tuomas, shuffling over the layers of birch twigs on the floor until she was kneeling before him.

"You should stay," she said quietly. "It's too dark out there now, too cold."

"I've gotten this far," Tuomas replied. "And the demon's gone now."

"But you know travelling in winter isn't a good idea," Alda insisted. "Do you really want to go out again now the Long Dark is at its longest?"

Tuomas placed a hand on her shoulder.

"No, I don't *want* to. But this is something I *need* to do. It's why I set out from Akerfjorden in the first place. I can't stop now."

Alda pursed her lips and threw a concerned glance at his hands. He still hadn't taken off the mittens, and the bulge of a bandage was clearly visible under each one.

"Are you sure you'll be alright?" she asked.

Tuomas nodded. "Yes. Thank you so much."

"I'll look after him," Elin promised. She smiled at Tuomas. "We'll go tomorrow. One more night isn't going to hurt."

After a fitful sleep, Tuomas let Alda dress his hands one last time before he and Elin began loading the sleigh. It was awkward with his bandages, but he was determined to not let Elin do all the work. He threw the reindeer pelts and sleeping sacks into the back, then manoeuvred the shelter poles in beside them with his wrists. Even though his fingers were healing well, too much pressure on them still brought forth a wave of pain.

Aino, Birkir, and a few others came out to see them off. To Tuomas, it was an eerie reminder of the last time he had left Einfjall, heading to the Northern Edge of the World.

But now, they were two people down. Only he and Elin would be facing the easterly journey.

Not for the first time, he wondered about Lilja. Had she gone to Poro too, to seek shelter with her father? He hoped not. He didn't know what he would do if he saw her again.

When the sleigh was packed and Tuomas's reindeer hitched up, he and Elin shared an embrace with Sigurd and Alda. Then Birkir and Aino approached to bid them farewell. The sight tore Tuomas – it felt like leaving a whole new family.

"I hope I'll see you again in the spring, on the migration," he said.

Sigurd smiled and laid a hand on his shoulder. "I'm sure you will. We'll look out for you."

He passed a lit torch to Elin and gave her a kiss on the top of her head.

"Go in peace," Birkir said. "Take care of yourselves."

Elin smiled at her parents as she climbed into the sleigh.

"Stay in peace," she replied.

Tuomas threw one final look at the village before sliding in beside her, covering their legs with the blanket. He wedged his drum between them, then Elin grasped the rope attached to the reindeer's harness and gave it a snap.

The sleigh moved away, through the protective circle; once more, Tuomas felt its tugging pressure on his skin. Then they picked up speed and headed out into the open tundra. The snow-covered huts disappeared into the darkness.

They rode in silence, conserving their energy, huddling close in an effort to keep warm. Alda hadn't been exaggerating: the air was terribly cold, and every inhale tore at Tuomas's lungs like a thousand needles. His eyelashes turned white and saliva froze on his lips. And in the flat plain, with nothing to hinder the wind, his body soon grew as icy as the earth below. He could almost feel the chill working its creeping fingers down to his bones.

He tugged his hat further down and wrapped a scarf around his entire face. He left only his eyes exposed, so he could look at the stars and judge their direction. The constellations were a little different this far north. Patterns normally high in the sky in Akerfjorden were now skimming the horizon. But he quickly deduced where they needed to head, keeping the North Star on the left, and let the reindeer trot along at its own speed.

Elin pulled some jerky from her pack and offered him a strip. He took it with a grateful nod. It was dry and salty, but gave him a much-needed burst of energy. Elin, however, soon fell asleep, her head resting against his shoulder.

Holding the torch in one hand, Tuomas wrapped an extra blanket around her and drew a reindeer skin across the both of them, fur-side down to trap more heat.

Hhe glanced down at her. The torch didn't give off much light, but the ice crystals on her eyelashes sparkled in its glow.

How many hours' sleep had she lost looking after him with her mother? She didn't have to do that. And she and Sigurd had come to save him on the mountain; she had shot the arrow which brought down the demon.

Then something in the distance caught his eye. A small smile traced his lips. Too far away to make out, a tiny aurora was sweeping along the snow.

He couldn't see her, but he knew Lumi was there.

*Lumi.*

It was a funny name to have given her, now he thought about it. He had needed something to call her, and settled on the word for snow. But what was her real name?

She had never uttered it. She was known as the Spirit of the Lights, the aurora… but somehow, he felt that held about as much weight as the name he called her. Even White Fox One, as Lilja and the Earth Spirits had addressed her, seemed more a title than a name.

Maybe she had no name. Maybe she had reacted so strongly to hearing his not because it wasn't his true name, but because Spirits were nameless, just as much as they were formless. He had forced her into a physical body, bound her to the laws of the World Between, and branded her with a label – one which spoke of how she was seen rather than who she was.

Perhaps, just by doing that, he had helped to destroy her. And now she had discovered the ability to feel: the final straw which would spell her undoing.

Beneath the blankets and furs, his hand closed around the pouch. The carved fox inside pressed into his palm.

Mihka and Lumi were both there. Once, they might have been enemies to each other. Now, both were just as important to save.

A few hours later, Elin woke up, and Tuomas took the opportunity to catch some sleep while she steered the sleigh. He tucked his hands inside his coat to keep them warm, then let himself drift away.

He dreamed. He was at home, at his hut in Akerfjorden, whittling patterns into an antler. It was harder to work than bone, but he was patient. He had all the time in the world.

He laughed as Paavo cracked a joke. His brother was bent over a spit at the hearth, cooking a fresh cod fished from the Mustafjord. Its delicious smell filled Tuomas's nose.

*Paavo...*

Something hard pushed into his ribs and he jumped awake. Elin was jostling him with her elbow.

"Is everything alright?" he asked, trying not to think about the dream.

"We're here," she hissed.

That got his attention. He rubbed his eyes awkwardly with the tips of his mittens and looked up. Sure enough, a group of huts were just visible on the horizon, lit by the occasional fire and nestled against the dark smudge of the forest.

The simple sight of trees was enough to fill Tuomas's heart with relief. He hadn't realised how much he had missed them out on the tundra.

He and Elin sat up straight, preparing for the final stretch. The reindeer noticed the village too and gathered speed, spurred on by the promise of the food it knew would be there. By the time they had drawn close enough to the huts to pick out details, Tuomas noticed a few people standing there, waiting to see who the visitors were.

One of them came forward: a middle-aged man with a shock of blonde hair. His coat and hat were decorated with the same patterns Tuomas had seen on Lilja. But there were antler and bone beads stitched to the fabric too. This man was a village leader.

Tuomas gritted his teeth as he thought of Lilja. This was her and Kari's home; where the two of them grew up and became mages. All these people would have known them as children. He imagined the two of them running around the huts, hiding in the trees, Lilja lying at death's door as the Great Bear Spirit was formed in her breath…

Elin pulled on the reins so the reindeer drew to a halt.

"Poro?" she asked.

The man nodded. "Yes. I am Stellan."

"My name's Elin; this is Tuomas."

"Welcome. Now, hurry, come in. There's talk of a troll or something on the loose."

"There's no troll," Tuomas assured as he and Elin clambered out of the sleigh. He checked the rope binding the drum to his belt to make sure it was still secure.

"How do you know?" asked Stellan.

"We've come from Einfjall. It attacked us there," Tuomas0 explained. "And it wasn't a troll. It was a demon."

A collective gasp flew up from the crowd.

"Please tell me it's not still out there," Stellan said in a hushed voice.

"It's not," replied Elin. "It's dead. And so is the mage who made it. There's nothing to worry about."

"Then why are you here? Who travels this deep into winter?"

"We need to see your mage, Enska. It's an emergency."

"Why not see your own mage?"

"We were told to come here," said Tuomas. "Aino recommended him for our... problem."

"Will you tell me what your problem is?" Stellan asked.

"I am."

Another gasp went up at the new voice; some people screamed in fright. Tuomas and Elin spun around.

Lumi had appeared from behind the sleigh, as seamlessly as though she had stepped out of the air. Her eyes were shining violet, ears droopy but unmistakable.

Everyone immediately bowed their heads, several dropping to their knees in respect. Lumi watched in silence, moving only to wipe more water off her arms.

Then, with a jolt, Tuomas noticed she had left footprints behind her. That never happened.

"Are you in pain?" he whispered.

Lumi didn't reply. She was struggling to stay upright.

Tuomas's heart thundered. She could run for miles at speeds to match a reindeer and never even gasp for breath. But now it looked as though the wind itself threatened to blow her away like a flurry of snowflakes.

Why hadn't she ridden with them in the sleigh and saved her energy? Even now, she was too prideful for her own good.

Another man came to the front of the crowd and strode past Stellan. He was tall and clean-shaven, with a pair of sharp intelligent eyes peering out from beneath a hat of white reindeer fur. Around his chest was a leather thong, and a drum hung from it, bouncing against his hip.

Tuomas looked at him hopefully.

"Are you Enska?" he asked.

"I am," said the man, and Tuomas saw the resemblance to Lilja and Kari at once. He had the same sandy blonde hair, the same build; the same way of speaking.

"You do seem to find yourselves in quite a predicament," he noted, eyeing Lumi. "And... is this who I think it is?"

"Yes," said Lumi, managing to keep a shred of irritation in her tone.

Despite the situation, Tuomas couldn't help but smile. No matter it had only been one word; that was more like the Spirit he knew.

Enska instantly lowered his head.

"My apologies, White Fox One," he said. "Please, you are all very welcome here. You can stay in the hut next to mine. It's been empty all winter. Can I give you any food or supplies?"

The rest of the village began following his lead. Stellan and the other leaders offered to bring logs to the hut so they could start a fire. Elin accepted it all graciously while Tuomas stepped forward to speak to Enska.

"I'm sorry, I know it's late," he said, "but we need to see you. It's urgent."

Enska's eyes flickered from him to Lumi.

"Fine. Come with me."

Tuomas nodded, turning to Elin. "Can you get our stuff into the hut?"

246

"Yes, leave it to me," she said. "You go with him."

Tuomas followed the mage, the villagers parting for them with awed mutterings. Lumi tried to walk with her head held high, but her knees buckled and she fell into the snow.

She reared up, shocked at herself.

Tuomas stopped beside her.

"Are you alright?"

Her entire body shuddered. She wouldn't admit it, but her weakness was unmistakable.

Tuomas offered his hand.

She glared at him for a moment, then her eyes softened, and she allowed him to help her to her feet.

# Chapter Twenty-Three

"Are you going to be alright in here?" Tuomas asked Lumi as they stepped into Enska's hut. "There will be a fire."

"Don't worry about that," said Enska.

He picked up a pail of water and poured it over the embers. A plume of smoke filled the hut, but was quickly swept out through the hole in the ceiling.

"I can light it again later," he said. "Come. Sit."

Even though the source of the heat had disappeared, it was still warm. Lumi limped to the side of the hut and slid down the wall, hugging her knees to her chest.

It was almost like being back in Henrik's hut. This one was practically the same size, with the same bundles of dried herbs and flowers hanging from the beams. The aromas of angelica and roseroot filled his nose, mixed with the mustier smell of burned wood and slightly damp reindeer fur from the skins underfoot.

Enska settled across the hearth. His eyes were the same as his children's: widely-spaced, brilliantly blue. His kindly face was creased with age, laugher lines etched deeply like the channels of a river. He was nowhere near as old as Henrik, yet Tuomas sensed he knew just as much.

Enska removed his hat and mittens and urged his guest to do the same. When Tuomas pulled off his own mittens, Enska's brows lowered in concern.

"What happened to your hands?" he asked.

"Frostbite," said Tuomas.

Enska clicked his tongue. "Nasty business. Have you lost anything?"

"The tips of a couple of fingers."

"I'm sorry. At least it wasn't worse. This is one of the coldest winters we've had in years."

Tuomas nodded, then changed the subject. He needed to put his anxiety to rest.

"Lilja isn't here, is she?" he asked.

Enska looked surprised.

"Lilja? No. I haven't seen her in about five years."

Tuomas breathed a sigh of relief.

"Why do you ask?" Enska frowned. "You've met her?"

"And Kari," replied Tuomas. "He tried to kill me. And Lilja is in league with him."

A flash of alarm passed across Enska's face, then he closed his eyes. His lip quivered, and for a moment Tuomas thought he was going to cry, but he held back the tears with a sharp sniff.

He straightened his shoulders and pulled his drum onto his lap, gently caressing the skin with one hand. Near the Great Bear Spirit in the centre were the figures of two children, hand in hand, a painted drum surrounding them in harmony.

"So they have both fallen," he said, his voice heavy with resignation. "I hoped they would be stronger than this. Especially Lilja. She had such potential... such power."

Tuomas swallowed, painfully aware of the healing wound on his chest.

"I know."

Enska looked at him with newfound interest.

"Who are you, boy? The *taika* I sense coming off you is even stronger than Lilja's. But it's unlike any I have felt, too.

You're more than a mage in training, aren't you? How else would you have a Spirit with you like this?"

Tuomas faltered. But before he could answer, Lumi spoke up.

"He is the Son of the Sun," she said.

Tuomas glared over his shoulder at her, and she matched it.

"What is the point in pretending? If you want help now, tell the truth," she snapped.

"The Son of the Sun?" Enska gasped.

His knuckles went white on the drum. His eyes roved as he tried to absorb the news.

Tuomas watched him warily. What if he had been lying about Lilja and Kari, and now the two of them would jump out of the shadows to capture him again?

Enska noticed his discomfort.

"No, no, don't look so frightened," he urged. "I won't harm you. It seems you've been through enough of that already. And I suppose it's been at the hands of my children."

He looked down sadly. "I'm so sorry. I thought I had raised them better. The least I can do is try to help you both."

"He speaks the truth," Lumi said, wiping water from her chest.

But Tuomas still couldn't help glancing at Enska's throat for evidence of a scar.

Enska gave them a smile still tinged with sorrow.

"Well, it makes sense for the Spirit of the Lights to be here, in a way. It explains how we have gone so long without seeing the aurora. People have been asking me to check on their ancestors, to make sure they are still dancing somewhere, but I haven't been able to connect with any of them."

Lumi let out a long sigh.

Tuomas lowered his head in shame. Being away from home was hard enough for him, but for her, it must be terrible. Her entire purpose for existing was to enfold the ancestors in her Lights and spin her fires through the night.

"That's my fault," he said. "I was stupid, and now everyone's paying for it."

"You pulled her out of the World Above, and now you need to send her back," Enska guessed.

"Lilja tried to, but she couldn't do it," said Tuomas. "She told me only I could."

"She was right," replied Enska. "Magic begets magic. What is done needs to be undone by the same mage. Just like if you sing yourself into a trance, you must be the one to return to your body afterwards – if anyone interferes, then the mage is the one who suffers."

He scratched at his forehead thoughtfully.

"I think that instead of trying to put the Spirit back now, we should seek guidance for how best to do it. In a way that won't harm her further."

He readied his drum on his lap and drew the protective circle with his finger. Tuomas frowned. He had extinguished the fire; how was he going to warm the skin for work?

"I was in a trance shortly before you arrived. It will still be fresh," Enska said, recognising Tuomas's surprise.

"But how am I supposed to warm mine?" Tuomas asked. He felt the skin on his own drum. It was tight, but not enough; and he had learned his lesson about making sure it was warmed enough to be ready.

"No need. You won't be able to hold the hammer."

Tuomas winced, remembering the state of his hands. Even though he'd tried not to use them to load the sleigh with Elin, it hadn't occurred to him that he wouldn't be able to drum.

"Then how am I supposed to beat it?"

"Just follow my lead and keep it close to you," said Enska. "Just set your intention: that's the most important thing. Every time you drummed before; you had an intent in your mind. Concentrate on that, don't let go of it."

Tuomas hesitated, but nodded.

"Alright."

"You can do it," Lumi whispered behind him, so quietly he had to look around to check he had heard her right. She gave him a tiny nod, her eyes shining a sheer periwinkle blue.

Enska struck the drum. The sound was deeper than the ones Tuomas had heard before; less refined – each beat seemed to melt into the next. He closed his eyes, letting himself relax, pressing his own drum to his chest as though he could absorb it into himself.

He became very aware of his heart. It was a second drum within his own body: steady, never-ending, shining like the Sun Spirit. He tasted ripe lingonberries on his tongue and felt the warmth of summer on his back as his *taika* swelled.

The surroundings seemed to dissolve. He gritted his teeth and almost lost focus – what was he doing? Did Enska seriously think he was strong enough to enter a trance without drumming himself?

He fought back a surge of panic. He wasn't doing this for himself – he was doing it for Lumi, and by extension, Mihka and everyone in the Northlands who were worrying about the missing Lights. He thought of them, of Mihka's white hair in the pouch at his belt, of the water which he could practically hear dripping off Lumi's fingers…

There it was. His intention.

He focused on Enska's beat. The air became thick with *taika*. He felt as though he was underwater, but there was no need to hold his breath. The power supported him gently, like he was floating on a cloud.

His souls began to loosen. He opened his mouth and let a chant spill out, mingling with Enska's. Behind his lids, his eyes rolled back in his head.

Then he felt himself leave the ground, peeling away from his body, drifting up like smoke towards the hole. Before he could even pause to think, he was out in the night, the dark sky opening around him, cocooning him in its peculiar silent bubble. Somewhere nearby, he sensed Enska, and their life-souls floated away from the snowy land, until he broke through the invisible barrier between realms.

Into the World Above.

He found himself in a place where time and form had no meaning. There was no weight, no gravity. Everything and nothing existed side by side. The stars stretched on forever, and he thought he heard a strange music coming from them.

Somehow, he knew Enska couldn't hear it. It was a tune not for human ears, but for Spirits: choral and ethereal, with instruments he could not name.

Up here, he was no longer the boy called Tuomas. He was something more, which transcended that earthly flesh. He was a life-soul unlike any other: that which had dwelled in the Great Mage from generations ago. The life-soul of a Spirit, not a human. And it brought a flood of peace unlike anything he had felt before.

He realised he was not alone.

*Who is here with me?* he asked.

He didn't need to open his mouth to form the words. They had no sound or order. They were the dapple of light on a pool; of whispering leaves in a breeze; of cool rain on its journey from cloud to river. It was a language of silence and beauty and life and death, all together; none greater or lesser than the other. And he knew, instinctively, that he was the only human who could speak it.

After a brief silence, a giant figure emerged from the darkness. It was made from starlight and cloud, ever-changing, shifting like ripples upon the surface of a lake. It looked at him with huge black eyes. Had he been physically standing, their gaze might have been enough to drive him to his knees.

It was more power than he could comprehend. More than Henrik, Lilja, Kari... more even than Lumi. And in that instant, he knew who was in front of him.

The Great Bear Spirit.

The glittering face drew close. He could feel its immeasurable strength: the source of everything, the guiding hand of all who had gone before.

*I do not come to many*, said the Bear. *But I come to you, as I came to Lilja.*

*You honour me*, he replied.

*There is no honour in this, Red Fox One. Only the need to set things right.*

The Bear regarded him for a moment; so long, it felt like an eternity. He was stunned by its appearance: neither male nor female; and old – so old, all other Spirits seemed like children in comparison.

*The ancestors cannot dance while the leader of the aurora is gone*, it said. *Without the White Fox One, they cannot look down and see you, and you cannot look up and see them.*

*I know what I must do*, he said. *I promise I'll put her back. But I don't know how to do it.*

The Bear sparkled before him.

*The solution is simple. You have tried to put her back in the wrong places, and asked the wrong people to attempt it. You must return her to the World Above at the same place you took her out of it.*

He was taken aback. *So, after all of this, I just need to go back to Akerfjorden?*

*To the frozen Mustafjord, where the water meets the land.*

*Do you mean I never had to go north in the first place? When I summoned her, if I'd just stayed there, I could have put her back in the sky there and then? All this has been for nothing?*

*Everything happens for a reason,* replied the Bear.

As the words reached him, he realised the truth of them. On the Mustafjord, hadn't he frantically tried to send Lumi back, and failed miserably? He'd only managed to hone his power by seeking Lilja out, and if he hadn't done that, he never would have met Elin and her family, or learned the truth about his life-soul – or about the connection between him and Lumi.

*You care for the White Fox One,* the Bear said, *even though she caused you pain.*

*I caused her pain too,* he replied.

The Bear gazed at him with its celestial eyes.

*The path of a mage is never easy, Son of the Sun.*

It circled around him, its formless voice washing over his mind like a soft river current.

*I know you gave your sister a humanoid form, because that is how you perceived Spirits. But your perceptions have widened since you brought her out of the sky. You need not see her as a human girl any longer. I shall give her a less vulnerable body, closer to her true form. At least that way, she will conserve her energy until you reach the Mustafjord.*

*Will that work?*

*She is weak, but not defeated. She does not know how to be defeated,* said the Bear. It brushed its nose against him. *Go in peace.*

*Stay in peace,* he replied.

Heaviness overwhelmed him. He became aware of a heartbeat somewhere below, and breathing, and the strict shape of a human body. For a moment, he wanted to fight it, to stay free and formless, but he came too close and fell back into it.

Tuomas opened his eyes with a gasp.

He was lying on his side; he had obviously tipped over while in the trance. His drum was still clutched to his chest.

He sat up and inspected himself. It was strange to see his own body again. Even though he knew it was his, it almost felt as though he had slipped on a coat belonging to someone else.

"How long was I away?" he asked.

"A few hours," said Enska.

"*Hours?*"

"I woke up not long before you, but I've looked outside at the stars. A fair amount of time has passed."

Tuomas rubbed his face groggily, gritting his teeth as pain fired through his hands.

"Did you hear everything I did?" he asked.

Enska nodded. His eyes were wide with reverence.

"Yes," he replied, barely above a whisper. "And I felt it as well. It is true. You *are* the Son of the Sun."

Tuomas breathed deeply. At last, he believed it, as sure as he knew his own reindeer among a herd several hundred strong. He could sense his own power, swelling within him like boiling water: a *taika* not of this World.

He turned to look at Lumi, to tell her what had happened. But then he saw her and froze.

The girl was gone, and in her place sat a small white fox. But it was more ethereal than any fox he had ever seen. Its ears were erect and turned towards him, eyes shining with the aurora. The end of each strand of fur glittered and its entire body glowed from the inside, as though filled with starlight.

The fox stared at him, the same way she always had. She padded forward and pressed her nose to his hand. Then she sprung to the door, pushed it open with her front legs and ran out into the dark.

Tuomas bounded after her, but by the time he stumbled into the snow, she had disappeared.

Elin was outside, walking towards the spare hut with her arms loaded with firewood. She frowned when she saw Tuomas.

"Was that Lumi?" she asked in disbelief.

Tuomas managed to nod, then his head swam from standing too quickly. Elin dropped the logs and only just managed to catch him before he fainted.

# Chapter Twenty-Four

When Tuomas awoke, he was inside a hut, but the herbs were missing from the beams so he knew it wasn't Enska's. He presumed it was the spare one which he and Elin had been offered.

Somebody had put him in a sleeping sack and taken off his coat and belt, so he was just in his tunic and leggings. His belongings laid beside him on the twig-covered floor, including the drum.

He looked around. Elin was in her own sleeping sack, her face turned away. Embers smouldered in the hearth. He laid twigs and bark over them, to catch the flames before they burned out.

His mouth was dry from sleep and cold, so he fetched water from the bucket by the door, poured it into a pot, and set it to heat over the fire. When it was boiling, he dug around in the supplies left by the villagers until he found some herbs, then tossed them in. In no time at all, the wonderful smell of tea filled the hut.

He went to pick up his cup, but paused when he looked at his hands. They were still bandaged. It would be very difficult to handle tea like that; and he knew it would be best to take them off. His skin would need cleaning.

Praying there would be no more damage, he carefully unwound the strips of fabric, gritting his teeth as the flesh stung. Eventually, he got the last bandage off, and inspected his fingers.

His left hand had come through the frostbite mostly unharmed, but his right was truly frostbitten. As he'd known, he had lost the tips of two fingers, and his thumb was still puffy, the nail black. He wouldn't be surprised if that one fell off, too.

He shuddered at the sight, testing his range of motion. He was able to wiggle everything, but his bones still ached. It might be weeks yet before the extent of the injury was really known.

Elin moaned, the smell of the tea stirring her. She peered over at him; black hair tangled wildly about her face.

"Hello," she greeted sleepily. "How long have you been awake?"

"Not long," replied Tuomas. "I'm sorry about yesterday. I think I passed out."

"You did." Elin rubbed her knuckles into her eyes. "Are you alright now?"

"Yes."

Elin sat up in her sleeping sack and rested her back against the wall. Tuomas fetched a second cup and filled them both with tea. She took one with a grateful nod and the two of them drank in unison.

Tuomas gingerly lowered his cup. He was using his left hand. In the past, he had always relied on his right.

*Not anymore*, he thought. *You'll be using the left for everything now.*

"Happy midwinter," Elin said.

Tuomas looked at her. Was it midwinter already? Where had all that time gone?

"And to you," he said. "I can't believe it's here."

"Me, neither," Elin admitted. "This feels like the longest winter ever."

Tuomas glanced at the sky through the smoke hole. As always, night stared back at him, the stars pinpricks against the darkness.

But after today, the Sun Spirit would start to spin closer. She would cast her warmth and light upon the earth once more; the snow would melt into the ground and the days would be never-ending.

His heart skipped a beat. The Sun Spirit... *his mother*.

He remembered that fever dream back in Einfjall, of himself with fox ears like Lumi. But they were red, not white.

*Red Fox One...*

Desperate for distraction, he turned his attention back to his fingers and flexed them again.

"Could you help me put some fresh bandages on these, please?"

Elin peered at his hands.

"I actually think you'll be fine without them now. Let the air get to them. Just make sure you wear your mittens when you go outside."

Tuomas smiled with relief. He understood the importance of the bandages, but they had been starting to annoy him.

Elin heated some more water and set the pot down in front of him. Tuomas gently eased his hands under the surface. It was hot, just short of the boil, but didn't burn him. The heat didn't even register. He wondered if the frostbite had stripped his ability to feel it.

"I take it there'll be a ceremony for midwinter?" he said, not expecting Elin to reply. The answer was obvious. Ceremonies to mark the solstices and equinoxes were as normal as sleeping.

But this one felt strange, to not be celebrating it in Akerfjorden. To think that it had been almost two whole months since he had last set foot in his own village.

"We should go along," Elin suggested, taking another sip of her tea. "It would be rude not to, after they've made us so welcome."

Tuomas nodded, running one finger thoughtfully around the rim of the pot.

"Elin, did you see where Lumi went last night?"

"No. Was that fox really her?"

"Yes. I went into a trance with Enska, and I managed to... You're going to think I'm mad."

Elin cocked an eyebrow. "Compared to the things I've seen since I met you?"

She had a point.

He paused, unsure about whether to tell her about what Kari had revealed to him on the mountain. He was struggling to take it all in himself. In the end, though, he decided it could wait. That revelation wasn't as important as saving Lumi.

"Alright," he said. "I managed to speak to the Great Bear Spirit. It told me that Lumi needs to be put back in the sky at the same place I pulled her out of it. On the Mustafjord."

Elin didn't blink.

"You saw the Great Bear Spirit?"

Tuomas nodded. "It was just as amazing as you'd imagine."

"I don't know if I can even imagine it," she admitted. "So, we're going to Akerfjorden now?"

"You don't have to," he insisted. "You can go home. I can get back there fine by myself."

"Don't be stupid. You know I'm coming. I've been away from Mother and Father for a whole month in the past. This is nothing."

She drained her cup and set it by the hearth before kicking her legs free of the sleeping sack.

"We'll go tomorrow morning. For today, let's just try and relax; celebrate midwinter. From this moment, the Sun Spirit will be on her way back to us."

Tuomas nodded in agreement. Lumi was a fox now; the Bear had transformed her so she would be less vulnerable. He supposed it was because in human form, the human emotions were much closer to her; so close, they could hurt. As the fox, she could conserve her energy. A few more hours' rest wouldn't make her any worse than she already was.

"Good idea," he said. "Come on. Let's go and be merry."

He wiped his hands on a square of wool and Elin stacked the logs to fall safely on the fire. Then the two of them pulled on their outdoor layers and stepped into the night.

The villagers welcomed them heartily. The whole of Poro was lit by dozens of torches, making the trodden snow between the huts sparkle, as though it was dusted with tiny diamonds. Everyone was busy: gathering wood for a large fire, pooling together tea and spices from the last summer trades, and picking cuts of meat off the racks.

Tuomas and Elin helped where they could, making conversation and soaking up the relaxed atmosphere. It was such a relief after all the hardship and travelling to finally be able to unwind.

When everything was ready, the fire was lit, its yellow tongues flickering high and sending sparks flying towards the stars. Everybody joined hands and danced around it, chanting and laughing. The heat prickled Tuomas's face, but he didn't step away. It was wonderful after spending so much time travelling through the cold.

After the dance, they all sat down to a banquet of reindeer and ptarmigan meat, salmon cakes and roasted char. Everyone tucked in heartedly, even splitting the bones to get at the marrow inside. This was the one day in the Long Dark when they could afford to be frivolous. There was enough food in the storehouses to last until the spring thaw, and now was the time to feast.

Tuomas couldn't help but remember the ceremony on the Mustafjord, when they had bid farewell to the Sun Spirit. That seemed so long ago now. Mihka had been his typical foolish self, Lumi had been dancing in the sky.

And Paavo had been alive.

Tuomas held a hand to his mouth and choked back a sob. The char he'd been eating suddenly tasted as horrid as ashes. Paavo would have done it so much nicer.

Would have, once.

Elin noticed his expression and put a hand on his shoulder.

"Are you alright?"

Tuomas nodded woodenly. "I'll be fine."

Before she could question him further, silence fell across the crowd and Enska came forward. He was wearing his white reindeer hat and had tied an impressive pair of antlers over it, cutting an amazing silhouette against the flames. As he walked, a wind blew past him and lifted the aroma of heady herbs from his clothes. He had daubed the ceremonial ash across his face, turning his pale skin grey.

Even though he knew he could trust Enska, the sight turned Tuomas's stomach. He looked so much like Kari.

He shuffled in discomfort. So much for relaxing and enjoying the evening.

Enska held his drum close to the fire and walked around the pit to form the protective circle. Then he began beating and chanting, asking the Spirits for protection and favour to see them through the rest of the winter. He called to the Master Spirits of all reindeer, fish, ptarmigan and hare, so their children could feed the people until summer. Then he sang to the ancestors, the Great Bear, the Earth Spirits, the Moon, the Sun, and the Spirit of Death... but not the Spirit of the Lights.

Tuomas averted his eyes. He knew why Enska was omitting her. There was no sense in addressing her if she wasn't there. But it was a little unnerving to not hear of her in this most sacred part of the midwinter ceremony. Tuomas was surprised concerned men and women hadn't chased after Lumi, to check their ancestors were safe.

They were probably too scared of her. He only had to remember his own reaction when he first met her – he didn't blame them.

The sob rose again in his throat and tightened like a noose. He had to leave.

He glanced around, making sure everyone was preoccupied by Enska, then slipped away silently. Not even Elin noticed he was gone.

He crept between the huts until he was out of sight. When he reached the one he and Elin were staying in, he walked over to his sleigh, still covered by tarp, the reindeer lying beside it. He stroked the bull's nose affectionately, ran his gloved fingers over the mark he had cut into its ear. Then he perched on the rim of the sleigh, looking out towards the snow-capped forest.

It wouldn't be long before he was home. Just over there to the south lay the river which ran into the Mustafjord: a dark black ribbon snaking through the pale snow. But would it really feel like home, after everything he had seen and done? After his last blood relative was dead, and his newfound sister returned to the sky? After what he had felt in the World Above?

He grasped the pouch on his belt and carefully removed the lock of Mihka's hair. It was so white, it almost blended in with the snow. Then he let the fox figure fall out too and held it in his other palm.

"What's that?"

Tuomas clamped his fingers over the hair in fright. Elin appeared at the edge of his vision.

"I'm sorry. I shouldn't have crept up on you like that," she said. "Can I sit with you?"

In reply, Tuomas shuffled over to give her room. She rested beside him and pulled her hat further down over her ears.

Tuomas quickly slipped the fox carving back into the pouch, but kept hold of the hair. It was so fine, he didn't want to risk any strands escaping by stuffing it away.

"You haven't seemed yourself since you went to see Enska," Elin said. "Is something wrong?"

Tuomas didn't look at her.

"It's just hit me, how mad this all turned out to be. All I wanted was to save my friend and become a mage."

Elin looked between him and his hand, still closed.

"Is that his hair?"

Tuomas peeled back his fingers so she could see it.

"It's black, really. Like yours. But Lumi attacked him before I summoned her into human form. He insulted her Lights."

Elin couldn't hold back a snort. "Well, she isn't the type to ignore insults."

"No Spirit is," said Tuomas. "It's part of their pride."

"Sounds like someone else I know," said Elin pointedly.

Tuomas frowned at her. He had never mentioned who he was in front of her – how had she guessed?

But then he realised she didn't know. It was simply a comment. Yet, deep down, he supposed she was right. Even before finding out he was the Son of the Sun, it had always been so easy for him to get angry. It was that very anger which had ripped Lumi from the World Above: the raw energy of his otherworldly *taika*.

Kari flashed in his mind, the image of a bloodied heart in his hands.

He shuddered.

The emotion finally overcame him.

A sob burst out of his mouth and he wept like a child, Elin put an arm around his shoulders before he could block her.

He didn't bother fighting. He let the tears come, allowed them to wrack his body like a tree in a gale. Each sob burned the wound on his chest. The water froze on his cheeks, and his lashes iced over, but he didn't care. It needed to come out.

He didn't know how long he cried for. When he managed to get himself under control, Elin's arm was still there. She hadn't left him.

"Do you need anything?" she asked gently.

Tuomas shook his head. He swallowed hard, trying to loosen his throat.

"What's the matter? You can tell me."

He screwed his eyes shut.

"Kari was wearing my brother's skin, when I found him in the World Below," he choked out. "That's how he tricked me into freeing him."

Elin looked at him in alarm. "*Wearing his skin?*"

Tuomas clenched his hands into fists, not caring that it made his frostbite hurt.

"He told me Lilja killed Paavo, and took his skin. I should have known back then."

"How could you have known anything?" Elin countered. "You hardly knew a thing yourself."

"I was trusting and stupid," Tuomas hissed. "We ran into her at a frozen river and she took us to her campsite. I fell asleep on the way so I don't know which direction we travelled in. She said she was heading towards Akerfjorden to find me, to protect me. More likely she was there straight after I left, killing Paavo, and then intercepted me on purpose, to make it look as though she was coming from the other way!"

Elin shook her head. "That sounds really farfetched."

"Would you put it past her?"

"Tuomas, I never saw this side of Lilja. The last time I laid eyes on her before you drove her off was when you went to the Northern Edge."

"So, you don't believe me?"

"I never said that! I only mean I can't judge what she did or didn't do, because I wasn't there."

Tuomas turned away, pinching the bridge of his nose between his thumb and forefinger.

"I'm sorry," he breathed. "I'm just so confused, and… Elin, I miss Paavo so much! I miss Mihka too, but Paavo's dead!"

He bit his lip so he wouldn't cry again.

"He wasn't just my brother. He raised me. He was my mother and father too; the only family I had. And now he's gone!"

He kicked out at the snow, but as soon as he did, all the energy left him. He buried his face in his hands.

Elin offered a small smile. She shuffled nearer to him, her arm still around his shoulder.

Tuomas looked at her. She'd never sat this close before.

Elin noticed his stiffness and hurriedly let go, wiping her hands on her thighs as though nothing had happened.

He patted her arm to get her attention.

"Thank you for coming here with me," he said. "And for coming to the mountain. You saved me."

"It wasn't just me."

"You killed the demon."

Elin shrugged, but it wasn't very convincing. "I got lucky."

"You're too good for that to have just been *lucky*," Tuomas said.

A thought crossed his mind. She had risked her life to rescue him, volunteered without hesitation to accompany him to Poro. And all because of what? She didn't know anything about who he really was.

He chewed his lip for a moment, then gave in. He would tell her. After everything that had happened, she deserved to know.

"Listen, Elin…"

"Look, don't worry about anything," she said quickly. "I'll be here to help you until you and Lumi are safe."

She cleared her throat and stood up.

"I'm going to head back," she announced. "Are you coming?"

Tuomas kept his eyes on her. "In a moment."

She nodded, and threw him one last sheepish smile before disappearing. He watched her go, wondering if the redness in her cheeks was from the cold, or something else.

Once she had disappeared from view, he let out an explosive exhale and kicked at the snow again. Why couldn't he have just hugged her back? Then he could have avoided all the awkwardness and still have her sitting here with him.

*Stupid idiot*, he cursed inwardly.

Then he heard bells – broken, jingling. The sound of running reindeer.

He stared out into the forest. Sure enough, barely visible against the trees, was the shape of an approaching sleigh, pulled by two animals. It grew larger; the bells sounded louder. It drew close to the village, and as it halted, Tuomas saw the rider.

His breath caught in a strangled gasp.

It was Lilja.

# Chapter Twenty-Five

The sleigh slid to a halt and Lilja tumbled out, landing face-first in the snow.

Tuomas's hand went to his knife, but he didn't draw it.

"Don't come any closer," he warned.

"Where's Enska?" Lilja demanded. Her voice sounded even more cracked and broken than before.

She grabbed at the sleigh and used it to haul herself upright. She staggered forward, then stopped when she recognised him.

"What are you doing here? No… it doesn't matter. Just run," she said. "Keep away from me, boy."

Tuomas frowned. *She* was telling *him* to keep away?

He decided not to take any chances and shouted over his shoulder.

"Enska! Elin! Come here!"

He kept his eyes on Lilja until he heard footsteps behind him. A few of the villagers arrived, along with Elin. Her bow was on her shoulder – Tuomas supposed she must have fetched it from the hut when she heard him yelling.

When Elin saw Lilja, she pulled an arrow out of her quiver and drew it back on the bow, ready to shoot.

"Put that down," Lilja snapped.

In response, Elin narrowed her eyes. She didn't move.

The villagers began muttering to each other.

"Is that *Lilja*?"

"What's wrong with her?

"Where's Kari?"

"Let me through!"

Everyone parted at that last voice. Enska ran forward, his drum still in his hand. His eyes were a little glazed from being in trance, but they widened in alarm when he saw who had come.

A myriad of expressions chased each other across his face. Tuomas could tell he wanted to run to her and embrace her like the daughter she was.

Enska wiped the ash off his skin and removed the antler headdress. He only took a single step towards her.

Lilja looked at him beseechingly, one hand on her throat. She was horribly pale, her eyes sunken, her hair wan and dry at the ends. It was as though she had died and clawed her way back to life.

"Please, I need your help," she begged. "You wouldn't turn me away, would you?"

Enska hesitated.

"No," he said slowly. "But neither will I welcome you with open arms. If you've come seeking shelter, then don't think we'll let you wander about."

"Father –" Lilja protested.

"No," Enska said again, his voice close to breaking. "I know what you've done."

Lilja's gaze shifted to Tuomas.

"What have you told him?"

"The truth," Tuomas said coldly.

"What truth?" she growled. "I told you, I had nothing to do with it."

"Lying to me again?" Tuomas set his teeth. "What's wrong with your throat? Why don't you tell everyone the truth of that?"

Lilja trembled.

"Listen, I know what this looks like. But I swear, I'm not here for you. That's what Kari wants, but I won't listen."

Tuomas faltered. He threw a worried glance at Enska, then at back to Lilja.

"What are you talking about? Kari's *alive?*"

Lilja nodded.

"Barely. After you unceremoniously threw me out, I went up to the mountain, looking for clues. I found him there, I thought he was dead. And monster or not, he is my brother."

"So what did you do? Nurse him back to health, so the two of you could come after me again?"

"Shut up and let me talk," Lilja snapped.

She shuddered again and collapsed onto her knees. Her hands curled into pained fists.

"Father, get the boy away from me," she groaned. "Now!"

Enska put a hand on Tuomas's shoulder and steered him behind Elin.

"Why are you so concerned?" Enska asked.

Lilja's breathing rattled.

"Listen… I went to perform funeral rites on Kari, but he was still alive. Just alive enough to pull his life-soul back, and force it into me."

Tuomas stared at her. Was she saying that Kari had somehow bound her to him, the same way he had done with the demon?

"Is that even possible?" he whispered to Enska.

"I don't know," Enska said warily.

Lilja searched the mage's face.

"Please, help. He's inside me. If you can't get him out, then kill me. I don't know what I'll do if this carries on."

Enska's face paled.

"Did he send you here?" Tuomas asked. "Did he tell you to come here for me? Where is he?"

"Tuomas, please," Lilja whimpered. "Someone, get him away!"

Tuomas stood his ground. "Where is he? Tell me!"

He strained to see Lilja's eyes in the low light. They were normal, not hollow like Kari's, but that brought little relief. For a moment, it even crossed his mind that this might not be Lilja at all – it could be Kari, wearing her skin like he'd worn Paavo's, trying to trick him.

*No*, he thought. *Kari would know that wouldn't work. He was the one who told you about Lilja in the first place.*

Before he could ponder any more, Lilja screamed.

The sound was bloodcurdling. Everyone stepped back in horror.

"*Get him... away from me!*" Lilja bellowed through gritted teeth.

She ran forward in great loping leaps, jaw straining, the scar on her throat red and angry.

Tuomas cried out. It was like the demon all over again.

Elin released her arrow. It hit Lilja's shoulder and she crashed into the snow.

Enska ran over and snatched Lilja's arms, pinning her where she landed. She thrashed and kicked like an incensed wolf. A few other men hurried to grab her legs.

After a several horrible seconds, the struggle flowed out of her. She lay still, struggling for breath.

"I told you to get him away," she murmured.

Enska looked up, his grip not slackening for an instant.

"Go back to your business, everyone," he said firmly. "And Tuomas, you go to my hut. Now!"

Elin took Tuomas by the elbow and steered him away, shouldering her bow with her free hand.

She led him to the mage's hut and pushed him inside before he could protest. The fire was low and what little light was left threw strange shadows across the walls.

Tuomas sat on the reindeer skins. Beneath his coat, his heart hammered.

"Are you alright?" Elin asked.

"I'm fine," he assured.

"What was that all about?"

"You heard her. Kari's inside her."

Elin went to the log pile and threw a new batch on the fire. It spat noisily, the wood not catching. To help it, she took another log and stripped the bark off before wedging that close to the embers.

It was a while before she spoke again.

"Why all this fuss over you?" she asked. "If Kari wanted anything, I would have imagined Lumi was more tempting. She's a Spirit, after all."

Tuomas swallowed nervously. It was now or never.

"She's not the only Spirit," he said in a small voice.

Elin stared at him. A frown creased her brow.

"What do you mean?"

"Do you remember the story about the Great Mage? The one who was the Son of the Sun? A Spirit in a human body?"

"Yes... why?"

"Well... that was me."

Tuomas kept his attention on the floor. He knew that if he looked at Elin now, saw her reaction, he wouldn't finish what he had to say.

"Up on the mountain, Kari tried to cut out my heart, because that's where a mage's *taika* is. He was going to eat it, to take my power for himself. When he realised who Lumi was, he decided to go after her too. We're equals, her and me. I'm the only one who was able to withstand her Lights."

He took a deep breath and glanced at Elin.

Even in the low light, he could see her face had turned white. He couldn't tell whether she believed him or not.

"Let me get this straight," she said shakily. "You're a Spirit too?"

"I think so. My life-soul is from the World Above. It's not a normal soul, like everyone else's. It's not really a soul at all. It's a Spirit."

"The Son of the Sun?"

Elin stared at him. He worried that he'd said too much. What would she think of him now? It had been difficult enough for him to take in, let alone anyone else.

Unable to bear her eyes any longer, he got to his feet.

"I'm sorry. Forget it," he muttered, heading for the door.

"Tuomas," Elin said. "Wait. Please."

She snatched his wrist. Her silhouette cut sharply against the orange glow of the fire.

"Why didn't you tell me sooner?" she asked.

Relief washed through Tuomas's veins. This was a much better response than he had expected.

"I didn't believe it myself. Not at first," he replied. "And I only really believed it after we got here."

"Is that why you were so long with Enska?"

"Yes. Please don't tell anyone. Not yet, anyway."

"I promise, I won't."

She pulled him around to face her fully.

"Son of the Sun or not," she said, "it will take more than that to drive me off. I'm still helping you. We'll save Mihka, get

Lumi home. If anyone tries to stop us, they'll have to go through me."

"Through your arrows, you mean?" Tuomas grinned.

The two of them chuckled, then he stepped close and hugged her. The soft fur of her coat tickled his nose.

Footsteps crunched outside. It was a group of people, walking close together – and there were pained groans and gasps for air.

Tuomas let go of Elin and inched the door open.

Three men had Lilja restrained between them, her hands tied behind her back. Her coat had been pulled back, revealing a bandage around the shoulder where Elin had shot her.

Lilja's eyes whipped around and locked onto him. She bared her teeth and her nostrils flared, as though she was sniffing him.

She leapt towards the hut, but the men kept tight hold of her and bundled her away.

A hand appeared on the door. Tuomas stumbled backwards as Enska entered. The mage was wide-eyed and flustered, but otherwise seemed unhurt.

He trudged to the other side of the hearth, pulled off his hat and threw it into a corner. He put a pot on the flames and began making tea, his hands trembling as he worked.

Tuomas and Elin looked at each other uncertainly, but didn't press him.

When the water was simmering, he finally spoke.

"What Lilja said is true. Kari has somehow gotten his life-soul into her."

"How?" Elin asked. "I shot his demon. I killed it myself."

"I saw the life-soul go into the sky," added Tuomas.

"He must have found a way to hold onto it. He won't have been able to recover the blood he put into a demon, but my son is powerful. Such a feat obviously isn't beyond him."

Tuomas stared at Enska.

"So what do we do?"

"Lumi can take souls, can't she?" Elin suggested. "She could pull his life-soul out of Lilja."

Tuomas shook his head. "She's too weak."

Enska jabbed the fire fiercely with another piece of wood.

"Well, we're putting Lilja in a hut at the other end of the village for now. And I've confiscated her drum."

Tuomas's eyes went to Enska's side. For the first time he noticed the mage had brought in another drum alongside his own. The smear of blood on the skin looked black in the firelight.

"What if we destroy it?" Elin suggested. "Would that do anything? Strip her of her power?"

"No," Tuomas said immediately. "Henrik told me that's the worst thing to do. A drum can be passed on, but you can't destroy it."

"That's true," said Enska as he stirred the tea. "Stripping her *taika* away will only leave more room for Kari to control her. It would be like stripping one of her souls. She's fighting against it enough now."

Tuomas shuddered as he said that. It made sense – after all, Mihka had fallen into a deathlike sleep without his life-soul. Without her *taika*, Lilja would simply become an empty husk.

Then he frowned.

"Wait, she's *fighting* it?" he repeated. "Kari didn't send her here?"

"From what I can gather, he did send her," said Enska. "When she charged, she went for you. But she's using all her energy to not obey him."

Tuomas exchanged a glance with Elin.

"Does that mean she *isn't* in league with him?" Elin asked tentatively.

"No," Tuomas snapped, more forcefully than he meant to. "Kari was wearing Paavo's skin. She got that for him!"

"And you believe what he said to you? Just before he tried to cut out your heart?"

"Well, he had me right where he wanted me. It's not like he had anything to hide."

"Or maybe he just said that to break down your defences and make you weaker," Elin argued. "As far as I saw, Lilja never did anything to hurt you."

Tuomas opened his mouth to remind her how little she had actually seen, but quickly bit it back. The last thing he needed now was to lose Elin's friendship.

Enska watched him closely, waiting until he was calmer before speaking again.

"Personally, I think she's innocent in all this," he insisted. "I don't say that as a father hoping for the best, I say it as a mage. And I know her. She's a good person. She knows sacrifices deeper than most will ever dream of."

"Are you sure you're not biased?" Tuomas said coldly.

Elin glared at him. A muscle twitched in Enska's jaw.

"Of course, I'm biased. But I resent the accusation that I don't know what I'm talking about, boy."

Tuomas quickly lowered his head.

"I'm sorry. That was very rude of me."

"Yes, it was," said Enska. "But you're forgiven. I can't blame you for not trusting her. Even though she's my daughter,

I don't trust her completely in these circumstances. She can barely control herself."

He loosened his belt and pulled his coat off with one hand, continuing to stir the tea with the other.

As he looked at the intricate carvings on the ladle, Tuomas's heart skipped a beat. It was practically identical to Lilja's. Had she made that for him, years ago, before she and Kari abandoned their village for a life of solitude?

"I believe she's innocent," continued Enska. "But if I'm wrong, and she has followed Kari's lead, it ultimately makes no difference. Nobody should be subjected to what he is putting her through. We should get him out of her, before he does any permanent damage."

"Can you do that?" asked Elin.

"I think so. I might need help."

Enska looked hopefully at Tuomas.

"I'll reserve my judgment for now," Tuomas replied. "My main concerns are Lumi and Mihka. And to help them, I need to be in Akerfjorden. On the Mustafjord."

"Then let me come with you, and bring Lilja along," suggested Enska. "I understand you not wanting to get involved after all you've been through, but perhaps Henrik will. Then you can put the Spirit of the Lights back, I can help Lilja, and we all accomplish something."

The two of them held the other's gaze for a long moment. The very idea of travelling with Lilja again was enough to turn Tuomas's stomach. But, he supposed, he should give her the benefit of the doubt. Elin was right: he had no solid proof. All he had to trust for her treachery was the word of her corrupted brother.

The more he thought about it, he wondered if Paavo's skin had just been a clever illusion by Kari, like Lilja had claimed. That would be incredible – it would mean his brother was alive after all. But at the same time, he couldn't bring himself to hope.

He was surprised at his own spitefulness. Was he really eager to find Paavo dead, just to prove himself right about Lilja?

He let out a long sigh of defeat.

"Fine. But I'm not riding with her."

"I wasn't expecting you to. She can come in my sleigh," said Enska. "Tomorrow?"

"Tomorrow," Tuomas agreed, running a tired hand over his face. "This was not how I imagined spending midwinter. I'm sorry."

"There's nothing to apologise for," Elin said. "But how about that tea?"

In reply, Enska pulled the pot onto the hearth stones. He only paused in pouring it long enough to wipe the last of the ash off his face.

# Chapter Twenty-Six

She hung back as the humans celebrated the winter solstice. This was a time she always looked forward to. Every midwinter, she shone bright so they could gaze up at her in reverence, honour her and bow their heads.

This was the first time she hadn't done that, in hundreds of years. She didn't even enter the village to receive their respect.

Yet again, she found herself secretive, keeping back from the heat and the festivity. No matter she had finally let them see her. It was too much to bear, coming too close to... was it a heart? Had Tuomas given her one of those when he summoned her?

Now she thought about it, she wasn't sure exactly what lay under this physical flesh. Were there bones? Did blood flow beneath the snowy skin?

She refused to know. It didn't matter. Soon she would be free of it all, never to come to the World Between again.

More water flowed over her pointed nose and a small whine escaped her throat.

The fox form was a little more freeing than that of the girl – still binding, but not as heavy. When she ran, her feet barely skimmed the snow. The air smelt crisper. She saw every flake of snow lying atop and beside its neighbours, sparkling in light so low it was barely noticeable. It was like she was floating somewhere between this realm and her own, barely held to the earth.

The water was still flowing, making her fur damp, but it wasn't as strong as when she had been a girl. Maybe because the human form was gone, she was less susceptible to their emotions. Maybe it was because it put her further away from Tuomas. Yet every time she thought of him, she felt herself weakening: a phantom pain which seemed to tear her from the inside out.

It was that pain which had made her run. She wasn't sure if he'd really had time to take in what he was seeing, to accept that the fox was still her. He was barely out of his trance when he'd looked at her.

But she knew she needed to get away. She had heard what the Great Bear had said to him. She had to make sure she kept enough strength to reach Akerfjorden.

She lay down, curling her bushy tail around herself, and closed her eyes. She had never been able to sleep – that was something for living creatures, with a body-soul which needed rest. But she still closed her eyes, let her mind be filled with the endless beauty of the World Above.

And how endlessly empty it would seem when she returned.

The next day, she hung back as Tuomas and Elin loaded the sleigh. Then the mage man, Enska, started walking towards them, pulling someone along by the arm.

Was he coming too?

She squinted, trying to make out who was with him, and let out an involuntary yip of surprise.

It was Lilja. Her hands were bound behind her back, and she was snarling like a wolf.

What was she doing there? Hadn't she been driven away?

The fur on her back stood on end. Lilja's *taika* was still there, but it was tainted, fouled by the same wrongness which had been in the World Below.

She wasn't taking any chances. She trotted over to Tuomas and curled back her lips warningly.

Lilja looked straight at her. Her eyes were heavy and bruised, the shine in them disappeared like stars behind a cloud.

"Well, this is a change, White Fox One," she said. Her voice was hoarse, as though she had been screaming. Or crying.

That wicked mage had infected her somehow. She could tell Lilja was fighting it, but it was like struggling against a rushing river when its ice broke in the spring. How long could she hold on in the face of such power?

Lilja was lifted into another sleigh by Enska, who then joined her and tied her down so she couldn't jump out.

"Lumi?" Tuomas said in an undertone. "You won't be able to run all the way back to Akerfjorden."

Pride prickled her thin skin. It was terrible to admit, but he was right. She doubted she could have even run back to Einfjall, let alone across the entire tundra.

She wished she could respond in the human words he had given her, but in this form, it was impossible. So instead, she swept her tail slowly in defeat.

He understood though, because he bent down beside her.

"Can I pick you up?"

She dropped her snout: the closest to a nod she could manage.

Tuomas was quick, remembering how much she disliked being touched. He slid his arms under her belly and lifted her into the back of the sleigh. Then he and Elin climbed in and took the lead, guiding the reindeer south.

Even though she wasn't on the ground, she let her tail dangle over the edge of the tent tarp. The tip touched the faint spray flung up by the runners, and a tiny trail of light drifted behind her.

Yes, this was more like it. This was the closest she had felt to her formless self in weeks.

They reached the forest and followed the treeline, staying clear so the sleighs wouldn't catch in the bumps and hidden roots. Soon they arrived at the frozen river outside Poro. Tuomas urged his reindeer onto the ice and began a route down it, using it as a natural path which wound its way through the land.

They didn't even stop to pitch a shelter for the night. Elin simply took over the reins while Tuomas slept. Enska tethered his own reindeer to the back of Tuomas's sleigh so it wouldn't wander and, making sure Lilja was securely bound, pulled his hat over his eyes.

They travelled hard and fast. The stars rolled overhead: the only way to track time. But already she could feel a shift in the air. Midwinter was gone; the Golden One had passed her furthest distance from the Northlands. Now she was waxing, preparing for her return. The Long Dark would pass, and following that, spring would come. The snow beneath them would melt away, leaving nothing to mark it ever having been there.

After two days, they passed the bank where she and Tuomas had faced off against the wolves. She had to stop for a moment, overcome with alarm. To her, a Spirit, time was almost meaningless; centuries could pass as quickly as seconds. Yet she found herself unable to believe that it was here that the two of them had stood, just weeks before, angry and fearful and barely tolerating each other's presence.

The river became narrower, more erratic in its frozen formations, and the sleighs were forced to abandon it in favour of solid ground. Then the ice spread into a huge body, stretching out as far as the eye could see, flanked by the sheer sides of towering mountains and cliffs.

She had never set foot here, but she had seen this place from the sky. She knew exactly where they were.

This was the great fjord which opened out into the sea. Where her dear brother, when he first descended into a physical body, had died.

And there, tucked away on its shore, she saw it: Akerfjorden. It looked just like all the other villages; a little larger, perhaps. But as soon as it came into view, she sensed Tuomas's heart speed up; heard it in her ears as keenly as a drumbeat. His relief and happiness flooded into her as though they were her own emotions.

She understood: he was coming home.

Water washed down her face and her ears drooped. She let out a whine of pain and lowered her head, deliberately not looking at the sky.

The sight of Akerfjorden lifted Tuomas's mood in a way he'd have never thought possible. After all he had been through, to be coming back here was the sweetest feeling.

He glanced at Elin. She was fast asleep, exhausted from her latest turn at the reins. Her head was resting against his shoulder, one eye hidden by the thick fur of his coat.

A smile traced his lips. She looked so peaceful, her eyes fluttering as she dreamed.

He wasn't sure if he had expected her to come this far with him. She had fallen into all this madness; she never would have been involved if he and Lilja had put up their shelter quicker in that blizzard.

*Funny*, he thought, *how one little action can impact everything.*

His eyes strayed over the edge of the sleigh. The ice on the Mustafjord was covered by a thick layer of snow, but he couldn't help but be aware that beneath it lay the Black Water. Down there, sometime long ago, he had drifted, gasping for air, felt his lungs straining as the life was choked out of him… only to come back now, in this body, as this short-tempered orphan.

He wondered, *what would it have been like to drown? To lose all those memories of another life? To have my life-soul ripped out…*

Movement stirred on the bank as people emerged from their huts to see who was coming. They would have heard the reindeer bells by now.

Tuomas looked at Lumi, still perched in the back of the sleigh. It was strange to see her like this, after so long spent with her in human form. But the celestial fox suited her, and he could still recognise certain facial features even behind the thick fur and pointed snout. The ears and tail were unchanged, but so were her eyes. The otherworldly colours were still there.

He felt like saying something to her, but held back. No words were needed.

Instead, he jostled Elin to wake her. She let out a groggy moan.

"Are we close?" she asked.

"We're here," Tuomas replied, and steered the reindeer up the bank.

A crowd of people instantly swarmed forward, grinning widely as they recognised who it was. Tuomas kept one eye on Lumi as she ducked behind the sleigh, concealing herself as best she could between the runners. Then he climbed out and fell into the arms of his neighbours.

He breathed the old familiar smell of them, almost brought to tears. There was Aslak, Sisu, Maiken, Anssi, Henrik...

He almost fell over in shock.

Standing next to the old mage was Paavo.

# Chapter Twenty-Seven

Tuomas forgot to breathe. He grabbed the sleigh to steady himself.

Paavo's smile dimmed into a frown.

"Hey, What's the matter?"

Tuomas swallowed hard, trying to get his tongue to work.

"You're... you're alive?" he managed to blurt out.

Paavo glanced at Aslak in confusion.

"Uh... yes," he replied. "Why wouldn't I be?"

Tuomas struggled to compose himself. He looked at Elin, then at Lilja. She was still tied in Enska's sleigh, but she had her head raised, watching the exchange with eyes glazed by fatigue.

"I told you I didn't have any part in it," she snapped.

Tuomas turned back to Paavo and tentatively approached him. He pulled off one of his mittens and held out his hand. Paavo gave him a perplexed look, but stayed still as Tuomas touched his cheek.

It was warm, not an illusion at all. There was a small scar on his temple, freshly healed from the night Lumi had struck Mihka.

He was alive.

Barely able to contain himself, Tuomas leapt into his brother's arms.

The force of his jump sent them both flying into the snow. Paavo let out a winded gasp, and the impact sent pain through Tuomas's chest, but he didn't let go. He buried his face in Paavo's shoulder, not even trying to hold back his tears.

"I thought you were dead!" he whimpered. "Kari had your skin... I thought..."

"Wait, what are you talking about?" asked Paavo, trying unsuccessfully to dislodge him. "I'm fine. Is this because I missed you leaving? I was out fetching reindeer moss for the herd – I didn't think you'd be gone by the time I got back! And what happened to your hands?"

It all made perfect sense. Kari admitted on the mountain that he had been spying on Tuomas long before he even made the demon. He would have known about Paavo from that – seen enough to be able to make a convincing illusion. The show in the World Below had all been a trick. And Tuomas barely cared anymore that it had worked to horrifying effect. None of it had been real.

But Paavo... *he* was real. He was here. Still breathing.

He eased himself away so he could see Paavo's face, but didn't let go of him. Part of him worried that if he did, his brother would somehow fall apart in front of him, and it would all have been a dream.

"So, nothing happened?" he asked. "Nobody came here?"

"No, everything's been the same as normal, except the lack of Lights," Sisu said. "What's going on? Should we be concerned?"

"No, nothing to worry about," Enska said as he dislodged himself from the sleigh. "Just an unfortunate misunderstanding."

Tuomas lowered his eyes in shame. He had been proven wrong, after all. Lilja had never said anything but the truth.

He released Paavo and wandered back to the sleighs. He had to apologise to Lilja.

But when she saw him coming, she wrenched herself away so fast, the reindeer snorted in alarm.

"Stay back!" she warned. "I'm serious, boy! The closer you get, the harder it is for me not to come after you."

Tuomas stopped in mid-step.

"I'm so sorry."

He meant it. He had wronged her and cast her out, when she was innocent in all this. And now, because of that, Kari truly had got his hooks in her.

Behind him, Enska strode up to Henrik, and the two mages embraced fondly.

"Hello, old friend," Henrik smiled. "What trouble are you bringing to my door today?"

"I'm sure you recognise my daughter?" said Enska, motioning to Lilja.

Henrik followed his gaze, and his grey brows lowered when he saw who was in the sleigh. Tuomas remembered how distastefully he had spoken of Lilja and Kari's power, how he felt they had too much of it.

Now, Tuomas finally understood why. Henrik hadn't said that out of any jealousy, or because she was a woman, but because of how easy it could be to slip into darkness.

The two mages muttered between each other, discussing the predicament. Tuomas left them to it and returned to the sleigh. He released his reindeer from the poles and Aslak looped a lasso around its neck, offering to take it back to the Akerfjorden herd. Then Tuomas freed Enska's reindeer, but tied it to a nearby tree so it couldn't mingle with the other animals. Trying to find one reindeer with a single different earmark among hundreds of others would be a nightmare.

Elin appeared beside him, but he avoided looking at her. The last thing he needed was for her to say she told him so.

But she didn't. Instead, she said: "I'm glad your brother is alright."

Tuomas smiled.

"I can't believe it. I seriously thought…"

"I know." Elin drew close and whispered in his ear. "But he's fine. And Lilja's innocent. So… do you think you might help her now?"

Tuomas gritted his teeth. He hated the way she said it, but she was right. He nodded and trudged over to Enska and Henrik.

He cleared his throat. "I'll help you get the life-soul out of her."

Henrik glanced at him. "You feel you can, boy?"

"You know he can," Enska muttered, so nobody else would hear. "Come on, Henrik. You know very well who he is. So do your leaders; you knew from the moment he was born."

Henrik's eyes widened. "How do you know about it?"

"It doesn't matter. But you knew, and now he does as well. He had to find out the hard way; harder than you can imagine."

"How do you tell someone a thing like that, Enska? How can anyone reckon with such a legacy?"

"He might be barely a man, but he's not stupid. Why didn't you tell him when you took him on as your apprentice?"

Henrik flustered. "Well… there was never a right time."

Tuomas felt the old irritation boiling inside him, but he held it in check. There were more important matters to deal with now.

"You know what, it doesn't matter," he said. "I know now, you know; there's no need to fuss. We need to help Lilja."

He paused, finding Sisu among the crowd. "And I'd like to see Mihka. How is he?"

"The same as when you left," Sisu replied, weariness tugging at his words. "Come with me."

He began leading Tuomas towards Henrik's hut. Tuomas had barely taken a step when Lumi shot out from beneath the sleigh and hurried to his side. A small aurora appeared behind her as she ran.

The villagers gasped when they saw her, and Henrik's eyes grew so wide, Tuomas thought they might fall out.

"What...?" he choked.

"I'll explain," Enska said calmly. "You go, Tuomas."

Tuomas gave him a grateful smile, then followed Sisu through the door. Lumi pressed herself against the wall, walking as close to it as possible to keep away from the fire.

The familiar smell of Henrik's hut flew up Tuomas's nose: a mixture of herbs, old man, and overly-brewed tea. Everything was exactly as he had left it.

He knew, deep down, that shouldn't surprise him – he had only been gone for a couple of months. But it felt like an entire lifetime. And he supposed, in a strange way, it was.

Mihka was in the corner, lying on his back inside a sleeping sack. His face was thinner than before, his white hair standing out harshly. Tuomas knelt beside him and touched his forehead to feel his temperature. He was cold, but not uncomfortably so. That was a relief. He hadn't deteriorated in the weeks since the attack.

Lumi padded over, limping slightly as the heat worked through her. She regarded Mihka for a moment. Tuomas could almost see an expression of disdain on her face.

She leaned in and pressed her nose to Mihka's cheek, as though in apology. Tuomas could barely contain his shock. Was she actually finding it in herself to let her pride go?

Before he could question her, she turned and ran back outside, clearly overwhelmed by the fire. Tuomas watched her leave, a small smile at the corner of his mouth, before whispering to his friend.

"I'll help Lilja first, so she can't try and kidnap me. And then I'm bringing you back," he said. "You're going to be alright, you stupid idiot."

There wasn't enough room for all of them in Henrik's hut along with Lilja and Mihka, so Enska suggested they go to the shore of the Mustafjord. While Henrik fetched his supplies, Tuomas moved his belongings into his and Paavo's hut.

He regarded the space for a moment. His old sleeping sack lay in its usual spot on the left side of the hearth. The same birch twigs lined the floor; the familiar smell of damp reindeer fur and Paavo's cooking lingered in the air.

But it didn't bring the respite he thought it would. After so long out in the Northlands, with his life turned upside down, could things ever really go back to the way they had been before?

He pushed that question to the back of his mind. It was too uncomfortable to address now. So instead, he grabbed his drum and headed outside.

Elin and Paavo were waiting to walk him down to the shore. As they descended the slope, fat snowflakes began to drift from the sky, and stuck to his eyelashes like feathers.

Henrik and Enska had made a fire at the edge of the ice. Lilja was sitting next to it, her wrists still tied together as a precaution.

When she saw him, she stiffened, as though bracing herself for a blow. She began shaking with the effort of holding back the urge to attack him. Enska had given her back her drum, tied it to her belt, and her fingers grazed it, seeking comfort from its presence.

She held up her bound hands.

"This isn't enough," she breathed through gritted teeth. "You need to strap me to something. Please!"

Enska wasted no time and quickly grabbed some more rope from his sleigh, which was sitting nearby. Then he wound it around her waist and tethered the other end to one of the runners. Tuomas sat opposite her, so he was furthest away, and would stay out of distance should she leap at him.

He glanced at Henrik. The elderly mage had done as he said he would: on his lap was a brand-new drum, the symbols on its skin dark and bold from fresh paint. It was smaller than his old one, but Tuomas could still feel the *taika*. He remembered what Henrik had said: *it will cross over to my new one. Drums can be passed on, just not destroyed.*

The two of them shared a knowing smile, and Tuomas took the antler hammer in his left hand. It was awkward to hold, but he managed well enough, and nodded to Enska to show he was ready.

Enska drew a protective circle around the four of them, then settled on the other side of the fire.

"Are you alright, Lilja?" he asked gently.

Lilja whimpered. She was trembling. Tuomas could tell it was taking all her power to keep Kari at bay.

She locked eyes with him.

"You can do this, boy," she said, her voice tight.

Tuomas took a deep breath. "Please do your best to stay there."

Lilja raised a sarcastic eyebrow, but didn't reply. She was too busy trying to keep control.

He set his intention and began beating the drum steadily, allowing his heart to slow. The warmth of his power welled up and his eyes rolled back in his head. He felt Enska and Henrik beside him, hovering above their bodies, as the chanting and drumming became deeper and more powerful.

His souls loosened. The taste of lingonberries and smell of summer flowers encircled his senses.

This was so easy now. He wondered how he'd ever had trouble with it before. This was who he was... *what* he was. Pure, unbridled *taika*, contained in a form of flesh and bone. And now it was free, it soared higher than any bird, leaving the two earthly mages in his wake. If he had only known this power from the first day, from the moment Henrik took him on as an apprentice...

*But you know it now.*

The voice inside him was strong; it vibrated straight through him, neither male nor female. He floated in the timeless void between Worlds, listening, searching.

Then the stars and mist drew together, forming paws, fur, ears, eyes deeper than the deepest lake. The Great Bear Spirit appeared before him.

*Will you help Lilja?* he asked.

The Bear looked at him unblinkingly.

*I have helped her before. I brought her back from the edge of death. There was a task she had yet to do, and she needed power to do it. I bade her bring the Son of the Sun into his new body, and so she did.*

*And now I need to help her. I have wronged her.*

*You have wronged many in your time in the World Between*, the Bear noted, swimming around him.

*So I want to fix it,* he insisted. *Please, help me. Give me the strength to help Lilja.*

The Bear surrounded him in its starry form. He spun like a fallen leaf caught in a river's current, feeling himself fly everywhere and nowhere, completely unbound by physical laws. It was bliss… perfection.

*Her brother's influence must be removed from her body,* said the Bear. *Two life-souls cannot exist together. It will tear her apart.*

*I'll get him out of her. Henrik and Enska are here too. We should be able to overpower Kari together.*

*You can overpower him yourself. You are strong enough.*

He faltered. The Bear came so close, he could have reached out and touched its sparkling snout.

*All mages are tested. But only they know when they pass the test*, it carried on. *You know who you are. There are no limits anymore. And no time to lose. Free Lilja, and then put the White Fox One back where she belongs.*

As he thought of Lumi, realisation struck him like lightning. Even though he needed to send her home, he truly didn't want to see her go. He didn't know if he could bear it. He loved her, like Lilja had loved Kari.

*No matter what happens, I'll be in pain*, he said. *Mihka is saved when she returns, but she'll be gone forever.*

*And so you are faced with the same dilemma as when you led your people into the south, long ago, in your first life here,* the Bear replied. *When you walked this World then, you were the first mage to ever exist. This is the price you pay. More than the loneliness and the unease you suffer, what is more important? Your happiness, or that of all the others around you?*

Sadness overwhelmed him. He couldn't cry here; there was no way for tears to form without a body. But the weight of it all was almost enough to break him out of the trance.

The Bear seemed to soften, and drew alongside him. Its power seeped through him, like lying on a warm rock in summer.

*I will give you my assistance, Red Fox One*, it said. *I will be by your side.*

And then he was falling away, spiralling down. He didn't fight it. His time with the Spirit was over. He felt Enska and Henrik somewhere close by and joined them in the descent, letting himself become heavier.

Tuomas slipped into his body and opened his eyes.

His breath misted before him: a white cloud in the frozen air. But as he exhaled, it twisted and spun into the shape of the Bear, and hung there for a moment before disappearing.

He blinked hard – had he imagined that? But then he saw Lilja in front of him, a small smile on her face. Elin and Paavo were standing there too, their eyes wide with shock.

"Did you see that?" Paavo whispered. Elin nodded slowly, not looking away from Tuomas.

Lilja was the only one who didn't seem unnerved.

"It came to you," she said. "Just like when it came to me."

Tuomas glanced at Henrik and Enska. They were still returning from their trances. Snow had built up on their heads and shoulders from sitting for so long.

He looked at where the Bear had been, and then down at the drum in his hands.

"Are you alright, Tuomas?" Elin asked.

"I'm fine," he replied quietly.

"Well, do what you need to do, boy," said Lilja. "Get him out of me. I don't know how much longer I can resist."

She did look worse than when before. Her skin was as pallid as a corpse, and her hair had started to freeze, leaving white streaks weaving through her braids. Her blue eyes were dim, like the life was slowly being sucked out of them. The only thing which still held some colour was her scar, the flesh around it angry and enflamed.

Tuomas waited a few more moments, until Henrik and Enska looked closer to waking up. When they began to stir, he braced himself, called on the power of the Great Bear, and raised the hammer above his drum.

Before he could strike, Lilja shrieked and ran at him.

He propelled himself backwards, dropping the drum. The rope pulled taught and she fell into the snow, but didn't stay down for long. She reared up on her knees, eyes bulging. Her mouth opened so wide, he was shocked her jaw hadn't dislocated.

She snarled, drool spilling from her lips. Tuomas trembled. It was like looking into the demon's eyes again. Behind Lilja's face, he could almost see Kari, cheeks grey with ash and teeth ready to take a bite out of his heart.

The commotion instantly woke Enska and Henrik. But it had come too quickly. The two of them struggled to focus as their life-souls still hovered above their bodies.

Enska managed to make sense of what was going on though, and made a grab for Lilja. Still disorientated, he only caught her by the belt and yanked her backwards, away from Tuomas. But the thong around her waist broke and sent her drum flying. It landed at Elin's feet and she quickly snatched it.

Lilja screamed and spun around, turning her attention to Elin. She strained against Kari's power.

"Help me!" she managed to get out before he overcame her again.

She lunged back at Tuomas, and this time, she pulled so hard on the ropes, the sleigh moved. Tuomas skidded away from her, fear lending him new speed.

Paavo saw the terror on Tuomas's face and wrenched the drum from Elin's grasp. Then he strode towards the fire.

"What are you doing?" Elin shrieked, trying to get it back.

"Enough is enough," snarled Paavo. "If this doesn't make her stop, I don't know what will!"

Hearing that, Tuomas looked up from Lilja for long enough to take in the scene. Paavo was heading for the fire, Elin clawing helplessly at his arms.

He knew instantly what his brother meant to do.

"No!" he shouted. "Don't!"

Paavo didn't listen and threw the drum into the flames.

The tight skin and dry wood caught instantly, sending a foul-smelling smoke blooming into the sky. The painted symbols bubbled and curled away.

Lilja screamed again, but it wasn't a sound of mere pain. It was as though a part of her had been ripped away.

And, in a way, something had. Tuomas knew she would have had that drum since she was even younger than him. It was her one prized possession, which had always been with her through her mad nomadic existence.

And now it was destroyed.

Her eyes became dark and hollow; her flesh turned a horrible shade of grey. The scar in her neck tore slightly and began to bleed.

Tuomas's heart sank. That one stupid act by Paavo had trampled Lilja's *taika*, and allowed her brother to swim in and claim her.

The fire spat loudly. Sparks burst out from the smouldering drum. The air took on a heavy, sickly taste… it was saturated with wickedness. It wormed its way into Tuomas's mouth and he turned over, retching into the snow.

When he looked back, he froze where he lay.

Kari was stepping out of the flames and coming towards him.

# Chapter Twenty-Eight

Tuomas crawled away frantically. He had heard tales of mages being able to travel through fire, as he'd heard of beating drums letting out shockwaves. But of all the powers, that was one he never thought he would see. The spectacle of Kari standing there, his body covered in red ashes, was like something out of a nightmare.

Kari snatched his coat and threw him back towards the sleigh. The circle broke and disappeared as he fell through it. His head slammed against the wood and black spots flashed before his eyes.

Elin hurried to his side. She paused for long enough to check he was alright, then drew an arrow and aimed at Kari. But before she could release it, Kari grabbed it by the shaft and wrenched it off her bow.

"Not this time, girl," he snapped, and struck her across the face. She fell to the ground, dazed.

Paavo bolted towards them. But Kari simply looked at Lilja, and as though a command had been spoken, she leapt like an animal and sent Paavo flying onto his back. She jumped on top of him, her knees on his chest, pinning him down.

Kari produced a knife from his belt and cut through the ropes around Lilja's wrists and ankles. She instantly grabbed Paavo's throat with one hand.

"No!" Tuomas cried. "Don't hurt him!"

Kari smiled at him. "That would be sad, wouldn't it? Now you're so relieved he's alive after all."

Tuomas looked at Paavo and Lilja. There was nothing left of her now, no shred of the fight which she'd shown. All that had gone when Paavo threw her drum on the fire.

Tuomas cursed him for being so rash – how could he have thought that was a smart thing to do? But then he remembered how ignorant Elin had also been on the subject. Paavo wouldn't have known. And now, because of that, he might have gotten them all killed.

If Kari had looked close to death the last time Tuomas had seen him, now he was practically skeletal. The twisted *taika* had warped his body into nothing more than wan skin draped over bones. His hollow eyes roved; one red, the other white and blind. The flesh around them was as dark as a storm cloud. Blood seeped from the wound at his neck and his hair hung long and unkempt, dirt clogging it at the roots. More blood had gathered around a hole in his leg: where Elin had shot him on the mountain.

At that moment, alerted by the noise, the villagers began streaming down towards the shore. Several had knives drawn, ready to face whatever had caused the upset. Sisu and the other leaders were at the front, but when they saw Kari, they drew to a horrified halt.

Henrik and Enska were lucid now, finally staggering upright, their drums in hand. Henrik didn't stay still for long though, and ran forward, reaching a hand out for Tuomas.

Kari grabbed Tuomas and spun him around so he was facing the mages. Then he held the knife under Tuomas's chin.

"*No!*" Paavo screamed.

Tuomas fought not to retch again. This close, the smell of Kari's corrupted power was overwhelming, as though he was a rotting corpse rather than a man.

"How did you find me?" he choked out. "How are you not dead?"

"Thank Lilja," Kari hissed in his ear. "She gave me her body to make a new demon and led me straight to you."

"That's not going to work this time," said Tuomas. "You're lying. I know she's on our side."

"Not anymore," Kari replied. "Because of her, I managed to hang onto life. And once she let me take over her completely, it was a simple matter of bringing myself to you through the flames. I might only be half-alive now, but my power was still strong enough for that. And once I have your *taika*, Red Fox One, I'll be whole again!"

He moved the knife until it was over Tuomas's chest, and pressed firmly.

It wasn't enough to draw blood, but it was right over the previous wound. Pain leapt through Tuomas's flesh and he fought back a blaze of panic.

"Don't!" shouted Henrik. "Don't hurt him!"

"Let him go!" Paavo yelled, followed by a feral snarl from Lilja.

"No," Kari smirked. "I wish no harm upon any of you. So, you all surrender, and I will take only him."

He cocked an eyebrow at Tuomas. "Or is your sister here as well? I haven't seen any Lights in the sky since I was last with you; I know she hasn't been sent back. Is she still around here somewhere?"

Tuomas's heart pounded so hard, he heard it in his ears.

"I take it by the sudden tension that she is here," Kari said. "Where is she? The two of you together will be perfect."

"I don't know where she is," Tuomas hissed. "And even if I did, I wouldn't tell you!"

"It doesn't matter. When I have your heart, and your *taika* is mine, I'll find her."

Enska approached, his hands held out as though trying to calm an animal.

"Kari," he said softly. "Son, listen to me. Let the boy go."

Kari looked straight at him. "It's nice to see you again too, Father."

"Let him go," Enska said again. "Just let him come to me, alright?"

"Don't you understand, Father? He's just a boy, he has no idea how to use the power he's been given! He never will! Think of how much better it will be in my hands!"

"That's not the point of being a mage, and you know it."

Kari shook his head, anger building in his bloodshot eyes.

"Why doesn't anyone understand? This is for the greater good!"

"It's not," Enska insisted. "Please, think about what you're doing. You're better than this."

"Better, worse, what does it matter?" Kari snapped. "I've been after this brat all winter. If I'd been smarter fifteen years ago, I'd have taken him then."

He snapped an order at Lilja. She withdrew herself from Paavo, but stayed close, like a hungry wolf. Paavo hurried away from her, visibly shaking.

"If you all leave, I'll tell my sister to stay where she is," Kari continued. "If any of you take a step closer, I'll have her kill you all. Starting with your loyal little friend."

He hissed those last words in Tuomas's ear, and swept the point of the knife towards Elin, who was still lying in the snow.

His rancid breath turned Tuomas's stomach.

"Please," Tuomas said. "Just take me. Don't hurt anybody else."

"That's up to them." Kari nodded at Enska. "Last chance."

But still nobody moved.

Tuomas stared at Enska, silently willing him to take charge and get everyone away. If the stalemate continued for much longer, he knew Kari would lose what little patience he had left.

There was a flash of green, and something came at them. Tuomas only manged a glimpse as Lumi clamped her jaws around Kari's wrist.

Kari howled and let go of Tuomas. He thrashed violently, trying to dislodge Lumi, but she hung on with an incensed fury. She clawed at his face, leaving deep scratches.

Then, with a snarl of anger, Kari spun in a circle and sent her flying.

Tuomas saw her fall as though in slow motion, heading straight for the fire.

She landed in the middle of the smouldering logs. There was a pained yelp, and she tumbled away in a heap and didn't move.

Something snapped inside him. Barely thinking, he threw himself at Kari and tackled him to the ground.

Kari slapped him across the face and rolled on top of him, forcing his wrists either side of his head. Somehow, he had kept hold of the knife, and positioned it so the tip was pressing into Tuomas's cheek.

Tuomas hissed in pain. His chest burned from the impact; he felt sticky blood under his tunic. The wound had opened.

"Nice to know where she is," Kari leered. "I'll get her heart later, once I've had yours!"

"Not likely," Elin snarled.

Tuomas twisted his head. She was standing just a few feet away, all daze gone from her sharp eyes. A fresh arrow was nocked to her bow.

"Spirits, forgive me," she muttered, and let fly. It went over Tuomas's head and straight into Kari's chest.

The force of it knocked Kari backwards. Tuomas wasted no time; he shoved Kari off him and grabbed his drum. Henrik ran to him and the two of them laid down a circle as fast as they could.

Lilja went to attack, but the energy of the circle repelled her, and she bounced off it like a stone hitting ice. Paavo quickly forced her arms behind her back.

Kari gaped at the arrow, as though unable to believe it was there. Tuomas could tell from its position that Elin had just missed his heart – if she'd hit there, like she had with the demon, it would all be over.

She noticed it as well, because she advanced on him, another arrow aimed and ready.

"No, leave him be," Tuomas called to her.

She gave him an incredulous look.

"You don't think I'm going to let him walk away from this, do you?"

Tuomas met her eyes evenly, letting her see his anger. It was a fury beyond him, something greater, more powerful than a mere human body could hold.

He gritted his teeth, channelling it all down his arms and into the drum. Then he struck it.

Kari was yanked to his feet like a puppet on a string. Through the pain, he managed a condescending smirk.

"The Spirit of the Lights didn't have it in her to take my life," he said. "What makes you think you can?"

Tuomas threw a glance at Lumi. She still wasn't moving.

"Neither of you can do it," Kari sniggered.

"Lumi knew you weren't worth it, and so do I," said Tuomas. "I'm not going to kill you. I'm sending you back to where I found you."

He took a deep breath, letting his *taika* flow, until it felt as though it might lift him off his feet. In his mind, he sensed the warmth of the long Sun on his shoulders; smelled the berries and the flowers and the call of the birds.

He raised the hammer high and brought it down on the drum, his focus completely on Kari.

A bright light shone from the centre of the Mustafjord, and a phantom herd of white reindeer spilled out of it. They galloped towards the shore, bearing the Earth Spirits in their wake, leafy hair waving in the wind. The air above them rippled, like heat in summer. And from the flying snow, the unmistakable face of the Great Bear Spirit appeared.

Henrik covered his mouth and fell to his knees in awe.

Kari's his smug expression transformed into one of fright.

"This is your doing!" he raged at Lilja.

"No," Tuomas said calmly, and struck the drum again. "It's yours."

The reindeer reached the shore. The Earth Spirits reached out and snatched Kari, hauling him onto the frozen fjord. At once, Tuomas became aware of everything around him: the still water, the ice sheet on top of it, the frigid air; the unique intricacy of every falling snowflake. He let it flow through him, feeding his power, and poured out his intent in a chant.

*This is the end.*

The Great Bear Spirit gazed upon Kari with its fathomless black eyes. Kari fell into a bow so low; he was almost lying down.

"Forgive me, I beg you!" he cried. "Please!"

The Bear didn't move, didn't even blink. It only stared at the disgraced mage for a long moment. Then, in one swift movement, it grabbed him in its jaws and dived into the ice.

The ghostly herd streamed back, disappearing the way they had come. And then there was only the snow, drifting down onto the empty Mustafjord.

Tuomas's vision spun. His knees wobbled and Enska grabbed his shoulders to steady him.

Lilja let out a huge gasp. She wrenched one arm free and clutched at her throat. When she opened her eyes, the hollowness was gone. There was only her own familiar blue.

She shuddered, exhausted, and collapsed back against Paavo. He wasn't prepared for her weight and the two of them tumbled over.

Lilja didn't even bother to roll off him. She just lay there, panting as though she had run for miles.

Enska approached, watching her cautiously.

"Are you alright?" he asked.

Lilja managed a small smile.

"Smart boy."

A relieved grin spread over Enska's face.

"She's fine! Kari's out of her!"

Tuomas nodded. He knew there would be nothing of her wicked brother left now. He had felt the Bear drag him back to his prison in the World Below. There would be no escape, not when the greatest Spirit of all had taken him.

Then he remembered Lumi.

He shoved past Henrik and ran to the fireside, wedging his drum under his arm in mid-stride.

She was still lying there, saturated with water. Tuomas wasn't sure whether it was from the heat or something else. Her fur, once a flawless white, was blurred at the tips and growing more transparent by the moment.

He slipped his arms underneath her and held her to his chest. She was lighter than a feather. He could see his hands through her body.

She was fading away.

He hurried to the shore. When he stepped onto the Mustafjord, his shoes sank through the snow and slipped on the ice beneath, but he managed to stay upright. He didn't stop running until he reached the spot where Kari had disappeared, then he crashed to his knees.

"Why did you do that?" he snapped, choking on tears. "You're so stupid!"

Lumi opened her eyes and growled at the insult.

He truly began crying then. Even though she was barely hanging on, she still couldn't hold back her pride. Nothing would take that away from her.

He buried his face in her wet fur, sobbing freely, and she curled her tail around his neck.

"Thank you," he whispered.

He laid her down on her side and drew the protective circle around the two of them. He knelt in the snow a few feet from her, balanced the drum on his lap. He held the hammer just above the skin, his hand shaking.

Could he do this? Was he strong enough?

He knew he was.

He hit the drum.

That single strike snapped him into action. He hit it again, finding a beat, one deeper than he had ever made before. He let himself be swept up in it, and a chant formed in his throat, bursting free with flawless execution.

It was the complete opposite of how he had felt when he'd summoned her. Back then, he'd been furious and vengeful... but now, there was only sorrow.

As his souls loosened and his power spread like a rushing summer river, he heard the words of the Great Bear Spirit echoing in his memory.

*What is more important? Your happiness, or that of all the others around you?*

He felt her fragile body coming apart; the cold fire of the Lights twisting inside her. He steeled himself, harnessing all the *taika* he could, and struck the drum one more time.

Lumi rose into the air, glowing from the inside out, and a river of green aurora poured from her body. It flowed across the fjord, surrounding him; close, but not quite touching. Then the Lights shot up into the sky, forcing the snow clouds away to reveal an inky sky laced with stars. There were greens, reds, purples, other colours which he couldn't think to name... waving like fabric in water, expanding until they reached the horizon.

They started dancing.

As he looked, Tuomas swore he could see shadowy figures just out of focus within the glowing curtain. He sensed them: the souls of all who had gone before, finally able to look down again on the living.

She was back.

The drum slipped from his grasp. From one of the green tendrils, something fell, like a shooting star against the night.

After a moment so long it felt like forever, a hand appeared on Tuomas's shoulder. He looked around to see Elin smiling at him. She helped him to his feet and pointed with her bow.

Tuomas looked towards the shore. While he had been out here on the fjord, the entire village had gathered on the bank. And now the sound reached him: clapping and cheering. They had seen what he'd done, witnessed the aurora erupt out of Lumi's failing body.

Elin shouldered her bow, then picked up the drum and handed it back to him. It felt heavier than before, as though the weight in his heart had somehow fused itself with the curved birch frame.

They walked off the ice. As they drew closer, the crowd parted, revealing Sisu. There was a figure cradled in his arms, wrapped up like a babe. The only distinguishing feature was a shock of white hair.

Mihka turned his eyes on Tuomas. They were a little misted and unfocused, but they were open.

"You're awake!" Tuomas smiled.

Mihka cocked an eyebrow. "Miss me?"

"You have no idea, idiot."

Tuomas sighed in relief. That hadn't been a star which had fallen from the World Above. Just as he had fulfilled his promise, Lumi had also made good on hers, and sent back Mihka's life-soul.

Clarity struck him; too perfect to be any mistake, and he looked down at the drum.

He had done it. The hardship was passed, things were set right, and he had come through it all. He had passed his test.

311

Overhead, the Lights blazed with newfound fire, as though they had never been gone at all.

# Chapter Twenty-Nine

Tuomas stared blankly at the smoke hole. Across the dying embers of the hearth, Paavo was asleep on his back, snoring softly as he did every night. Elin was lying on his other side. As usual, her hair was an unkempt black mess, spilling across her face like a spider web.

But for Tuomas, restlessness and unease gnawed at his insides. He couldn't even be bothered reaching over to grab another log for the fire. Instead, he snuggled deeper into his sleeping sack and rolled over in an attempt to get more comfortable.

How could either of them sleep so soundly? He had lost count of the amount of times he'd woken, each time feeling more drained than the last.

He pulled open his tunic and looked at his chest. The wound had stopped bleeding, and a fresh bandage and poultice had been applied by Henrik. It would leave a nasty scar. But he was lucky. A scar and two shorter fingers were nothing. At least he was still alive.

He had barely set foot on the banks when the celebrations began. After Enska and Henrik confirmed he was alright, he had been practically lifted off his feet and taken to the centre of the village. A chorus of cheers and applause quickly turned to joyous laughter. He was sure he'd danced with every single person in Akerfjorden – even Lilja had been thrown into it at one point. She had avoided his eyes, and before he could get a chance to speak to her, Maiken appeared and took her place.

Even though it had only been that evening, it was already beginning to blur. His mind hadn't really been there, among his people. It had still been out on the Mustafjord, feeling Kari's knife on his throat, and Lumi's soaking fur against his cheek…

He heaved a sigh. There was no point trying to sleep. He needed to get some air.

He crawled out of his sack; pulled his shoes and coat on in silence. Then he slipped outside into the frozen night.

The Lights were still drifting in the sky. Tuomas looked at them as he walked between the huts. Lumi was making the most of her returned freedom.

What must it be like for her up there, back in her realm, in that place where form and time had no meaning?

Before long, he reached a conical tent, which stood out starkly from the turf shelters around it. Enska had set it up earlier in the day for himself, and now he and Lilja were inside.

Tuomas crept past it and rested his back against the turfed wall of Henrik's hut. A small smile crossed his lips – the last time he'd been here was when he had sneaked over to eavesdrop.

He didn't linger outside, and eased the door open a crack. The musty smell hit his senses like a wall. Once, he might have wrinkled his nose at it, but now, it was oddly comforting. It was the smell of all those lessons he should have listened to, of all the memories of Henrik weaving illusions with his drum – the same drum Tuomas now called his own.

Henrik was asleep in his usual place, and in the corner was Mihka, eyes closed softly. If Tuomas hadn't known better, he might have thought nothing had changed. He had to remind himself that he'd seen those eyes open just a few hours earlier.

He sneaked over and slid down the wall until he was sitting. Mihka stirred. Tuomas stayed still, hoping he would settle. But Mihka yawned and looked at him, squinting in the low light.

"Who's that?" he mumbled.

"Me," Tuomas replied. "Go back to sleep."

"I've had enough sleep," Mihka said. His voice was cracked from so long without use. It reminded Tuomas of Lilja.

Mihka propped himself up on his elbow and looked straight at Tuomas. He still wasn't completely lucid, but managed to focus well enough.

"I heard them talking," he said. "I've been here for *two months?*"

Tuomas nodded. "Do you remember what happened?"

"Yes. The Spirit of the Lights didn't like what I had to say."

"That's one way to put it."

"It was so strange. When I was up there... I was stuck in the Lights, with all the dead people. She was so angry with me. I didn't think she'd let me come back. And then she just... disappeared. I couldn't see anything else."

Tuomas frowned. "You remember what it was like up there?"

"It was like being awake, but not really; like my body had turned to water," said Mihka. "But then the Spirit vanished, and it all went black. All the souls were around me, wondering what had happened."

Tuomas bit his lip guiltily. "That was my fault."

Mihka raised his eyebrows.

"It sounds like you got in even more trouble than I did."

"I don't think anyone could get in more trouble than you."

"Well, I've got to have some fun, haven't I?"

The two of them smiled, but quietened when Henrik tossed in his sack. Tuomas silently urged Mihka to go back to sleep, but his friend reached over and clasped his wrist.

"You went out there for me, didn't you?" he whispered. "I saw you leaving in a sleigh… that happened before the Spirit left us. You went to find some mages."

Tuomas nodded. "I found them. They weren't what I was expecting."

"Neither was she," Mihka admitted. "The Spirit. She was so mad at first. But then she let me come home."

"She promised me she would," said Tuomas.

Mihka smiled, his eyes becoming heavy.

"Thank you. I don't know what you did while she was gone, but she was different when she came back."

He slumped down into his sleeping sack.

"Don't be expecting me to be a pushover now though, just because I've got hair like Henrik's."

Tuomas snorted a laugh, watching as sleep dragged Mihka back under. Then its hooks spread to him too, and he dived deep, grateful to not surface.

He woke slowly, finally feeling rested. He was still sitting against the wall, but a heavy blanket was wrapped around him. He supposed Henrik had found him there and tried to make him more comfortable.

Stray reindeer hairs were stuck to it, and they tickled his nose as he breathed. He pushed the blanket away and stretched his arms above his head. Mihka was still asleep next to him, but Henrik's sack was empty.

He looked through the smoke hole. The Lights were gone. Now the snow clouds were back, and a handful of small flakes were drifting down into the hut.

He eased himself to his feet and walked outside. The torches had been lit, and fresh prints told him that some people were already up. He gathered from the direction of most of them that the villagers had gone to the herd. Everyone else was still at home; he could smell the aromas of stews on the crisp air.

He knew he should eat something – he couldn't remember the last time he'd had a proper meal. But his hunger had receded to a dull ache in the pit of his stomach, easily ignored. So instead, he scooped up some snow and took a mouthful, letting it melt on his tongue. He swallowed the water, then touched the pouch on his belt.

How many times had he done this, thinking of the white hair and carved bone inside? Both of them had stood for something greater than what they were, and now both were done. How was everything supposed to go back to normal now?

Or wasn't it supposed to? Was this strangeness his new normal now? Had normality ever really existed for him at all?

He knew who would tell him.

He trudged towards Enska and Lilja's tent. A pair of footprints were leading away from it. He guessed Enska had left to have a meeting with Henrik, because the tracks intermingled with ones coming from the hut and then disappeared in the direction of the Mustafjord.

Lilja was still there though. He could see her silhouette against the stretched tarp.

He pulled back the flap and peered inside. Lilja jumped at the sound, but when she saw who it was, she relaxed.

Tuomas didn't wait for her to speak and let himself in, settling on the opposite side of the fire from her. A piece of antler was in her hand, the start of a new carving etched into the brown surface. She hadn't done much, but already it looked stunning.

She put it down and withdrew a strip of salted meat from a bag. She cut it neatly down the middle with a knife.

Tuomas regarded the blade with interest. It was one of her own. Enska obviously trusted her enough to have given her back her belongings.

Lilja held out half of the meat. Tuomas took it, but didn't let his fingers touch hers. No matter that it was a peace offering, tension still hung in the air.

"How are you feeling?" he asked.

Lilja didn't answer straightaway, taking a sizeable bite out of her share.

"I'm not sure about being back in Akerfjorden," she admitted. "Last time I was here, I ended up playing midwife."

Tuomas gave her a half-smile. "I suppose I should thank you for that."

"And I should apologise to you," said Lilja with sudden sincerity. "I never meant you any harm. What I did, out there on the fjord... that wasn't me."

"I know," Tuomas replied. "I'm sorry too, for thinking you were with Kari. You had nothing to do with him."

Lilja cast her eyes down and picked her teeth.

"I tried to stop him in the beginning. When I saw what he'd done, when he created that demon... My brother died that day. I was just too foolish to see it."

She touched her scar with one hand. It had stopped bleeding, but still looked tender.

"He set that monster on me. I did what I could. I didn't have it in me to kill him."

"You're a mage," said Tuomas. "We don't rule and we don't kill."

Lilja grinned at his words.

"So, you've passed your test."

"Yes. I know I have. I felt it."

"And you've accepted who you are at last?"

"I'm starting to," Tuomas admitted. Then he shifted his weight and looked straight at her.

"Why didn't you tell me? You knew all along who I was. Wouldn't things have been so much easier if you were honest with me? Were you even going to tell me?"

Lilja sighed.

"I'm no Spirit reborn, but I know what it's like to have knowledge like that hanging over your head. When my village found out I'd been touched by the Great Bear, I never got a moment to myself again. That's why I left, decided to become a wanderer. Kari just followed me, because he was older than me. He wanted to make sure I wouldn't be alone. He wasn't bad, not at first. He was kind. He was all I had."

She threw another log on the fire and it flared, casting shadows on her face.

"I wanted to spare you that isolation for as long as I could. I'd take you to the Northern Edge, get you help, so you could put the Spirit back in the sky. And then I'd go on my merry way. That was what I hoped. It was my plan. Henrik knew about your life-soul too, and he was your teacher – I was going to leave it to him."

She took a few more bites of her meat. Tuomas regarded her as she ate, wondering how he had been able to mistrust her so much.

"I shouldn't have thrown you out of Einfjall," he said in a small voice.

"You were scared and delirious," she replied.

"But they cast you out because of what I said."

"And you think I had a problem being on my own?"

"I'm still sorry," said Tuomas. "If you're on your own, it should be because you choose it, not because you're unwelcome."

Lilja shrugged.

"How can I make it up to you?" he asked. "I feel awful for what I did. Even when you came back, I still didn't want to believe you weren't wicked. What can I do?"

"For starters, you can eat the peace offering," Lilja said, finishing off her half.

Tuomas realised he hadn't touched his, and forced himself to take a small bite. It was a good cut, but tasted sinewy, not quite right in his mouth. He swallowed it after barely managing three chews.

"In all seriousness," Lilja carried on, "you don't need to do anything. I know you're honest, and now you know I am – I always have been. So, if you really want to make things up to me, just do me a favour."

"What?"

"Take care of yourself. You're a mage now. Everyone thinks passing the test is the most important thing, but that's just the beginning. This is a long and lonely road, even when you're surrounded by others. I think you're starting to realise that now. You will live to serve the Spirits and keep balance. So whatever you do, do it because you choose it. I know I'm going to keep doing that."

Tuomas looked at her curiously.

"What does that mean?" he asked.

"It means," said Lilja, "that I'm going back to Poro with Enska. It's been too long since I've had a true home. And enough time has passed since I was last living there. Hopefully they'll accept me back and won't come asking me for favours every other day."

She sighed, staring into the fire.

"And it will be good for my father and me to grieve together. No matter what Kari became, he was still family."

Tuomas nodded. He couldn't help but recall the thoughts he'd had in the World Below: that once their escapades were over, he would offer Lilja a home with him in Akerfjorden. It was clear, however, that she had made up her mind. He would respect it.

And it wasn't as though she would never be able to travel the Northlands again. Once the Sun Spirit came back, all the villages would be on the move, following their herds on the migration paths and setting up their summer camps.

After a long silence, he spoke again.

"I'm sorry about your drum."

"Mm."

For the first time during the conversation, Lilja's expression darkened, but she shook it off.

"I won't waste energy being annoyed at your brother. He didn't know what he was doing. I guess he's just lucky I didn't rip his face off because of it."

Tuomas shuddered, remembering the hollowness which had spread over her eyes when Kari took control of her.

"I'll make another drum," she said. "It can mark a new beginning for me. I'll rediscover my *taika*. I'm content to not run away from it anymore."

Tuomas smiled at her. "I think that's a good idea."

"Of course it is."

Lilja put a pot on the hearth and filled it with snow, then fished around for some tea herbs.

"The Great Bear really is something, isn't it?" she said wryly.

Tuomas smiled, but it was quickly chased away by a frown.

"Lilja… when I met the Bear, it didn't call me Tuomas. It called me Red Fox One."

A grin spread across Lilja's face.

"Because it's your Spirit title, that's why," she replied. "You and the Spirit of the Lights are equals and opposites. She's the White Fox One, Daughter of the Moon. Don't you think it makes sense for you to be the Red Fox One, Son of the Sun?"

Tuomas settled back against the tarp wall, Lumi's spectral eyes flashing in his mind.

"Perfect sense," he said.

# Chapter Thirty

The midday twilight slowly grew longer and longer, until the time came for the night to finally end. Everybody in Akerfjorden hurried to the bank of the Mustafjord. Children played and poked each other with twigs, and the adults shared hearty conversations over shared bowls of sautéed reindeer.

A sense of relief and celebration hung in the air. At last, they could welcome back the Sun Spirit. But this year, there was more to celebrate. Perhaps more than there would ever be again.

Tuomas sat with Paavo and Mihka, as he had since he could remember. Elin was with them too – she had decided to stay in Akerfjorden to make good on the promise to Alda, and care for Tuomas's hands. The frostbite had done its damage now, and while he had lost the thumbnail, as he thought he might, it luckily hadn't spread any further.

Tuomas was just grateful he could still work with it. When he'd come down from the mountain a month ago, it was difficult to tell whether the limb could be saved. It was only thanks to Elin and Alda that he still had it.

"Is it hurting?" Elin asked, noticing how he was looking at it.

Tuomas shook his head. "No. It's just taking a while to get used to it. It feels like I have phantom fingers!"

Elin smiled. "I've heard of that happening before."

"Only you would leave the village and come back with frostbite," Mihka chuckled, earning him a shove from Tuomas. But that didn't dissuade him and he carried on.

"At least you're not walking like a... what was it, Paavo?"

"Angry moose?"

"That's it!"

"Fine. If you're going to insult me, I'll just help myself to this," said Tuomas, snatching Mihka's bowl. "You can only use your big mouth for one thing at a time!"

Mihka grabbed it back and went to respond, but then silence fell over the crowd. Tuomas twisted around.

Henrik was walking towards the shore, drum tied onto his belt. This time, however, instead of going straight past Tuomas, the old mage motioned for him to join him.

Tuomas got to his feet and threw a small smile at his friends. Henrik led him to the edge of the ice, took up a bowl of ash and daubed it on his face in the ceremonial patterns. It was coarse and flaky; its bitter scent filled his nose. Henrik swept it across his cheekbones and forehead, down his chin and nose.

Then he untied his drum. Tuomas copied him, holding his own in his hands.

"Are you ready, boy?" Henrik asked under his breath.

Tuomas nodded.

Without another word, they both raised the antler hammers and struck the skins.

Tuomas began the chant first. The warmth of his *taika* twisted and rolled inside him, and he let it out in an ululating stream of song. He didn't think on it, didn't try to force it to sound like anything except what it was. It combined with Henrik's, swirling towards a horizon of pale blues and faint pinks.

He could feel the Sun Spirit, just beyond the edge of the World, working closer, opening her bright eye once more. Her magic and love entered him as he hovered above his body, formless and endless, floating in the space between realms.

When the chant drew to a close, and he drifted back to the World Between, the Sun Spirit had broken through, the top of her shining face just kissing the earth. The villagers erupted into applause and song.

Tuomas lowered his drum and Henrik placed a proud hand on his shoulder.

At last, the Long Dark was over.

As he dreamed, Tuomas found himself sitting on a hilly tussock, watching the herd forage in the snow. Paavo was there with Aslak, as the two of them usually were, tossing down some food and checking to make sure no bells had broken loose from around the animals' necks. The females' bellies were fat with unborn calves. When spring came, those young ones would drop, and then would be a frenzied few days of herding them all into the corral for the earmarking.

Tuomas found his own mark within moments of looking. There weren't many reindeer bearing it, but it didn't take him long to pick out the bull which had accompanied him on the long journey. It had lost weight while they had been away, but now it was filling out again. It would be a strong one in the next rut, he knew it.

A smile traced his lips, but disappeared just as quickly. How was he supposed to pick up the threads of this old life?

After fifteen years of knowing nothing but this, everything had happened so fast. Could he truly return to it as though nothing had changed? When he stood there, slicing his mark into the ears of his new calves, making burr-cups, following the herd on the migration… would things really look and feel the same?

He heard Lumi's voice in his memory.

*"I would give anything to take you back there. Back home, with me."*

He blinked, and when he opened his eyes, he was lying on his back in his sleeping sack.

Paavo was snoring, Elin kicking out in her sleep. The fire was still going strong, and filled the hut with delicious warmth. A hare, fresh from the day's hunt, hung by its feet from the central beam.

He sat up and peered out of the smoke hole. The sky was clear and dark, spangled with thousands of stars. Then the unmistakable shimmer of iridescent green drifted by.

Careful to not make any noise, he dressed himself and eased outside, closing the door as softly as he could.

The village was deserted. The quiet sound of snores came from the huts as he passed them. He pulled a pair of mittens on in mid-step, letting himself wander to the edge of the Mustafjord.

He walked out onto the ice. The Lights blazed above him, filling the sky, leaving the cold landscape awash with colour. They reflected off every surface, dancing to an otherworldly silent tune. But Tuomas could remember it: that celestial sound, inaudible to human ears, so welcoming and pure.

When he reached the middle of the fjord, he dropped to his knees. In the aurora's floating curtain, he could just make out the swaying shapes of the ancestors. Then, running through the veil, he saw a white fox, her face turned towards him.

He heard footsteps behind him and looked over his shoulder. Elin was standing there, her hair a mess, eyes still heavy with slumber. She hadn't even put on a hat.

"Sorry if I woke you," he said.

"It's alright. I wasn't having a good sleep anyway." She came closer and knelt beside him. "What are you doing out here?"

In answer, Tuomas turned his eyes back to the sky.

Elin gazed up at the Lights.

"Are you missing her?"

"More than you think," he replied. "It feels like a part of me went away with her."

Elin hesitated for a moment.

"Listen, I can tell you haven't been yourself since you went into that trance in Enska's hut," she said carefully. "Why?"

"No. I'm more myself than ever," Tuomas said. "I don't really know how to explain it. But everything just feels so... different now."

"Because you know who you are?"

He nodded. "Nobody else – apart from the Great Mage – has ever had a Spirit for a life-soul. And I don't know what to do with that. When I was up there, in the World Above, everything felt so right. Like I'd come into a second home."

Elin was silent for a long time, her hands clasped in her lap, fingers weaving together agitatedly.

"You're going up there, aren't you?"

Tuomas gnawed on his lip.

"Not for long," he whispered. "I just want to feel it again. See what it really feels like to be a Spirit."

"Nobody's done that before."

"I know. That's the point."

"How do you know you'll be able to get back?"

"I walked physically in the World Below. This can't be any different."

He looked into her face. It was flushed from cold, and a few tears had started to roll down her cheeks. He wiped them away so they wouldn't freeze, but she grabbed his hand.

"Promise you won't be gone too long."

"I promise," Tuomas said. "Besides, I need to come back. It will be time for the migration before we know it."

"You'd better," Elin said. "I've gotten used to getting you out of trouble."

Tuomas smiled. "I'll be back. I don't break promises."

He put his arms around her and pulled her into a hug. She held him tightly, her fingers digging into the fur of his coat.

"Thank you," he said. "I couldn't have done any of this without you."

Then he pulled away from her, turned his eyes to the sky, and held out a hand.

He barely needed to summon his *taika* before the aurora extended down to the earth. Its colour lit up the snow and millions of flakes across the fjord sparkled like diamond dust. It shifted and twisted, and a familiar face appeared in its curtain: pointed ears erect atop a head of white hair.

Lumi grasped her brother's wrist.

The Lights spread into Tuomas's body, and he was lifted away. Elin's hands closed around empty air. The two Spirits drifted into the World Above, curling around each other, new branches of magic spreading across the night like limbs on a tree in summer.

A few heartbeats later, Elin was alone in the middle of the Mustafjord.

"I'll see you soon," she said.

Then she laid down in the snow, ignoring the cold, and watched the dancing Lights until morning.

The drumbeats continue…

# The Mist Children

## The Foxfires Trilogy
## Book Two

Read on for an exclusive sneak peak!

# Prologue

At the outskirts of Poro village, the sound of friendly jeering carried over the frozen surface of Lake Nordjarvi. On the banks, three children – two boys and a girl – ran about with lengths of rope in hand. They had stuck a pair of antlers into the snow, and were testing how far away they could get before the lassos landed short.

The girl tossed her rope and it fell pathetically, three feet from the antlers. The boys shrieked with laughter.

"What kind of throw was that?" one of them snorted.

The girl glowered.

"Shut up, Niko. Mine was better than any of yours!"

"Alright then, let's try something else, and see who's best," said Niko. "Boden, get the antlers and pretend you're a reindeer, and then Inga and me will try to catch you! Whoever lassos first wins!"

"Fine!" Inga snatched her rope with newfound vigour.

Boden dug the antlers out of the snow and held them against his head. He loped around, kicking and snorting like a calf. Inga and Niko tossed their lassos, but both missed, and they gave chase.

"Come on!" Boden shouted. "You can do better than that, can't you?"

Niko shoved his way past Inga and threw his rope. It snagged on one of the antler points, but slipped off before it could tighten.

"I'll get you!" he cried, the words broken with laughter.

Excitement overcame them and Boden soon gave up impersonating a reindeer. He sprinted towards the Nordjarvi. The others ran after him, giggling wildly, slipping as they left the bank and emerged onto the lake. There was still a layer of snow lying on top of the ice, but their shoes sank straight through it, all grip gone.

Boden lost his footing completely and went flying onto his backside. The antlers fell from his grasp and skittered across the surface.

A lasso landed neatly around his torso.

"I got you!" cried Inga triumphantly. Then she turned on Niko. "I win!"

"Shut up," Niko glowered. He glanced uneasily at the antlers.

"Why did you throw them?" he demanded.

"I didn't throw them. I dropped them," argued Boden as he disentangled himself from the rope.

"We've got to get them," said Niko hotly. "My Papa will be so cross if I lose them. He said he needed them later to make new knife handles."

"Well, go and get them," said Inga. "The ice is still thick enough to walk on."

Niko nodded – more to himself than the others. He had never liked being out on the water in the middle of winter. Even though he'd crossed lakes every year on the migration, and sometimes came ice fishing with his family, there was something about doing it which unsettled him.

It was a frozen purgatory; water, yet solid: a thin skin which he could crash through at any moment. Eevi, his older sister, had told him: if you fall under the ice, the cold would kill you before you could drown, before you could even shout for help.

He shuddered. He couldn't wait for summer.

But he couldn't let Inga and Boden see he was afraid, either. They were his friends, but they would still tease him.

So he straightened his back, and headed towards the antlers.

They were several feet away, but the distance seemed like miles as the anxiety tightened his muscles. The soles of his shoes were made from the fur of a reindeer's head; and the strands, sticking out in all directions, gave a fantastic grip. But he still moved slowly, listening for the slightest crack.

After a few tense seconds, he reached the antlers and snatched them up. He let out a small smirk of relief and turned back to his friends.

But they weren't looking at him. Their eyes carried on past him, wide with alarm. Inga's mouth had fallen open and her breath fogged in the air.

"What is it?" Niko asked.

They didn't reply. Niko slowly turned.

A boy was standing on the ice, just out of arms' length. He looked about the same age as them, or perhaps a year younger, with sandy blonde hair reaching to his shoulders. Ugly burn scars shone on his cheek. He was dressed in a baggy coat, decorated with the patterns of Poro, but Niko couldn't remember seeing him before. He was dripping wet from head to toe, clothes clinging to his skinny body. His eyes were closed.

Niko shivered just looking at him. How had he not frozen solid, soaked as he was? Where had he even come from?

"Uh… hello," he said tentatively.

The boy didn't reply.

Niko threw a confused glance at Boden and Inga.

They were muttering between themselves, still staring at the newcomer. But they didn't come closer to investigate. No matter that the ice was still sturdy; they all knew that too much weight in one place was never a good idea.

Niko fidgeted, rocking back and forth on his heels.

"What's your name?" he asked.

The boy tilted his head slightly. The movement was strange and fitful, more like a bird than a human. He kept his eyes closed.

"I'm Aki," he said, barely above a whisper. When he opened his mouth, water spilled out and dripped down his chin.

Niko fought the urge to recoil.

Inga took a tentative step forward. "Is everything alright?"

"I think so," Niko called back.

"Do you want mc to get my Mama?" she offered.

Niko refused, then addressed Aki again.

"Hey… aren't you cold? Do you know you're not supposed to go out in wet clothes?"

Aki didn't say anything. The only movement was another twitch of his head.

The silence began to get uncomfortable, and Niko went to ask something else, to break it. But then Aki murmured something, so quietly, he had to lean in to hear.

"It's my birthnight."

Niko hesitated.

"Happy birthnight," he said. "How old are you?"

"I'm five."

"Uh… well, do you want to play with us?"

Aki nodded woodenly, but didn't take a single step.

Then he opened his eyes.

Niko screamed. They were completely white and clouded over, with no hint of colour at all. It was like they belonged in a corpse.

He bolted for the shore, for his friends, but they were screaming too. Niko slipped, arms flailing frantically as he tried to stay on his feet. Dense mist spread around him, as though a giant being had let out a lungful of breath into the winter air. It enveloped him first, then Boden and Inga as they tried to run.

There was a slippery sound, like fish squirming over each other, followed by the gnashing of teeth. And then, as though the icy layer had given way beneath them, the children disappeared from view.

On the hill nearby stood the Poro mage, Enska. He had heard the commotion and arrived just in time to see Inga fall.

His eyes strayed to the little boy, standing in the middle of the lake, and his blood ran cold.

There was nothing to be done for the youngsters now. He turned back and ran towards the village.

"Lilja…" he muttered under his breath. "Lilja, what have you done?"

Printed in Poland
by Amazon Fulfillment
Poland Sp. z o.o., Wrocław

64464867R00200